Cat About
Town

Cat About Town

CATE CONTE

St. Martin's Paperbacks

NOTE: If you purchased this book without a cover you should be aware that this book is stolen property. It was reported as "unsold and destroyed" to the publisher, and neither the author nor the publisher has received any payment for this "stripped book."

This is a work of fiction. All of the characters, organizations, and events portrayed in this novel are either products of the author's imagination or are used fictitiously.

CAT ABOUT TOWN

Copyright © 2017 by Liz Mugavero.

All rights reserved.

For information address St. Martin's Press, 175 Fifth Avenue, New York, NY 10010.

ISBN: 978-1-250-07206-1

Our books may be purchased in bulk for promotional, educational, or business use. Please contact your local bookseller or the Macmillan Corporate and Premium Sales Department at 1-800-221-7945, ext. 5442, or by email at MacmillanSpecialMarkets@macmillan.com.

Printed in the United States of America

St. Martin's Paperbacks edition / August 2017

St. Martin's Paperbacks are published by St. Martin's Press, 175 Fifth Avenue, New York, NY 10010.

10 9 8 7 6 5 4 3 2

For Journey and Harry,
JJ's real-life rescuers.

Acknowledgments

There are so many people to thank in the creating of a book it's hard to know where to start. First, my agent John Talbot, for keeping me top of mind as the cat lady and helping dream up this series. My editor, Hannah Braaten, whose vision got this book to where it is today. And the fabulous designer at St. Martin's who came up with such a great cover, and all the other cogs in the publishing wheel that saw this book to fruition. Thank you all!

Still, this book wouldn't have been written without the help of two amazing writing friends, Barbara Ross and Sherry Harris, who both helped me out of numerous plot holes along the way. And without Sherry's master editing skills, the final version wouldn't be half as good.

I am forever thankful for my blogmates over at Wicked Cozy Authors—Barb and Sherry, along with J.A. Hennrikus/Julianne Holmes, Jessica Estevao/Jessica Ellicott, and Edith Maxwell/Maddie Day. Together, the six of us have truly found a lifeboat to help navigate the waters of both writing and life. I'm blessed to be part of this group.

To get the feel of an islander's life, I spent some time on Martha's Vineyard in Massachusetts. I want to give a shoutout to the local businesses out there—it's not as easy as it looks in the summertime. Thank you for all you do, and for welcoming so many visitors to your island.

The late, great Dr. Wayne Dyer deserves a mention here. I borrowed the name "Scurvy Elephants" from an anecdote he told during one of his motivational talks. Rest in peace, sir, and thank you for all the wisdom you shared with the world.

And for all the readers—keep reading. We writers would be nowhere without you. Thank you all.

Chapter 1

The main difference between a cat and
a lie is that a cat only has nine lives.
—*Mark Twain*

The cat's eyes had been on me during the entire service.
I'd seen him right away despite his attempts to remain
hidden behind a distant gravestone—I'm a sucker for an
orange face. Plus, he was the only spot of color in this bleak,
gray, sad day. Every time I glanced in that direction those
green eyes blazed a hole right into me, like I emanated
some kind of cat-attract radar. On second thought, I probably did. Cats were my weakness. I'd never met one I didn't
love instantaneously. Not even the one who had nearly
scratched my eye out at a shelter I'd volunteered at years
ago.

Now that most of the crowd here to mourn my grandma
had dissipated as everyone headed back to their cars with
the postfuneral luncheon on their minds, the cat seemed
to feel more comfortable. He—I assumed it was a he, given
his color and size—took a tentative step forward, big paw
moving gingerly as if still unsure of his actions. One of
his ears looked bent, as if he'd had an ear infection from
which he hadn't recovered well. Sadly, a common ailment
for strays.

I moved closer to his position and crouched down,
holding out one hand to coax him forward. I wished I still

carried treats in my purse. There'd been a time I never left my house without cans of cat food and Temptations treats packed in my oversized purse. I could see him pondering, assessing, then one paw started to move . . .

"Maddie!" My dad's voice rang out through the quiet. I sighed as the cat darted back to hiding; then I stood up and turned around.

"Yeah, Dad?"

"When Grandpa's ready, we'll be in the limo." He pointed to the sleek black car idling on the main path of the cemetery. My mother, sisters, and aunt were already safely tucked inside. "Take your time."

Which really meant, *We're on a schedule here.* I gave him a thumbs-up to acknowledge his request. He returned to the limo and I returned to waiting. Grandpa Leo still stood in front of my grandma's grave a few feet away, head bowed and hands clasped, saying the final good-byes he hadn't been able to say with the other mourners watching. I thought I'd give him another minute, which might give me time to coax the cat out again. Besides, I hated looking at the coffin poised over the hole in the ground. Even though I knew Grandma's spirit wasn't in it, it still seemed so final. And claustrophobic.

I tugged my black sweater tighter around me, wishing I'd chosen pants instead of a dress. Especially since I'd forgone tights. I hated tights. But even though it was almost June, the air still held a chill, exacerbated by the sea breeze ruffling through the trees. It was the reality of island living, being surrounded by water that hadn't completely warmed yet from the harsh New England winter. The damp weather today wasn't helping. Rain had chased us on and off all day, and thick moisture hung in the air. I wondered if the orange cat had found shelter.

Movement behind the gravestone perked me up. My orange buddy must still be there. I took a few quiet steps closer, buoyed by the sight of one cat ear poking out. "Come here, cutie," I called softly.

The cat eased around the stone in a one-sided game of peekaboo and looked at me curiously. I could see him weighing his options—*trust her? Don't trust her?* Once again, the minuscule movement. And once again, a voice rang out, startling both of us.

"Leo! I'm glad I caught you."

A curse on my tongue, I turned around in time to see a short, older man who looked vaguely familiar loping toward my grandpa, whose head was still bowed in front of the grave. His pasty face, thinning white hair, and glasses made me guess late sixties. He looked like he fought a good fight to keep the pounds from settling in his middle and was slowly but surely losing the battle.

Grandpa looked up from the casket, disinterested. "Frank," he said, nodding at the other man but making no move to shake his hand. "Thanks for coming."

I looked back for the cat, and he'd vanished again. Giving up, I trudged toward Grandpa, hoping to rescue him from the visitor he didn't seem eager to see.

"Ah, Leo, so sorry," Frank said, the hint of an Irish accent dancing through his words. "Lucille was one of a kind. Good Irishwoman."

Grandpa inclined his head in acknowledgment, his eyes suddenly wet. "You remember my granddaughter Madalyn," he said, nodding at me.

Frank turned his attention to me, smiled. "'Course I do. Though it's been a long time. Frank O'Malley, if you don't remember. President of the Daybreak Island Chamber of Commerce." He puffed his chest out a bit, then leaned over and bussed my cheek. I smelled wine on his breath, even though it was barely eleven in the morning. "I'm sorry for the loss of your gran."

"Thank you," I said.

Frank adjusted his glasses and turned back to Grandpa. "When things calm down, we need to get together. Continue our discussions about the house," he said. "We'll do it over dinner."

It almost sounded like a directive. I held the frown back as I watched Grandpa. I didn't know what they were talking about, but Grandpa wasn't usually on the receiving end of directives. If someone tried it, they got The Look—bushy white eyebrows drawn together in a wild slash, the usual twinkle in his brown eyes dimmed by dark storm clouds. He'd perfected The Look during his long tenure as chief of police of Daybreak Harbor, the largest of the four towns that made up Daybreak Island. I waited breathlessly for it.

But The Look didn't surface. Instead, defeat slouched his shoulders forward, exhaustion settling into the lines around his eyes. "Yeah," he said. "Give me a call."

Frank nodded. "You'll be hearing from me," he said with a smile. "We'll take care of you, Leo." He patted Grandpa's back, then lifted his chin to me in acknowledgment. "Madalyn."

"Maddie," I murmured, but he was already walking away. I glanced at Grandpa. "What was he talking about? What house? Who's taking care of you?"

Grandpa Leo looked at me, his mouth working. "I've been wanting to talk to you about something," he said finally. "But not now. Let's talk tonight over dinner."

I frowned, warning bells dinging in my brain. The tone of his voice sounded ominous even though he tried to pass it off as nothing. "Okay. But is everything—"

"They're waiting for us," he said, nodding toward the limo where my dad had reappeared out of the car, checking his watch. "We have to go." He started walking, not looking to see if I followed.

I didn't. Even though I wanted to race up to my grandfather, grab his arm and demand he tell me whatever secret he was keeping. Instead, my gaze slipped back to the gravestones by the tree line, one last-ditch effort to glimpse the cat again. But I didn't see anything beyond the stones. Disappointed, I started to walk back to the limo when I heard a squeaking sound. I paused and scanned the area. My eyes finally landed on the orange cat sitting a few feet away next to a different gravestone. His clear green eyes radiated calm and wisdom. He was the most handsome cat I'd seen in a long time, with his perfect ginger patterns. And he sat perfectly still, like one of those statues people put in their gardens.

I moved forward slowly, one hand extended to the cat. He watched me, unmoved. I'd almost reached him when my dad came up behind me, startling both of us. I wanted to cry out in frustration.

"Maddie? What are you doing? They're holding the limo for you. We need to get back to the house."

"Coming," I said. "One second."

My dad sighed, but didn't argue. Between me, my sisters, and my mother, he was used to being overruled.

I turned back to the cat, but I'd had three strikes, and I was out. He was gone.

Chapter 2

My mother cornered me in my old bedroom at the post-funeral gathering, foiling my attempt to steal a few minutes to check some e-mails. I'd been neglecting my business while I'd been home in Massachusetts. My fabulous business partner, Ethan Birdsong, would disagree. *You're at a funeral,* he would say. *Why would you care if the Grapefruit Pucker was no longer the best seller after the Spicy Green Apple beat it out?* But Ethan is much too accommodating.

We owned Goin' Green, an organic juice bar, out in San Francisco. We'd opened up shop over a year ago now, and it had been the smartest business move I'd made. Since we had a spot on Pier 39, we had constant foot traffic, an awesome location to hang out in all day, and fun, healthy offerings.

Basically, we had it made.

"I knew you'd be in here," she said, leaning against the doorjamb. "It gets to be a bit much, doesn't it?"

I tossed my phone on the bed and leaned back against my pillows. My mother had made my room into a lovely guest room, with decorative pillows and a matching comforter. I kind of missed the old iteration of my room, with my Nirvana posters and favorite red down quilt.

"It does," I agreed. "For you too?" Given my mother's extroverted personality, I wouldn't have imagined that. But it *was* her mother's funeral. That, I imagined, changed everything.

"Way too much," she said, entering the room and kicking the door closed behind her. She reached up and tugged out the barrette holding her mane of curly brown hair in a funeral-appropriate style, letting it fall around her shoulders. Her eyes were red-rimmed and tinged with exhaustion. She'd lost weight, and her flouncy black skirt reminiscent of Stevie Nicks in her Gypsy days hung off her tiny waist. She sat down next to me and I leaned over to give her a squeeze. "I'm glad you were able to come home for a few weeks," she said.

"Me too." Although I hadn't spent much time at my parents' house during this visit, choosing instead to stay with Grandpa. I knew he'd have a rough time after my grandmother died, and I wanted to be there to help him as much as possible. Grandpa was my favorite person in the entire world. Usually when I was home I had to divide my time between the two houses so no one would be offended. This time, my mother seemed relieved.

"I'm grateful that you've been with your grandpa. He needs you. You're his favorite, you know." She smiled at me, but it had a hint of sadness. "You're not to repeat that to your sisters, of course."

I smiled. "Of course."

My mother picked at a thread in the blanket. "Do you know when you're leaving?"

"I haven't made official plans yet," I said. "Ethan's got everything under control and told me to take my time. So I figured I'd see how Grandpa felt." I was looking forward to some quality time with him before I left. I'd been here for nearly three weeks already but given the circumstances, we hadn't had much down time. The first two weeks had centered around spending as much time with Grandma as possible, which was a blessing as much as it was heart-wrenching and difficult. After she passed away earlier this week, we'd then become engrossed in the arrangements, finding pictures, ordering flowers, and all the other logistical work that funerals demanded in order to create a fitting send-off. Most nights we fell asleep before nine, exhausted emotionally and physically. Ironic that death could be more grueling for the people watching than the person dying.

But I'm lucky. Being my own boss means I get a certain level of freedom, but having someone like Ethan to cover with a smile was the icing on the cake. Plus, he cared about the business as much as I did, if not more.

"Good," she said, still avoiding my eyes.

Something was up. My mother seemed way too subdued, even if it was a funeral. This wasn't her typical demeanor. My mom was the coolest person I knew. Not because she rocked out to better music than I did, always drove fun cars, and knew how to dress. She lived her life exactly the way she wanted it. She'd kept my father, the quintessential straight arrow, on his toes since the day they met in college. The way the story goes, my mother was involved in a war protest and my father had been one of the "dorm police" who had to break it up. Reportedly, my mother had taken a swing at him. He'd asked her out to dinner that night, and they'd been inseparable ever since. He'd been so smitten with her he'd even moved to the island—akin to another planet for my Pennsylvania-raised father. None of that could have happened without her bubbly, expressive personality. And I hadn't seen much of that personality while I'd been home. "What's going on, Mom?"

She hesitated.

"*Mom*. Just tell me."

"I'm worried about your grandfather," she said finally.

"Worried? About him being able to live without Gram? I know." I sighed. "It's going to be tough."

"Not just that. He's been having some . . . trouble."

Now she had my attention. "What kind of trouble?"

She dropped her hands into her lap and finally looked at me from under hooded eyes. "Small things, but they've become more noticeable over the past couple of months. Some of his friends have mentioned it, but I've seen it too lately. He's agitated a lot. He's become forgetful. Have you noticed any strange behavior while you've been with him?"

I hadn't, aside from his passive demeanor at the cemetery with Frank O'Malley and the evasive comments about needing to talk to me. Which I chose not to mention. But all of this seemed ludicrous since he'd been dealing with Grandma's illness and death. Who wouldn't be acting differently?

"No, and it doesn't seem like a fair question. He's been under a lot of stress, in case you hadn't noticed." I didn't know where this was going, but I immediately felt defensive. Grandpa Leo wasn't old and he certainly wasn't sick.

"Maddie. Honey." She reached out and squeezed my hand. "I know that's not good news to hear. I don't want to think about it either. I just lost my mother. But there've been little things. Bills that haven't been paid. I found an invoice on his counter from the landscaper. It was the third notice. Then he volunteered to help with the Food Stroll, but didn't meet certain commitments. Most recently it's related to your grandmother's illness, of course. But it's been happening for a while."

Bills that hadn't been paid? Commitments? That wasn't like Grandpa. His superpower was dependability. It was part profession, part character. I pulled away from her, got up and walked slowly around the room. My mother had kept some of my favorite childhood trinkets, which I always loved to see when I came home. A picture of me and my best friend, Becky Walsh, on the beach when we were around ten. My music box with the three cats that played "You Light Up My Life." I picked it up and wound it, let it play.

My mother got up too. She came over, turned me around, and took my hands in hers. "Look. I don't want to worry you. I just want you to keep an eye on him, okay? Please?" Her eyes were wet.

The song from the music box faded into slow motion, finally winding down into silence. I squeezed her hands. "Sure," I said, forcing a cheery note into my voice. "I'll keep an eye on him."

Chapter 3

Once the crowd had thinned out enough that we could make our escape, I kissed my parents good-bye and followed Grandpa to his car—my grandma's car, actually. He usually drove a beat-up pickup around town. Having a nice car had never been a big priority, because he'd always had an official vehicle.

We drove the ten minutes to his house in Daybreak Harbor in silence. My parents lived in Duck Cove, the town bordering Daybreak Harbor on the west side. In the dead of summer, this ride could take up to forty-five minutes as people crammed the streets, walking, biking, riding Segways, and packing onto tour buses. But tonight, thankfully, the traffic wasn't completely insane even though tourist season had already dropped onto Daybreak like a falling meteor—barely two weeks in and the population had tripled. Give it another week or two and there would be ten times the people thronging the streets, fighting for the best spot on the sand or the last umbrella at Grisham's General Store, determined to get everything they wanted and more out of this summer vacation. It made me glad I lived in San Francisco.

My mother's words weighed heavily on my mind. And

then there was the matter of whatever Grandpa wanted to talk about. I couldn't shake the bad feeling brewing and wished I could avoid the conversation. It felt like genie-in-the-bottle syndrome—once released, there was no stuffing whatever it was back inside.

I hadn't realized I'd been manically winding my long hair around my fingers until Grandpa glanced over. "How you doing, doll?" he asked. "You're going to rip your hair out of your head."

Self-conscious, I let my hands drop to my lap. "I'm fine," I said, forcing a note of cheer into my voice. I turned to look out the window so he couldn't see my liar's face. Grandpa was a human lie detector. I wanted to pour a glass of wine, grab a good book, and curl up under the covers. Then I'd be fine.

"What do you want to do tonight? I mean, after we chat," I said, keeping my tone light. "Clue? Or an Audrey Hepburn movie?" Audrey was our favorite. "Or we could have a reading session."

Since I was a kid Grandpa and I had had a tradition of reading to each other. He'd been a book fiend his entire life and passed the love on to me. Grandpa's house had the perfect place for cozy reading nights—a turret-shaped nook at the end of the second-floor hallway, with a full-length window overlooking the sea. Years ago when my parents and I lived in that house, before my sisters were born, Grandpa had installed a window seat for two and added built-in bookshelves on either side. We'd spent the early morning hours there every day, Grandpa reading Curious George and Danny and the Dinosaur to me when I was young, graduating to Nancy Drew, the Hardy Boys, and Trixie Belden mysteries as I got older. When I'd come home from college we'd read nonfiction together, an eclectic mix of everything from *The Diary of Anne Frank* to *Walden* to *The Autobiography of Malcolm X*.

"I'd love to," he said. "But I bet you'll fall asleep ten minutes in."

"I will not," I said, pretending outrage. We both knew he was right. Especially if we were reading in the nook—it was so comfy and cozy.

We turned onto Grandpa's street and I turned my attention to the change in energy. Shoreline Avenue was the busiest street outside of the downtown radius because of the ferry dock. Here, people jammed the sidewalks. The diehard island visitors weren't wasting any time getting to their vacations.

Grandpa lived across the street and down a quarter mile in a prime corner lot—the best location on the island, he claimed. He loved to watch the ferries belching out their passengers from his third-floor balcony. Heck, he loved being in the center of all the action. And Daybreak Harbor was the place to be, catering to the boatloads of tourists, with trolleys waiting to whisk visitors away on forty-dollar-an-hour narrated excursions, plentiful food, and high-priced boutiques fighting for storefronts.

He pulled into the driveway of his sunny yellow Victorian-style house with red trim. It looked the same as it had twenty years ago, albeit with some wear and tear. The house had originally been a dull olive color, but my grandma had insisted on upgrading to something "fun and welcoming." Grandpa had agreed, but with one condition—no pink or purple. They'd both fallen in love with the yellow. It complemented the architecture perfectly—the rounded rooms facing the street, the A-frame accent over the front door, the wraparound porch on the side facing the ocean. Two stone lions sat on either side of the front steps. When I was little, Grandpa and I used to sit on them and pretend we were riding into battle.

I followed him into the house. His movements were slow, almost painful. Once inside, he put the teakettle on.

"I got you potato chips," he said without turning. "And pumpkin pie."

"Aww, Grandpa." I felt a little misty-eyed. Those were our traditional snacks, mostly driven by my longtime obsession for potato chips and anything pumpkin. We had them every time I came home. Sometimes when we get especially silly, we crumble up the potato chips and sprinkle them on top of the pie. I suspected Grandpa thought it was disgusting, but he did it. For me. And even in the chaos of the last few weeks, he'd taken the time to get "our" snacks. "Thanks." I hoped my voice sounded normal. "We can have them in a bit." I leaned against the counter and waited for him to finish fiddling with the teapot. "So what's going on?" The suspense was killing me. "Is everything okay? Does this conversation have to do with that guy at the cemetery?"

Grandpa turned around to look at me. I couldn't quite read the expression on his face, but I didn't like it. "Yeah. Frank O'Malley. He wants me to sell my house."

Chapter 4

My mouth fell open. Whatever I'd been expecting, it wasn't that. I snapped it shut and frowned. "Sell your house? Why on earth would you do something like that? It's been in our family for generations." Grandpa's great-great-grandfather, Theodore Mancini, had built it by hand. It had more longevity on this island than the famous beach-front carousel down at Daybreak Harbor Town Beach, which had been around pretty much forever. "Maybe you misunderstood him?" I heard my mother's words in my head again but they sounded more ominous now on the replay. Was Grandpa confused?

Grandpa shook his head slowly. "No," he said. "I most definitely didn't misunderstand."

"Grandpa," I said, trying to keep my voice reasonable. "Why would he think you'd sell your house? I'm sure Frank doesn't want to live here. He has his own house, doesn't he?"

Grandpa scoffed. "Of course he does. He doesn't want to live here. He wants my land. The location. Believe me, I don't want to, Maddie," he said, winding the string of his tea bag around his finger so tightly I worried he'd cut off the circulation. "I've been . . . having some hard times.

Unfortunately, Frank found out about them. He's got a knack for that."

"Wait." I held up a hand, trying to process what he was telling me. Frank didn't actually want the house—just the location? What in the world for? "What kind of hard times?" If Grandpa was in trouble and he'd kept it from me because I was away, I'd never forgive myself.

"Your grandmother's medical costs were extensive, even with our insurance. That long in a nursing home . . ." He sighed. "And the house is old, Maddie. It needs a lot of work. More so now than ever before, it seems. You know the saying. When it rains, it pours. I needed to upgrade my electrical. The central air conditioning stopped working. My roof is leaking. Then there's all the regular maintenance. I do what I can, but it's a lot." Grandpa looked at me, his eyes watery. "It's a million things at once and I . . . can't afford it."

The kettle started a long, low whistle, adding to the sudden pounding behind my eyes. I'd anticipated an unpleasant conversation, but this bypassed unpleasant and went straight to nightmare. I could only imagine how the medical costs had derailed him. Grandma had spent the last six months of her life in a full-care facility—the best on the island. Grandpa wouldn't have it any other way. My father was the CEO of the Daybreak Island Hospital, so I wasn't naïve. I knew bills like that could drown a person, even someone with a decent pension who'd lived a fiscally responsible life. But how could it happen to Grandpa with no one noticing?

"Why didn't you tell someone?" I asked, at a loss for words.

He sniffed. "I'm seventy-four, Maddie. I shouldn't need someone to bail me out at my age." He looked disgusted at the thought. The kettle's whistle rose to a high-pitched scream, and he turned the stove off and poured the boiling water into our mugs.

I studied him while he made our drinks. The last time I'd been home was nine months ago. He looked a lot different now. His full head of thick, white hair—his trademark—had yellowed with age. He felt lighter next to me, as if the bulk of his muscle and his height had started to fade. An older, tired man had taken over his face. He looked more like his seventy-four years than I'd ever noticed before. Misery had certainly converged in this house, and the outlook was turning more bleak every day. I'd seen it in him and chalked it up to Grandma's illness and, ultimately, her death. I should've realized there was more to it.

"Everyone needs help sometimes," I reminded him gently. "What about Mom and Dad? Mom would never want to think about you not having the house. Or a home equity loan? Or Valerie?" My middle sister had married into one of the wealthiest families on the island. "The Tanners are lawyers, for goodness' sake. Even if they are cheap, they wouldn't turn down an opportunity to 'help' extended family so they can brag to everyone about it."

I had to hold my nose with the suggestion. I wasn't crazy about my sister's husband. Cole Tanner was one of those privileged boys posing as a man, riding on Daddy's coattails. Daddy was Erik Tanner, one of the top defense attorneys in the state. He'd defended some of the area's most notorious criminals, including members of Whitey Bulger's gang. Cole did have enough brains to pass the bar exam, and I guess he was good to my sister, but she could've done a lot better. But Val had a hard time thinking out of the box, so Cole had been a natural choice.

I suspected Grandpa felt the same way about Cole. He shook his head vehemently. "No. I don't want your parents or your sisters to know about my financial issues," he said, sounding like his fierce old self again. "I only told you because you're a problem solver, not so you would worry. And it's not about a loan. It's not just the money, Maddie. That just makes it an easier pitch. Frank wants this property. He has it all planned out. He came to me last week, right after your grandmother . . ." He wiped his eyes and smiled ruefully. "Right when the funeral costs started piling up."

"Planned out?" I think I screeched it, but I'd finally lost my cool. "This isn't his property to have plans for!" I grabbed my mug and paced the kitchen. I think I sloshed tea in my mad march, but barely noticed. Anyone who knew this island knew this house was part of the fabric of our lives. It *was* part of the family. Thinking about any of us living on Daybreak without this house in our universe made me feel sick. "What about his wife? Wasn't Grandma tight with Margaret?"

"Yes. But this doesn't concern Margaret. She doesn't get involved in his business dealings."

"Well, we should get her involved! She can stop him, can't she?"

Grandpa shot me a look I couldn't quite decipher. "I doubt that. Once Frank makes up his mind, he's ruthless about getting his way."

Disgusted, I set my mug down on the table with a snap. "Great. So the whole island is at this guy's mercy? I don't think so. I don't know who Frank O'Malley thinks he is, but he doesn't bully this family." I punctuated every other word with a finger jabbing the air. "There are plenty of other houses and plenty of land—"

"Maddie," Grandpa said, before I could get completely hysterical. "Frank has connections. And he can make things happen."

I paused mid-stride and turned to face Grandpa, hands

on hips. "He can make things happen, huh? Did he *threaten* you? Did he forget who you *are*? You were the police chief for nearly *twenty years*!"

"He says this property can be rezoned," Grandpa said, his voice sounding far away, echoing from the depths of despondence. "That I'd lose a lot of the current value. Eventually I'd be forced to sell and I'd get much less. That there was an amendment to the zoning bylaws—"

I could barely hear him above the fury pounding like a drum through my ears. That little weasel had threatened my grandpa to try to coerce him to sell his property. "What does he want the property for?" I asked, my voice alien to my own ears.

"His son wants to create a transportation rental center," Grandpa said, the contempt turning his tone bitter. "Cars, bikes, and mopeds. Combine them all into one and, I'm assuming, put the other people who already do those things out of business along with putting me out on the street." He looked at me, the anguish on his face ripping my heart to shreds. "Maddie, I'm at a loss. He's already started a campaign about how living in this house alone without your grandmother will ruin me. How I'm getting *older*. His talk's already reached your mother. She asked me if I'd ever thought about moving in with her. I can't lose this house. I can't fail my family."

My heart hurt for him. "Fail us?" I asked, going over and placing my hand on his back. "How could you ever think that?"

He spread his arms wide. "If I can't keep the house she loved? The house that every generation in my family took better care of than the last?" He shook his head, and I could see the self-loathing in his eyes. "My father was right. He always said that being a policeman was a noble profession, but that it wouldn't feed us caviar and steak."

My great-grandfather, who'd been a successful stone-mason. I hadn't known him, but I hated him at that moment. "Who wants to eat caviar anyway? Or steak for that matter? Gross." I leaned down and hugged him. "Grandpa. You were the best chief of police ever. And you're the best grandpa ever. You've never failed anyone—certainly not Grandma or any of us."

"I don't want to start now," he said. "Maddie, I don't want to leave my house. Can you help me save it?"

Chapter 5

Sun and brilliant blue skies welcomed me when I woke Saturday morning. I spent a few minutes staring at the ceiling in the room I'd lived in until I was nine. When my parents told me we were moving to our own house in Duck Cove, I'd cried and asked if I could stay with Grandpa and Grandma.

I had the best room. Not the biggest but the coolest, with its slanted ceilings, nooks and crannies, and best of all, an entire wall that Grandpa had converted into a bookcase. Many of my books were still here, at least the ones I couldn't fit into my suitcase when I'd left for college. I took a minute, running my fingers over their spines: *Little Women*, *A Separate Peace*, *Of Mice and Men*, *Go Ask Alice*. Books that had all, at one time or another, been read in the book nook right around the corner, under the special string of white lights Grandpa made sure wound around the inside of the window most of the year. He only removed them during the holidays, when he swapped them out for my favorite holiday treatments—orange lights at Halloween; a tiny tree, colored lights, and snowflakes at Christmas; red lights for Valentine's Day.

I could spend days curled up there with my favorite

blanket. Even now, after years of living on my own and creating my own sacred spaces, that nook still symbolized comfort, home, and family. I felt another surge of anger, followed by despair, at the thought of never reading a book there again. Of losing that sense of home to a person so disconnected with being human that they'd cause an already defeated person even more misery so they could turn a profit. Of someone selling out their so-called friend.

Those were the thoughts fueling my fire when I marched into La Rosetta a few hours later. The restaurant served the best Italian food in the Harbor, but I wasn't thinking about eating today. I'd called Frank O'Malley and asked him—no, actually I'd told him—to meet me there for lunch. He'd tried to decline at first.

"As much as I'd love to catch up, my dear, tonight is the chamber's Food Stroll," he'd said in that Irish brogue. "I'll be needing to spend time making sure everything's set up right. It's our biggest event, you know."

I persisted. In the end, I think he agreed out of curiosity, or perhaps he saw it as a game. Watch the pathetic granddaughter beg for mercy for her grandfather. It made me more determined to thwart his efforts.

I hadn't told Grandpa my plans. In fairness, I hadn't known what to do. I'd promised him I'd do whatever it took to save his house, then went upstairs and spent a sleepless night tossing and turning, looking for a brilliant idea.

This was the best I could come up with on short notice. I felt like a fraud. Grandpa thought I was so smart, but I was good at business planning, not thwarting-evil-schemes planning. I scanned the already half-full dining area for a glimpse of O'Malley.

"Can I help you?" the polite, young hostess inquired. She had long black curls, the kind of hair you'd see on models. I'd been blessed with great hair—long, thick, wavy, reddish-brown—but hers managed to make me a little jealous.

"I'm meeting Frank O'Malley," I said.

"Right this way." She tossed a curl over her shoulder and led me to a booth in the back of the restaurant. Frank looked like he'd been there a while, given his nearly empty wine glass. The hostess placed a menu in front of me and promised that Shakira would be right over to take our orders. Frank winked at her and she retreated, blushing. I successfully subdued an eye roll.

He turned his attention to me and smiled, motioning for me to sit. He hadn't risen from his chair. True gentleman.

"Madalyn," he said. "Good to see you again. How's everyone holding up without your gran?"

"It's Maddie. We're surviving," I said, my voice clipped. Shakira the waitress, a blonde whose arms were more toned than Serena Williams's, appeared at my elbow, her peppy smile dimming a notch when she saw the look on my face.

"Welcome!" she said. "Can I get you something to drink?"

I ordered a sparkling water with lime. Frank asked for another glass of wine. Shakira rattled off the specials then scurried away to give us time to decide.

Frank took the small-talk route. "Lovely day," he said. "Will you be at the Food Stroll tonight?"

"I will," I said. "Looking forward to it." Despite my current feelings about Frank, I loved the Food Stroll, where Bicycle Street, our main drag, was transformed into an endless food and beverage heaven. Local restaurants and bars occupy nearly seventy tents and offer tastings of special dishes or drinks. They did it twice every year, spring and fall. An island tradition, it had improved every year and now accounted for a good portion of tourist revenue. Becky and I had plans to eat our way through every single tent.

"Good," Frank said. "That's the chamber's signature event. You remember—your family's always been involved. Your grandpa is volunteering again."

He waited, but I said nothing else. Knowing my ten bucks was going to go to his organization made me want to reconsider my attendance, but I probably shouldn't say that.

"So. This was a nice surprise. What's on your mind?" he asked.

I leaned forward, cutting to the chase. "I think you know. But here's the deal. My grandfather is not selling his house to you."

Frank's eyebrows rose, then he chuckled. "Oh, Madalyn. I'm afraid that's your granddad's business." He sipped his wine again, his eyes doing a quick scan of the room. No doubt seeking out the waitress for the refill. "Did he send you here to talk to me?"

"No one sent me," I said. "He told me what you wanted to do. He doesn't want to do it. So I'm here to ask you to leave him alone."

Frank gazed at me over his glass. "Look, my dear. Leo's a smart man. He's starting a new chapter in his life. He doesn't need a big house like that dragging him down. He's been telling me about all the renovations that need doing. Unwieldy, for an older man who just lost his wife. And the location." He made a dismissing motion with his hand. "Us older gents don't need to hear all that noise. Screaming kids, arguing tourists, the ferries chugging in and out of the harbor. He'd be much happier in a quieter place. Like with your mother."

"Have you met my grandfather?" I asked, incredulous. "He loves his location. It fits him. More than that, he loves that house. It's been in his family—our family—forever. His family built it. Look," I continued, leaning forward on the table, the illusion of meeting him halfway. "Why don't you go ask the Murdochs if you really want property on that side of town? They're right down the street. I think their lot might be bigger than Grandpa's. And they want to get off the island. Jane Murdoch told Grandpa that just the other day."

A buzzing sounded. We both looked down. Frank's phone vibrated on the table. He hit a button to silence it and returned his attention to me. The distraction gave him the chance to mask his annoyance, but I saw a lingering flicker across his face.

Good. I was getting to him.

He adjusted his glasses. When he spoke, his Irish accent came through more strongly, another hint at his attempts to keep calm. Or his increasing drunkenness. He smiled, condescending. "Maddie, love. With all due respect, you haven't the first idea of what it takes to run a business on this island. The company I'm advising—"

I resisted the urge to point out I was not his love. "Yes. Your son's company, isn't that right?" I smiled, folding my hands together on the table. "What are they called again?"

Frank's smile vanished, but he ignored my comment—and my question. "The company has received advice from people who understand the needs of that industry, as well as location dos and don'ts. It's more complicated than sentimentality."

His condescending tone made my ears bleed. He may as well have patted me on the head, called me a little lady, and told me not to worry myself about something the men can handle.

"Plus," Frank continued, "you don't even live here, Maddie. Really, what does it matter to you? It's not like you'll give up your West Coast life to move back to Daybreak, even if someone handed you your granddad's house free and clear."

Shakira approached with a tray. She deposited the wine,

my water, and a basket of Sal's renowned garlic bread on the table then retreated. Frank sipped, savoring the wine, then smiled again.

I didn't want to pull the threat card—it felt too early—but he was doing a great job pushing all my buttons. "You know, Frank," I said, taking a sip of my water, "you're right about one thing. I've never run a business here on Daybreak. But I run a business in San Francisco. A place that has more competition than you could ever dream of. And my business is doing quite well." I set my glass down and returned his stare. "And my address has nothing to do with the fact that you're trying to throw around weight that you don't really have. I mean, who threatens the former chief of police and actually thinks they can get away with it?"

I guessed he'd thought Grandpa would leave that part out when he told me the story. Frank gripped his knife, his knuckles turning white with the effort. He managed to catch himself, but I'd seen his face pale and his jaw slacken as he tried to figure out how to respond.

He was good, I had to give him that. It took him less than a minute to recover. Frank sipped his fresh wine, smacked his lips. When he spoke again, he blew his sickly sweet wine breath at me. I tried not to recoil. "Your grandfather must have misinterpreted our conversation," he said smoothly. "But that's not surprising, given the . . . challenges he's been having lately."

"Challenges?" I asked skeptically. "What challenges are those?"

He sighed. "Of course he wouldn't have mentioned that to you. I'm sorry, my dear. Your granddad seems to be failing somewhat, especially in the memory department. Truthfully, I worry about him alone there. Even simple things relating to tonight's event that he used to do with his eyes closed, well, I'm afraid he's having trouble with."

I felt like he could see the smoke coming out of my ears. It all made sense now—my mother's concerns, the rumors about Grandpa being "not quite right." It went beyond simple hints that Grandpa wouldn't do well alone there. Frank was creating doubts about his well-being. Another tool in his arsenal to get the property. Drop enough comments to enough people, and word would get around. "My grandfather," I said through clenched teeth, "is not failing. And if I find out you're spreading that around, I'll have you sued for slander." Or was it libel? I could never remember. I'd have to ask Becky. Being best friends with the editor of the local paper had its perks.

Frank took his glasses off and rubbed them against his tie. "The truth is hard. I understand," he said. "But—" He held up his hand to ward off my next verbal onslaught. "I simply told him about the change to zoning laws that would permit that area to become a commercial lot." He shrugged. "It isn't a threat, my dear. It's a fact. I'm trying to help him get as much as he can in the face of a changing island culture. People don't want houses. They want industry. Jobs."

Shakira chose that moment to return. "Are we ready to order?" she chirped.

I smiled at her, sure my face resembled a glass mask that looked about to shatter. "I'll have a glass of merlot." My voice sounded shockingly normal.

"Excellent choice. Our house merlot is delightful. Something to eat?"

"No, thank you." If I had to sit here and actually try to choke food down in front of this man, I'd poke my eyes out with my fork.

Frank ordered spaghetti bolognese. Clearly this conversation wasn't ruining his appetite. I used the time to compose myself by taking a bite of garlic bread. Sal baked the best garlic bread in the entire world. It had just the right amount of garlic—a lot. Crusty on the outside, moist in the middle, buttered just right. Heaven. Too bad I felt sick to my stomach and could barely taste it.

Still, I forced the bite down, then focused on Frank again. He smoothed his thinning gray hair over the crown of his head and adjusted his chair, a smug smile tugging at his lips. I could hear his thoughts: *Checkmate!* Well, he'd underestimated his opponent.

"I'm not as dumb as I look, Frank," I said calmly. "And I know for a fact people want houses with ocean views. That house, needed repairs and all, is worth a fortune. Anyway, I have a meeting set up with Gil Smith." A fib, but the town selectman, also a good friend of my dad's, would get a call from me before the weekend was over. "If I have to, I'll meet with the zoning board. And an attorney. And the editor of the *Chronicle,* who happens to be my best friend. You know Becky Walsh, right?" I smiled. "I'm sure all those people would be interested in your tactics to get a pillar of our community to sell his house at a discount so your son can start up a business. I'm sure your board wouldn't look too kindly on it either." I picked up the wineglass Shakira set down and took a gulp, leaning forward so Frank wouldn't miss a word I said. "You won't mess with my family. Stay away from my grandfather, and stay away from his house. Or you'll regret it."

I stood up, jostling the table in the process. Frank's wine sloshed over the side of his glass and onto the cuff of his suit jacket. He jumped back in his chair, grabbing a napkin to dab at the spot.

"Have a great Food Stroll," I said, and strode out, leaving him to pick up the tab for my wine.

Chapter 6

I left the restaurant, still riding high on adrenaline and feeling smug even though I wasn't sure if what I'd said had changed anything. Frank would probably use his version of the conversation to tell anyone who would listen how aggressive I was, how crazy the Mancini-James clan could be. I'd probably given him greater motivation to go after Grandpa's house.

I squared my shoulders and marched away in case Frank watched out a window. As the rush wore off I tried to force my mind to quiet so I could think, but the town had already succumbed to the frenetic energy preceding a big event. The chaos contributed to my frantic stream of thoughts. I had to make good on my threats—call Gil, tell Becky, call the zoning officer. Cut this guy off at the knees. I walked fast, head down, lost in my mental list, until I turned the corner where Ocean Avenue ran parallel to Bicycle Street. Now I had to walk through the throngs of people setting up for tonight's festivities in order to get, well, anywhere. Police barriers were already in place. Most of the tents were up and people rushed around stocking them with cooking and warming paraphernalia, foil-covered food, bottles of liquor. Half-hung signs tormented their installers. Curse words floated past me on the ocean breeze. I moved out of the way seconds before a folding table hip-checked me.

I ducked out of the fray, slipping behind the tents to walk between the Dumpsters, trash cans, and tangle of extra supplies where I wouldn't get clocked. Or be noticed. Grandpa would be out here in this crowd volunteering. I wasn't ready to see him yet. He'd immediately see something was wrong, and I didn't want to explain. And I didn't want to give Frank O'Malley so much attention. After all, what could he really do? The property wasn't his. He could threaten all he wanted. He had no power over anything.

But fear had returned, and it churned in my gut. What if he did? Between his chamber career and his earlier political career, he knew everyone on the island. And both positions required major sucking-up abilities. The chamber of commerce was largely funded by local businesses, and in a unique setting like this island, he needed to make sure he had the biggest moneymakers—the potential benefactors—squarely in his pocket. Otherwise he wouldn't survive.

I mentally ticked off a list of influencers with whom Frank probably rubbed elbows: Saul Grayson, the yacht club owner, reportedly the richest man on the island; Lourdes Vaughn, owner of the country club with its fancy golf course, function rooms, and restaurant; Gareth Ward, who ran the construction company that built all the celebrity mansions that had popped up in the last decade. If that were true, Ward might even beat out Saul Grayson as the richest man in town and simply kept it undercover. Then there were the politicians, plus the others who flew below the obvious influencer radar—the owner of the private tour business on the island that catered to the rich, the woman who ran the jazz club in Turtle Point and owned clubs across the country, the guy who ran a network of seafood restaurants across the island.

I'd had enough experience out West with people like Frank to know they followed the money. In return, they got favors. Obviously it was smart to keep powerful people close. It also made sense to stay on the good side of the police, but Grandpa wasn't active with the police anymore. He represented someone who *used* to be in power—still deserving of respect, but not at the top of the priority list when you were thinking about surviving and thriving. Maybe I was reaching, thinking any of these people cared that much about Grandpa's property or Frank's ambitions, but I wasn't naïve enough to think alliances like this weren't built to make people's lives miserable. And even though it seemed like this had nothing to do with the chamber and was only about Frank's son, his connections would still come in handy to help him get what he wanted.

But Frank's personal financial situation also had to be considered. I didn't know the O'Malleys' net worth, but figured they were doing well. Could he pay someone off to do something underhanded and take Grandpa's house away if he declined to sell? Would he jeopardize his professional standing doing so, or would anyone even care?

My head hurt. Contrary to what Frank thought, this wasn't *just a house*. It had been my home for a while, when I was little. A real home, one with a foundation built on love. And once my parents had built their own house, it had been my second home.

This was an impossible situation, and I had no idea what to do. My next thought left me cold: *What if I couldn't figure this out?* Then *I'd* be the one who failed Grandpa. And I wouldn't be able to live with myself if that happened.

I walked aimlessly with no destination in mind, turning down streets randomly, each one bringing with it a childhood memory. Like Shore Avenue, where our old baseball field had been before they developed the area into some of the largest homes on the island. Instead of parents crowding around watching games, tourists now crowded the streets gawking at the houses, snapping iPhone photos and videos, hoping to catch a glimpse of Beyoncé or whichever celebrity had decided this was the cool place to be for the summer.

My subconscious directed me a few more blocks to the gates of the Sea Breeze Cemetery. Brushing away fresh tears, I made my way to my grandmother's brand-new plot. It looked different today without so many people around. Lonely. The freshly dug patch of earth that grass, and eventually snow, would cover, would soon be distinguishable only by the headstone that hadn't been finished yet.

I sank down in the grass and stared at the grave. I wasn't religious. If anyone asked, my parents would tell you they were Catholic, but the only time they saw the inside of a church was for a funeral. My sisters and I had never taken an interest either. We'd all followed our own spiritual path, which meant we didn't do much. My grandparents had been more prone to bouts of religion, like most people of their generation. There was space in the cemetery for Grandpa Leo, my parents, and my aunt Gail. I supposed there was a place for me and my sisters too, if we wanted it.

I sat for a long time, but no great revelation came to me. I needed some help. I focused on the fresh dirt covering what used to be my grandma. "People are trying to get Grandpa to sell the house!" I blurted out, then immediately felt foolish. I looked around, but I was alone.

No one answered me. I figured I'd continue the conversation anyway.

"He doesn't want to," I told her. "He asked me to help him. I have no idea what I should do, but I promise—" I broke off when I saw out of my peripheral vision two brilliant green eyes staring at me. Their gaze was familiar, and I felt a thrill of excitement. I turned slowly and there, sitting next to a stone a few feet away, was the orange cat who'd attended the services yesterday. I knew because of his folded-over ear. He didn't run away this time.

Still, I spoke softly. "Hello," I said.

He stared at me.

"It's nice to see you again," I told him.

He squeaked. The sound seemed odd coming from such a big cat. I cocked my head. "Was that really you?"

He glared at me. A warning: *Don't make fun of my voice.* I held up a hand in defense. "Sorry. You look tough. I'm sure you are tough. The squeak doesn't go with that persona. But hey, it's all good."

He squeaked again and came over to rub against my leg. I stroked his ginger fur. Softer than I'd expected for a street cat who hung out in a graveyard. He wore no collar. I glanced at my grandmother's grave again. Was this a sign? My grandma had always loved cats. But what was she trying to tell me?

I wasn't a big woo-woo type, but I couldn't deny the timing. I stood cautiously, hoping I wouldn't scare him off. "So, you want to hang out?" I asked him. "Becky and I are going to the Food Stroll tonight."

He blinked. I took that as a yes. "Well, come on then," I said. I didn't have an answer about the house, but for right now it didn't matter. Winging a silent thank-you to my grandma across worlds, I turned to go. The cat followed me out of the cemetery and down the street.

Chapter 7

I didn't want my new friend to feel pressured, so I didn't smother him as we walked. I kept a few feet in front of him. No coaxing, no cajoling. But he stuck with me like we'd been walking together every day for years. We turned into Seaside Park on our way downtown when an arm was slung around my shoulder. A voice purred in my ear, " 'And the cat will mew and the dog will have his day.' "

I turned, breaking into a smile. The man who stood behind me wore leopard-print clothing from his fedora all the way to his boots. Leopard Man, our island enigma. He'd been around as long as the cranberry bogs, but no one knew his real name. I'd taken to calling him that because as a kid I'd equated him with a superhero. He wore a tail sometimes—special days, I guessed. He also wore kickin' leopard boots, which I suspected were Louboutins.

I remembered pulling his fake tail once as a kid, when my father and I had run into him out in the park. My father had been horrified. Leopard Man had been amused. We became friends after that. Some people thought he was homeless. Others thought he was crazy. I wasn't sure about the homeless part, but I didn't think he was crazy. I thought he had a story and I'd love to hear it. I was surprised he recognized me. I hadn't seen him for the better part of a decade.

He swept off his hat and bowed at the waist. *"Hamlet,"* he said.

"Yes, that one I know," I said, proud of myself. I wasn't a Shakespeare scholar, but certain lines from certain plays could stir a memory even in an economics girl like me. Leopard Man spoke mainly in Shakespeare, which added to his endearing quirkiness.

"The wheel is come full circle," he said. "You are here."

King Lear, a variation. The original quote was *"I* am here." I knew that one too, even though *King Lear* hadn't been my favorite. "Just visiting," I said. "My grandma passed away."

He nodded. "I know. My condolences."

So Leopard Man kept up with the obituaries. "Thank you," I said.

He nodded at the cat, who'd stopped when I did and sat next to me. "Who's your friend?"

"He . . . doesn't have a name yet. We just met."

Leopard Man studied him. "May I pet him? He looks like my kind."

"Of course."

He got down to the cat's level, talking softly. He certainly revered cats. Maybe he wanted to be one. He seemed especially enamored with the cat's sleek tail. I smothered a giggle. Tail envy?

He finished petting my new friend and straightened. "Those who love cats have a special place in heaven," he said, tipping his fedora at me. "Tell Leo I said hello." Then he turned and walked off down the street, whistling. I was delighted to see he wore his tail today. It swung with every step.

Leopard Man was on a first-name basis with Grandpa. Who knew. I continued on, reaching the *Daybreak Island*

Chronicle offices just after five. The newspaper had a prominent position at the far end of Ocean Avenue near the police station and town offices. Becky waited outside, texting furiously on her phone. I surveyed the old brick building behind her while I waited for her to finish. It looked the same as I remembered, even down to the faded wooden sign over the door.

"Remember riding bikes here when we were little so you could pretend you were going to work?" I hadn't realized I'd spoken out loud until Becky looked up and laughed.

"Totally. Remember the time I made my mom come and take my picture near the sign for a press pass?" She sighed. "Those were the days."

"And now you're the big shot. Got a window seat yet?" I asked.

Still texting, Becky smirked. "Yeah, right. The city editors don't get anything but more work. If I'd known that when they offered me the promotion, I might've said no."

"I doubt it. You've wanted to run this paper since you were ten," I said.

She looked up and grinned. "Damn right. It's a thankless job, but I love it."

Not only did she love it, but she rocked the job. Becky could've gone anywhere to work and been successful, but she was an islander for life. Partly because of her dedication to her mom, who'd raised her as a single parent, but mostly because she simply loved it here.

"Did you know a cat's following you?" she asked, noticing my companion.

"Yup." I glanced down. Orange Guy sat at my feet like I'd leashed him there. "He was in the cemetery yesterday. And today when I went back. Guess he decided he wanted to be friends."

She tucked a springy blond curl behind her ears. Becky

looked like a walking American Girl doll—blond, blue-eyed, perfect pale skin. We'd always been complete opposites in the looks department. I had the dark hair and olive-toned skin, thanks to Grandpa's family. She was taller too. I didn't care much about that. I wore heels enough that my five-foot-three-inch frame suited me fine.

"Still the cat whisperer, eh? He coming to the Food Stroll?" she asked.

"Hey, I never plan it," I said, innocent. "They always come to me. He's been invited to the stroll, and I don't think he has other plans."

The cat squeaked at us. Becky raised an eyebrow. I shook my head. "Don't," I said. "He'll get mad."

I've had two very apparent talents since I was a kid. The first is entrepreneurial. At age eight, I raided my mother's makeup cabinet and convinced Becky to do the same. We created a sign with the moniker MJ MAKEUP (short for my name, Maddie James, since I came up with the idea) and sold the goods to ladies arriving on the ferry. We made $436 in three hours, before my mom found us and put the kibosh on our little venture. Unfortunately, we had to donate our proceeds to our moms' new makeup fund.

My second talent is communing with cats. I'd been born an animal rescuer and had put my talents to good use over the years with dogs, rabbits, possums, chickens. Once, a raccoon who wasn't grateful for the assistance. But cats had always been my weakness. I'd done in-the-trenches cat rescue up until a year ago when the juice bar opened.

"Like I said. You're the cat whisperer. So you ready to roll? We might as well get in line early." She tucked her phone in her pocket. "You know how long the wait can be." The Food Stroll opened at six, but the lines would reach all the way to the ferry docks if you waited until then to buy tickets.

"Sounds good. I'm starving." I realized I was, despite

the day's events. Maybe food would help me figure this out. Or Becky. Or both. "After the stroll want to go have a drink? I have a story."

"Oooh." Her eyes twinkled. "A publishable one?"

I considered that. "Maybe at some point," I said.

"Really." She studied my face. I tried to keep it neutral. "No hint?"

"No. I'll tell you later. It's not really a conversation for the side of the road."

She frowned but let it go.

"Are you covering the stroll?" I asked as we started walking.

"My features reporter is. With photo and video. Readers love video—especially of food." She rolled her eyes. "Exciting stuff, those cupcake close-ups."

We walked down Ocean Avenue and turned onto a side street that emptied out onto the main drag. I was surprised to see tents and barriers here too.

"They expanded the stroll area this year," Becky said when I asked. "Mostly because they wanted to separate the alcohol tents from the *family area*." She emphasized the words with air quotes. "People complained last year. The ones who can't accept the island's not dry anymore. So this side street and the next one have the booze." Her phone dinged again as we reached the corner where our street intersected with the real chaos. "Sorry," she said, fishing it out of her pocket and stepping out of the line of traffic heading down the sidewalk while she answered.

I moved over too, the cat sticking to me like glue. The number of people multiplied the closer we got to the action, from the setup crews to the vendors to the people scurrying to get a spot in line. The cat sat at my feet, surveying everyone who passed. I did the same, counting the familiar faces from behind the safety of my oversized sunglasses. I saw Grandpa farther down the street carrying a

box, evident by the red pants that had become his trademark at community events. He led a small group of people
and resembled the Pied Piper.

I knew nearly one out of every three people in some
capacity. There was Lilah Gilmore, resident socialite and
town gossip. Colin Hardy, who owned Death by Chocolate,
balanced a tray of fudge over his head. Pauline Crosby, island fixture and owner of the old-time coffee shop, hurried
by with two carafes of coffee. Gil Smith, first selectman and
the man at the top of my to-do list, strode by while deep
in conversation with a younger man I didn't recognize.
Seeing Gil jolted me back to the Frank/Grandpa dilemma,
but it would be bad form to corner him here.

Becky finished her conversation and pocketed her
phone. "Okay. You'd think this was rocket science or something," she said. "Go get a story about people eating. God,
I need a drink."

She started to walk again but I stood frozen, realizing
Orange Guy wasn't at my feet. Panicked, I looked to my
right and my left but saw no sign of him. "Oh, no," I cried.

"What?" Becky stopped and looked at me quizzically.

"The cat . . . he's gone!" I spun around, desperate to get
a glimpse of him. I didn't want him to take off. I already
felt like he was mine. Then I saw it: the tip of an orange
tail disappearing through one of the metal barriers keeping street traffic from wandering into the stroll without a
ticket. He'd snuck in on the bar side from the side street. I
hoisted myself over the barrier and tried to follow him, but
he'd already escaped my line of sight.

"Maddie," Becky called, but I ignored her and burst into
the nearest tent. The Four-Leaf Clover, an Irish pub. The
lone bartender slicing fruit looked at me, startled.

"We're not open yet. And tickets are that way," he said,
pointing.

I ignored him and raced to the next tent. Empty. The

bar tents were like mini ghost towns this early in the evening, set up with their liquor bottles, plastic cups, and freshly cut lemons and limes. The proprietors had less setup to do than the people actually hauling and overseeing fresh food, so they'd likely gone out to get early samples before the crowds rushed in.

The next two were also empty. Feeling frantic, I hurried to the last one on the side street before it emptied out into the park on the opposite side of the stroll. Jade Moon, a newish bar in the Harbor. I looked around. Empty of people, but from under the white tablecloth covering the makeshift bar, I saw the tip of the orange tail.

Relief flooded my bones and I dropped to my knees. "Hey, Orange Guy!" I called, feeling stupid, but he had no name yet. I made a smooching sound. He didn't budge. I could see his tail twitching. I moved closer and pulled back the tablecloth to see what the cat was doing, hoping he hadn't stolen a steak or something. And stopped, horrified, frozen to the ground, oblivious to the gravel grinding into my knees.

Behind the bar, well out of sight unless you were crawling on the ground like me, lay Frank O'Malley, head on his side so he stared right at me. And if the ice pick lodged in his back and his wide-open, unseeing eyes were any indication, he was seriously dead.

Chapter 8

"There was hardly anyone around," I said. *Anyone alive, anyway.* "Well, inside the bar area. There were plenty of people on the main street."

Officer Craig Tomlin of the Daybreak Harbor Police Department frowned at that. He'd been the first on the scene. He'd also been my high school boyfriend, which made this extra weird. Although he looked a lot different from high school. His face had thinned out and he had muscles now. His shoulders had broadened. He had biceps, even. Big ones. His hair was better too, not too short that you couldn't tell it was thick and blond and wavy. I forced my attention back to his face as he started firing questions.

"The vendors weren't around? It was almost time to open the gates."

I glared at him. "You think I'm making it up? I'd love to tell you I found someone standing over the body, believe me." I rubbed my temples, leaning against the makeshift bar in the tent next to Jade Moon. It would be a long time before I got the image of Frank's dead face out of my brain, even though I'd been removed from the area and couldn't see it—him—anymore.

Craig had escorted me away from the immediate crime

scene while the police swarmed around. He'd found me a folding chair and set it up in a nearby tent they'd commandeered. The Jade Moon tent and surrounding area had been blocked off with crime scene tape. I could see Jade Bennett, the bar owner, standing outside, white-faced. Official-looking people milled around. Someone from the medical examiner's office was here to remove the body. Crime scene techs too, although they looked nothing like the ones on TV. They'd all arrived in record time. After I'd realized what I was looking at, I'd screamed so loud I scared the cat away. Becky and a couple of the nearby vendors had come running as I scrambled out from under the table in a full on crab crawl. Someone had called the police, and everything from there was a blur.

Grandpa Leo leaned over and squeezed my knee. He'd rushed over as soon as he'd heard the ruckus, much to the responding officers' chagrin. Now he checked out the scene like he was still in charge. "You don't have to answer without a lawyer present, you know," he said.

A lawyer? Jeez. "It's okay, Grandpa," I said.

Craig immediately looked apologetic. "I'm sorry, Maddie," he said, glancing at Grandpa. "I hate to have to ask you these questions. Unfortunately you're our witness." He hesitated. "What were you doing inside the stroll area? It wasn't open yet."

Too shaken up to turn my glare into a full-on Look of Death, I settled for frowning at him, enough that he flushed. "Becky and I had come from her office around the corner. We took a shortcut down this street. The cat . . . took off through the barricade, so I followed him."

"Cat?" Craig looked around. "What cat?"

I looked around too, feeling bereft. My orange buddy still hadn't resurfaced. I remembered reading stories about cats with uncanny senses of smell who could detect imminent death. Maybe he had that talent. I blinked, trying to hold back the tears. I tried to tell myself I was crying about Frank, but honestly, I was more upset at the thought of the cat taking off. Then I immediately felt horrible. Someone was dead.

"There was a cat that followed me. He ran into the tent. I went to get him from under the table and found . . ." I shivered and looked up at Craig, searching his face for answers. "Who would've done this?"

Craig hesitated but before he said anything two other cops came into the tent, both men. One was older, lanky, bald, his nose slightly off center. He had sergeant bars on his sleeve and boots shined within an inch of their lives. The other one wore a state trooper's uniform and had a bushy mustache and the tall trooper hat.

"Tomlin," the sergeant said with a nod. "This our witness?"

"Maddie James," Craig said. "Chief Mancini's granddaughter." He inclined his chin in Grandpa Leo's direction.

Grandpa'd been silent until now. He held out his hand. "I don't believe we've met," he said. "Leopold Mancini."

"I've heard a lot about you, sir," the sergeant said, shaking his hand vigorously. "Sergeant Mick Ellory. New to the force, going on three months now."

I watched the interaction, choosing to focus on their politics rather than Frank's deadness. I could see Grandpa assessing this guy, trying on personas to see which one fit best.

"Her friend Becky Walsh called it in," Craig said into the moment of silence that followed.

Ellory's jaw set. "Walsh? From the *Chronicle*?"

Craig nodded.

"Great," Ellory said. "She get the scoop online before

you got here?" Shaking his head in disgust he turned to
Grandpa, not even acknowledging me. "Chief, we'll need
a word with your granddaughter," Ellory said.

Grandpa smiled. "She was giving Craig here a word already."

"Great. I still need to talk with her," Ellory said.

Grandpa shrugged. "Be my guest, but I'll stay." He sat
back down in the folding chair he'd pulled up next to me.

Ellory's face said he didn't love that idea, but he didn't
fight it. Having Grandpa here was probably better than a
lawyer sitting next to me. Instead, he nodded to the trooper.
"You and Tomlin can go speak to the other witness."

I presumed that meant Becky. If they had their way,
they'd keep her sequestered all night so she couldn't pub-
lish anything. I watched the trooper leave, Craig on his
heels, thankful Grandpa had stayed. As if he could read
my mind, he squeezed my hand.

Ellory waited until I'd turned my attention back to him
before he spoke. "Ms. James. How are you doing?"

My eyes inadvertently wandered outside the tent, trying to catch a glimpse of any activity. I forced them away.
"I'm fine."

"Do you need anything? Water?"

I shook my head.

"Tell me how you found the body."

I explained again about Orange Guy taking off, my barrier jumping, and subsequent discovery.

"Did you see anything out of the ordinary when you
were walking nearby? Hear anything?"

"No. It was just . . . normal. Everyone getting ready for
the stroll."

"Did you touch anything in the tent?"

"Like the body?" I asked, horrified. "God, no! I
pulled up the tablecloth to get the cat. That's when . . . I
saw him."

Ellory watched me, his face impassive. "Didn't you have a lunch meeting with O'Malley?" he asked casually.

I tried to hide my surprise. How on earth did he know that? *Stupid,* I scolded myself. That restaurant had had a dozen people in it. Grandpa stiffened next to me. "I did. Why?"

He shrugged. "Figuring out timelines, that's all. It would help to know if you were the last person to see him alive. Well, other than his killer, of course."

"No way." I shook my head. "I left him at La Rosetta hours ago. With plenty of customers and waitstaff."

"What time were you with him?"

"From twelve-thirty until about one, maybe a little after."

"You left together?" Ellory asked. "Or you left him there?"

"I left first. He was still finishing his wine." I didn't realize my comment had a derogatory edge until Ellory raised his eyebrows.

"Frank was drinking?"

"Sure. He ordered a couple of glasses of wine with lunch."

"Was he drunk?"

"I have no idea," I said. "I didn't know him well enough to know what he's like drunk."

"Were you drinking?"

"I had a few sips of the wine I ordered. I didn't finish it."

"What were you meeting about?" Ellory asked.

"A personal matter," I said. I was sure Ellory could hear my heart pounding.

Ellory frowned. "You just said you didn't know him well."

"I don't."

"Then why would you be discussing a personal matter with him?"

I felt the angry red traveling up my neck. I had no idea how to respond to that. I'd never been interrogated before. I opened my mouth but Grandpa cut in.

"Is it a crime to have lunch with someone?" he asked Ellory smoothly.

"Of course not," Ellory said.

"Then why does it matter what they talked about?"

"It doesn't, unless the conversation offers any information about how we got here," Ellory said. I could see calculations playing out over his face as he assessed Grandpa. *How much clout does this guy still have? Will I get slapped on the wrist if I throw him out?*

Before he could force me to answer, a shrill scream pierced the air. We all swiveled around to look outside the tent where Craig attempted to restrain a tall, bony woman with frizzy black hair. Things may have just gotten worse. I recognized Piper Dawes. These days, she worked as Frank O'Malley's vice president and top henchwoman at the chamber. Ten years older than me, Piper had an island-wide reputation. She'd worked in various capacities, usually high profile and for men she perceived as powerful. When I'd left the island she'd been working at the hospital in my dad's finance office. Apparently she'd seen more opportunity working for Frank.

"What do you mean? I need to see him! Frank!" Piper shrieked. I couldn't take Piper on a good day, never mind when she was in hysterics. "I told the chief something like this would happen! I told him . . ."

My head snapped up sharply at those words. She'd told the chief Frank might get killed? What on earth?

Craig spoke in low tones to her until she stopped yelling, her shrieks replaced with sniffles and sobs. Finally someone led her away.

Ellory turned back to me. "Your lunch conversation," he began curtly, obviously hoping I hadn't heard Piper's claims. But I got distracted by a rustling sound. Then Orange Guy careened into the tent and raced to me. He wound himself around my legs, purring. Relief flooded me. I reached down to pick him up, nuzzling his head with my cheek. Orange Guy settled on my lap, kneading his sharp claws into my thigh. He watched Ellory with interest.

"This the cat?" Ellory asked.

"It is." I stroked his head.

Ellory held out his hand. Orange Guy sniffed it. Ellory didn't seem impressed. "So back to Frank. Did he mention trouble with anyone? Any disagreements?"

"No," I said. Technically it was true. He didn't think he was having any trouble at all.

"What else can you tell me about your meeting? Did you leave on good terms?"

"Of course," I said, like it was the dumbest question I'd ever heard. I chose to forget about the spilled wine, my empty threat. *Stay away from my grandfather, and stay away from his house. Or you'll regret it.*

"Was he coming to the Food Stroll?"

"He said he was," I said. "It's a chamber event. He's the face of the chamber."

"He say when he was coming?"

"No," I said, then remembered the phone call he'd gotten. "He may have been meeting someone. He got a phone call when we were at lunch."

"From whom?"

I shrugged. "He didn't answer the call."

Ellory noted that in his book. "Can you think of anything else out of the ordinary?"

I shook my head. "No."

"Sounds like she's done," Grandpa Leo said.

Ellory gave us both a long look. "For now."

Satisfied, Grandpa turned to me. "Maddie, we need to get you home. You've had a day."

Still clutching the cat, I got up. I had no idea if he had any intentions of coming home with me, but I planned to force his hand.

"Before you go, Ms. James," Ellory said, "please make sure you leave us your contact information. We may have a few more questions."

"Sure, but that's all I know," I said. "I don't know what else I can help you with."

Ellory shrugged. "You never know what you may remember." He handed me his notebook so I could scrawl my cell phone number with a shaking hand. As I gave it back to him his eyes lingered on me a few seconds longer than necessary.

It hit me then, like a dive into the frigid Atlantic too early in the season. I'd been with Frank shortly before he died. We had witnesses to our ugly meeting. Then I'd found his body a few hours later. Any cop worth his or her salt would put me at the top of their suspect list.

Chapter 9

Grandpa Leo took my arm and propelled me away from the Food Stroll and the grisly scene still playing out a few feet away. Clutching Orange Guy, I tried to keep up as we hustled around the corner from which Becky and I had come hours ago, past the gawking crowd gathered on the street. I'd bet my juice bar half the island already knew Frank was the dead man in the Jade Moon tent. I scanned faces as we passed, trying to see if I could pick out a murderer. I wondered if they really did stick around at the scene of the crime like on the prime-time cop shows. But I had no idea who I'd be looking for. Who would want to kill Frank badly enough they'd stab him in the back with an ice pick on a public street, moments from a big event, in broad daylight?

I had to pick up my pace to keep up with Grandpa tugging me. He led me down a side street away from the circus, heading toward his house. I followed, too numb to protest. Finding a dead body had definitely messed with my head. In the category of firsts, discovery of a murder victim is one I'd rather have skipped.

Grandpa walked purposefully, but didn't lose sight of his surroundings. We didn't speak until we reached his house. Lights burned in the kitchen and from the upstairs hallway, a welcome sight. I didn't fully relax until we'd entered and locked the door behind us. I set the cat down. Immediately he began a sniffing tour of the kitchen, his body low to the ground as he crept around, familiarizing himself with his surroundings. We both watched him for a minute, then I sank down in a chair, trying not to cry.

"Grandpa," I said. "This is really bad."

"I know, doll," he said, grim. "I know." He put the kettle on, his movements slow and thoughtful. Or maybe it was age, starting to take its toll. I didn't like that thought and pushed it away.

"What did Piper mean, she'd told the chief something like this would happen?"

Grandpa's lips thinned. "I have no idea."

Grandpa's house phone rang, startling us both. He gazed at the cordless offender sitting on his counter, then snatched it up. "Hello. Yeah. She's fine, Sophie. She's here with me." Wordlessly he handed me the phone.

"Hi, Mom," I said, taking a deep breath.

"Maddie! I just heard," she said breathlessly. "Are you all right?"

"I'm fine. How on earth did you—"

"Lilah just called me. She said Frank is . . . *dead*?" Her voice dropped almost to a whisper on the word. "And that you . . ." She trailed off, the words hanging in the air between us. Lilah Gilmore. Daybreak's resident gossip. It figured.

"Technically, I didn't find him. The cat I found did."

My mother sucked in a breath. "How traumatizing. Is your grandfather all right? Was he there too? Brian," I heard her yell. "She's on the phone. She's fine."

I heard a rustling, then my father's voice sounding somewhat far away. They must be sharing the receiver.

"Maddie! What on earth happened? Is it true? Frank O'Malley is dead?"

I nodded. "Someone . . ." I swallowed. "Someone killed him."

My father whistled. "Murder. On Daybreak Island. My God. I can't remember . . . Sophie? Can you remember the last time something like this happened?"

"Hang on, dear, I'm leaving Samantha a message to come straight home," she told us. I could hear her pressing buttons on her cell phone. I closed my eyes and dropped my head against my hand, rubbing my temples as my mother left instructions on my sister's voice mail. She finished with, "You don't want to be out alone tonight." If that wasn't enough to freak Sam out, nothing was.

"What, dear?" she asked, returning to our call.

"Murder," my father repeated. "We haven't had a murder here in a long time, have we?"

My mother paused to think. "Well, there was the boy a few years ago. Drug deal," she said. "The culprit tried to swim off the island in the dead of night and ended up drowning. Aside from that, not in many years. People just don't do that here."

Well, they did it tonight. But it was mostly true. There were limited places to flee when you committed a serious crime on an island. If you could stay hidden long enough to melt away into a ferry crowd during a scheduled trip or get on one of the limited planes out of our tiny airport, you might have a chance. But really, you'd better have committed the perfect crime, or chances were they'd track you down.

"Mom, Dad, can I call you tomorrow?" I asked. "I . . . want to go to bed."

"Of course, honey, of course. Get some rest," my mother said. "Love you."

"Love you," my father echoed.

I assured them I loved them too, then hung up. Grandpa still fiddled with mugs and tea bags.

"What happened today?" he asked, his back still to me. "Why did you go see Frank?"

"I called him," I said slowly. How much should I tell him? I didn't want him knowing some of the ugly things Frank had said about declining home values and sentimentality, or worst of all, about Grandpa's mental state. "I figured that was the best place to start. We . . . had a discussion. It was mostly civil."

At that, Grandpa Leo turned to me. A ghost of a smile tipped his lips. "Mostly?"

I sat up straight, angry all over again. "I know he's dead and you're not supposed to talk badly about dead people, but Grandpa, what he was doing was wrong and I told him so!"

"I know, Maddie," Grandpa said. "And I can also guess some of the things Frank told you. We had a similar conversation last week. Before the funeral. That's when he decided to pull out the big guns and start talking about killing my property values."

The teakettle whistled. Grandpa took it off the stove, filled two mugs, and set one down in front of me. He passed the organic honey I'd put in his cabinet last week after a visit to the farmers' market. I added a liberal spoonful to my cup and sipped. "So you knew what he was up to," I said.

Grandpa smiled without humor. "I'm retired, Maddie, not stupid. My brain didn't go into retirement." He shook his head and sat down across from me. "O'Malley was a piece of work. There's no sugarcoating it. I wouldn't say it around town, but most people know it."

My hopes rose a bit. "They do?"

"Of course they do."

"I thought you were friends," I said. "Grandma and Margaret were."

"Margaret's a good woman," he said. "More than what Frank deserved. As for us being friends, well." He shrugged. "Sometimes, when you play a certain role in a small community, you have to play other roles too. Like keeping up friendly appearances with people you otherwise wouldn't look twice at. Frank's one of those people. He's got a reputation as a snake. But he's also got—had—enough pull that people listened to him. And he had friends in high places."

"Like how high?" I asked.

He shrugged. "High enough. Did you argue with him? Enough so people would notice and remember?"

I looked down at the table. "I was mad," I admitted. That feeling of dread curled back in my stomach. "Grandpa. You don't think the police actually suspect me, do you?"

I expected him to laugh, to chide me for asking such a stupid question. But his response was much more muted. "Of course not," was all he said.

Grandpa Leo's words had many nuances—a quirk that came from years of police work and learning how to effectively speak to different audiences. Often, a one-word answer had more depth to it than a Robert Frost poem, and I'd become adept at deciphering what he really meant. I wasn't quite sure why these three words, spoken in a very blasé voice, made me nervous.

"Craig knows me," I said with more bravado than I felt. "He's involved in the investigation." I pictured the cops at the scene, collecting evidence, talking to the reporter who'd surely showed up. I wondered if Craig still canvassed the area. I wondered if Becky would help write the story. If my name would come up.

"Craig hasn't been on the force long enough to be taken seriously," Grandpa said bluntly. "And they'll be more skeptical when they hear you were high school sweethearts."

Great. I curled my hands around my mug and stared into it. "So what now?"

He shrugged. "Nothing. If they have more questions, you answer them. They'll figure out who did this. They're good cops."

I knew they were good cops. I also knew they didn't have much experience working murders. Hopefully they'd look a lot deeper than Frank's lunch plans today, since I didn't kill him. And if Frank had some scheme going to hurt my grandpa, it wasn't a stretch to think there were other people to whom he'd been doing the same. Or worse.

Chapter 10

I barely slept at all that night. When I did I dreamt of Frank, in snippets. In the most vivid one we drank wine together in an otherwise empty restaurant. An ice bucket with an ice pick sat on the table. When I raised my glass to his for a toast it cracked and the wine seeped out, thick and red like blood.

I woke up at six A.M., my heart racing, and sat straight up in bed. I could hear Grandpa, always an early riser, moving around downstairs, the coffee maker grinding beans. Normal sounds. He must be getting ready to go out for his morning walk.

I flopped back down, the images from my dreams still fresh in my mind. I'd never look at wine the same way again. Orange Guy had draped himself over my pillow sometime in the middle of the night. It made me feel warm and fuzzy inside. Mim used to sleep on my head too. I'd missed that feeling of a purring cat curled around me. I resettled my head in the tiny space he'd left me and tried to go back to sleep, but ten minutes later I was still wide awake. I tossed and turned for another half hour and then I gave up. I wished I was across the country right now, still sound asleep in my cozy sleigh bed in my studio apartment, dreaming about a new root-vegetable juice and what band I would go see after work.

I flung the covers off and sat up, cringing at the thought of the day ahead. I tried to rewire my thoughts to positive. Maybe the police had worked all night and found Frank's killer. Or maybe whoever had done it had been gripped with remorse and confessed, and now everything would be set right again.

Holding on to that positive attitude without coffee would never work; so I dragged my long hair into a messy ponytail and pulled on a pair of yoga pants and a sweatshirt. I looked at Orange Guy. He opened one eye and observed me.

"Going to get coffee, then I need to go out for a bit," I said. "I have to get you some stuff. And pick out a name for you."

He rose, stretched, and squeaked at me, then raced to the bedroom door.

I cocked my head at him. "You want to come?"

He squeaked again.

"I don't have a harness yet to take you walking," I countered.

He glared at me now. I recognized the look. It said, *You best not be leaving without me.* "Okay." I sighed. "Let's go. But you can't take off. We're a team now, right? Plus I like you."

He purred. I took that as agreement.

We headed downstairs.

Grandpa was gone, but he'd left plenty of coffee with a note next to the pot that said, *Morning, doll. Out for my walk. Love you.* I tucked the note in my pocket and found some tuna for Orange Guy in the fridge. While he ate, I poured myself some coffee. The thought of food made me queasy. Coffee probably wasn't the best thing either, but given my lack of sleep it was necessary. And Grandpa had ordered my favorite dark roast from Peet's. I sipped, savoring the taste. Coffee wasn't supposed to settle an upset stomach, but I already felt better.

I searched the kitchen and living room for the paper, but didn't find it. Either Grandpa had stopped getting it, which I doubted, or he'd removed it so I wouldn't read about Frank first thing in the morning.

Grandpa's phone rang. The caller ID displayed a Massachusetts number, but I didn't recognize it. "Hello?"

"Maddie James?" the young, eager voice asked.

"That's me. Who's calling?"

"This is Jenna Randall from the *Chronicle*. I'm working on a story about the murder. I wondered if you and your cat are available?"

My cat? "I'm sorry, but did you say you want to talk to my cat?" I asked stupidly.

She laughed. "Well, no. But I heard he was the real hero in the story, so I wanted to make sure we featured him, if you agree."

"Hero?"

"Yes. He found the body, didn't he?"

I made a mental note to ask Becky if they did psych evals on their reporters. "He did."

"Right. So we want to interview you about your traumatic experience, but we want to feature him with photos and stuff. That okay?" Impatience had seeped into her voice. I was messing up her deadline, apparently.

"I guess," I said. "When do you want to do that?"

"Thank you so much," she said, sounding relieved that she didn't have to keep explaining. "I'll come to you. What time?"

I looked at the clock. "Maybe two?" I said.

"Sure. That's great. What's your address?"

I gave it to her. She thanked me and hung up. I looked at the cat. "Sorry," I said. "You're going to be in a photo shoot. That means you definitely need a name before two o'clock."

He looked at me quizzically but didn't seem to protest.

"Apparently you're a hero," I said. "Although I thought that only happened when the person's found alive."

He had no answer to that and went back to his breakfast. Once he finished his food, we left. I locked the doors and started down the steps, the cat keeping pace with me. As I reached the street, Leopard Man came around the bushes from the side of the house near the garage. He held something by his side, partially hidden from view. I froze. Why was he skulking around Grandpa's house?

Then immediately felt terrible when I realized he held a small bouquet of wildflowers. I recognized them from the small bed Grandma had planted years ago right next to the house. She'd never expected them to last more than one season but every year they returned, a bouquet of yellows, purples, and blues.

What was wrong with me? I was the first person to defend Leopard Man from the naysayers. Now I was letting fear get the better of me. I had a sudden, horrible premonition of the entire island behaving this way, suspecting each other of murder.

"Good morning," he said solemnly. He noticed me looking at the flowers. "Your grandmother," he said. "She granted me permission to pick a flower or two when I felt in need of color. And now, I feel she'd like nothing more than to offer that small token of color in memory of our deceased brother."

I tried to smile. "That's very sweet," I said. "Help yourself."

Leopard Man nodded. " 'All that lives must die, passing through nature to eternity,' " he quoted.

I wondered how well he knew Frank. He had to know him a little, anyway, since he was going to put flowers on the spot where he died. "So, were you friends with Frank?" I asked, trying to sound casual.

"Friends," he said slowly, as if tasting the word. "As the Bard said, 'Words are easy, like the wind; faithful friends are hard to find.' "

I had no patience for Shakespeare quizzes today, but didn't quite know how to say that.

Leopard Man tucked one of the flowers into the brim of his hat. "Everyone is my friend," he told me with a wink. "I only knew Frank from seeing him out and about. He always said hello."

"Were you downtown last night?" I asked.

He nodded. "I love Food Stroll night."

"Did you see Frank?"

"Fleetingly. He was still alive and well." Shaking his head, Leopard Man tipped his fedora at me. "I must be off. Good day, Maddie, and good sir." He nodded at Orange Guy, then shuffled away. "Stay safe."

I watched him go. No tail today. He'd dressed down, maybe out of respect for Frank. He didn't have leopard pants on today, just black ones. And no cape either, though he did still wear his cool boots. Mourning must have officially begun on the island.

Chapter 11

Orange Guy and I started down the street toward town.
The first ferry sailed toward the docks, which already
stirred with morning activity. I wondered if word had gotten to the mainland yet about Frank's murder. The Boston
TV stations would surely pick this up, as well as the pa-
pers. No wonder Becky's reporter had called me at the
crack of dawn. Becky would lose it if they were scooped
on any aspect of the story—especially an interview
with a witness. And an alleged hero, even if said hero was
feline.

I tugged my sweatshirt tighter around me as the chilly
sea air assaulted me from all sides. Orange Guy lifted his
head so his whiskers twitched in the breeze. I'd forgotten
how glorious the island was at this time of the morning.
The only people out were either arriving or departing on
the ferry, out for their morning walk or heading to work.
Weird how the world still turned after Frank's murder and
the uncertainty lingering over the island like a black cloud.
But despite the normalcy it felt strange out here, like last
night's events had changed the fabric of the island.

As we neared the ferry parking area, I saw a man setting up a sidewalk sign in front of a small shack restaurant.

FRIED CLAMS, it read. Underneath, LOBSTAH ROLLS, FRIES, KIDS' MENU. The roadside stand used to belong to the Rice family. Orange Guy wandered over to sniff the sign and the man's pants, which no doubt smelled like the afore-mentioned clams and lobster. I automatically went to scoop him up, not sure if the man would appreciate the visitor, but he bent down to pet the cat. He looked slightly familiar.

"Hi," he said. "You want some fish?"

Orange Guy squeaked.

"Sorry," I said awkwardly. "He doesn't have a harness yet."

The man gave me an odd look, but rose and held out his hand. As I got closer I realized where I'd seen him before. He'd been walking with Gil Smith last night at the Food Stroll, deep in conversation. He was younger than he looked from a distance, maybe mid-thirties. His khakis, dress shirt, and slightly beat-up loafers looked more Boston suburb than Daybreak Island. His pale blue eyes reminded me of the sky bleached out before a storm. He wore small, wire-rimmed eyeglasses. He'd gelled his sandy hair sternly into place. Clearly he wasn't hauling clams or lobster.

I shook his hand. "Maddie James."

"Damian Shaw." He motioned to the restaurant. "I bought this last summer."

"Really. From the Rice family?"

Damian nodded. "Yup. They were moving. Sold the house and the business as a package deal." He smiled rue-fully. "I'd always wanted to be an island beach bum, but the business has me working more than bumming."

I laughed. "That happens out here."

"Have you lived here long?" he asked.

"I grew up here. I actually don't live here anymore. I'm just home for a . . . family thing." I glanced down at Orange

Guy and scooped him into my arms. "I'm staying with my grandpa. He lives there." I pointed at the house.

He snapped his fingers as my name clicked. "Right! Leo's granddaughter. Your grandpa talks about you all the time." He smiled. "He's very proud of you. You run your own business, right?"

I squirmed under this stranger's praise. "I do. In California."

"Your grandma talked about you a lot too. I was very sorry to hear of her passing."

"So you knew them?" Well, duh. He'd just said that. Plus they lived on the same street on an island where everyone knew everyone—and everything.

"Yeah, they came to the shack a lot. Your grandpa more often, but he'd bring your grandma if she felt up to it." He trailed off into silence as we both thought of my grandma, and how she'd never get to eat another lobster roll. Damian nodded at the cat. "What's his name?"

I looked at the cat, feeling bad. He deserved a name. "He doesn't have one yet. He sort of adopted me yesterday. And I've been a little busy. That's on the agenda for today."

Damian nodded, as if my reason made perfect sense. "He's a nice cat. Can I give him some shrimp?"

"I'm sure he'd love that."

We waited while Damian went around the side of the shack and came back with a small plate of fish. I lowered Orange Guy to the ground, where he attacked the food like I hadn't just fed him ten minutes ago. Typical cat.

"I love cats," Damian said, reaching down to scratch Orange Guy's ears while he ate.

"Do you have any?" I asked.

He shook his head ruefully. "No time. This business is literally killing me. I'd thought it would be better to have an already established place, you know? I kept all the same staff, hoping things would just continue on as they had. But once people hear the management has changed—" He shook his head. "It's not as easy as I thought."

I totally understood what he meant about survival in this fickle island paradise. Life here could be wonderful and amazing and difficult all at the same time, and if the locals didn't know or trust you, chances were good that you wouldn't survive. It was easier with visitors and tourists. They just wanted a good sandwich. But if your competitor was better at marketing him or herself, or had gotten on a coveted "Best of" list, or simply had better food, there wasn't much you could do.

"And lots of the other business owners, they don't seem to like newcomers," Damian went on. "I mean, there's a few who are okay. Like Russ from the Dairy Bar. He shared his tent with me last night so I could have a spot at the stroll."

"How come you had to share?" I asked. "Don't all food establishments get their own tents?"

"I don't belong to the chamber. So I couldn't get a tent unless someone was willing to 'sponsor' me. Russ is great, so he did. It ended up not really mattering. The stroll . . . didn't turn out so well."

The understatement of the year.

"They let us stay open in the food area. I mean, we still got customers and all. The police did a good job blocking off the side street, and the guests didn't really know at first. Then word started to get around, especially when some of the vendors got freaked out and left." He shook his head, kicking at a rock with the toe of his shoe. "It's too bad."

I wasn't sure if he was talking about Frank or the Food Stroll being cut short. "Maybe you should get a cat," I said. "It might help your stress levels. I bet there's tons of them up for adoption." I stopped, catching myself. I tended to offer advice freely, and not everyone appreciated it.

But he laughed. "You're probably right. I'll think about it. I'm not sure I'd have enough time for one. You know what would be cool, though," he said, suddenly turning serious. "If there was a place to go and just play with cats. That way you don't have to feel bad for neglecting your own cat, if you didn't have time for one."

"Like Rent-a-Center?" I smiled at the thought. "It's a cool idea. You could always go to the animal control shelter. They have a shelter."

He shrugged. "I did that before, but it's small. And there's no good sitting area to play with the cats. Plus I think it annoyed the woman in charge."

I frowned. "That's crazy. They should be happy that people want to come in and visit with the poor animals."

"Not if they're not taking one home, I guess," he said.

I scooped up Orange Guy as he finished licking the plate clean and thanked Damian.

"No problem. Hey, come by for a lobster roll sometime." He looked at me hopefully. "I guess I should practice so it sounds real. Lob*stah*." He grinned as he accentuated the last syllable and dropped the *r*. "I'm from the Midwest," he explained, sheepish.

I assured him I'd come for lunch one day soon, hoping that he did actually have good food.

Chapter 12

Orange Guy and I continued on our way into town. The tents were still hoisted on Bicycle Street, although their guts had been emptied of all the food paraphernalia. Their fabric flapped in the wind. I couldn't see Jade's tent from here but ventured a guess that the crime scene tape remained. I shivered and kept walking, picking up my pace.

We made it to Jasper's Tall Tales in ten minutes. My friend Cass Hillaire owned the Ocean Avenue bookstore that also served as a tai chi studio, a treatment center for crystal healings, and an unofficial tea bar. Basically, all the woo-woo you wanted built into one shop. Despite my general lack of woo-wooness, I would stand upside down with incense burning between my toes if Cass suggested it.

Cass thought everyone should read. He also thought everyone should drink tea and do tai chi, which was why he'd merged the two ideas. It wasn't uncommon for an unsuspecting person to be shopping for a book and find themselves doing a tai chi move in the aisle at Cass's insistence. He was a born teacher and a true healer. Cass hailed from Haiti, but has been on Daybreak Island as long as I've been alive. The bookstore was named after his beloved childhood dog. He'd taken me under his wing when

I started visiting the bookstore as a toddler and became fascinated with what I then thought was a dance. As a result, I can do tai chi moves in my sleep.

Cass hovered somewhere between fifty and ageless. He stood around six feet five, built with solid muscle. His hair fell to his waist in intricate braids, and the wrinkles in his face told stories of experience rather than age. He wore huge silver rings on every finger and played Tibetan singing bowls every Monday night in front of his shop in the summer, inside in winter, for anyone who cared to listen. He was the gentlest, wisest person I knew and the only one I wanted to talk to right now.

I'd gambled that he'd be in the shop this early—it was a short walk from where he lived upstairs—and I was right. His door was unlocked and I followed the sounds of a crystal healing meditation into the studio where Cass did tai chi. Long form. I paused in the doorway and watched his graceful movements in silence. He looked like a vision.

His back was to me. I hadn't thought he'd heard me, but after a minute he said, "Maddie. Come in."

I slipped into the room and sat on a pillow on the floor. I recognized some of his moves—Carry Tiger to Mountain, Move Hands Like Clouds. Then my attention slipped to the newspaper on the floor near me. Like a train wreck, I couldn't look away, even though I had no desire to read the story.

I picked it up and scanned the headline—"Community Leader Murdered"—and cringed at the picture of police activity around the fateful tent next to a head shot of Frank smiling at some past event. The reporter, the very same Jenna Randall who'd called me first thing today, wrote about the "out-of-towner with ties to the island and a hero cat" who had found the body. I wondered if Becky had offered any input into that description. I didn't notice Cass had broken form until he stood in front of me. I glanced up and tried to smile, but it didn't work. I tossed the paper aside.

"You are still here," he said. Despite all his years in this country and on this island, Cass still had a thick accent.

"I am," I said.

Cass looked at Orange Guy. "Who's this?"

I stroked the cat. "My new friend. He needs a name." I glanced up at him. "You're good at that. Can you help me name him?"

Cass smiled. "Let me see his personality for a bit. Our names have to match us, you know. Tea?"

"Yes, please. You read the story?" I nodded to the paper I'd let slip to the floor.

Cass nodded. "Tragic." He moved to his tea table at the far side of the room and poured two small cups. He carried them over and arranged himself on a pillow facing me, then handed me one.

I sipped gratefully. Cass's tea was some special, medicinal blend from somewhere far away. He sent me some every few months to make sure I stayed healthy. "I met Frank for lunch yesterday," I said.

Cass also sipped his tea and waited for me to say more.

"Did you know him?" I asked.

Cass nodded. "Of course. He was like the mayor." He winked at me.

"Great," I said miserably. "The whole island's going to be in an uproar."

"Now wait a minute." Cass wagged a finger covered by a long silver ring at me. "I said they *knew* him, not liked him."

Chapter 13

"What do you mean?" I asked.

Cass shrugged. "He was like any other big shot. People loved him or didn't."

"So who didn't?"

"I could guess," he said. "But I was speaking generally. I'm usually here in my shop. I try not to get involved in the town gossip."

I knew that, of course. Worth a try.

"But," he continued before I could respond, "that doesn't mean I don't hear things."

I perked up. "What did you hear?"

"I heard there was some discord among the chamber's board of directors. One of them comes for my tea hour every week. Same problem—some agreed with him, some didn't."

"What did *you* think of Frank?" I asked.

He thought about that. "I understood what motivated Frank. Every year, he asked me to join the chamber."

"Every year? So you don't belong?" I thought every business on the island automatically joined the chamber, given that it was such a small community. Strength in

numbers and all that. But I guess not. Damian Shaw
had said he wasn't a member either.

"No." Cass set his teacup aside. "I think they do good
work, but it's not for me."

I had to smile. It's what I loved about Cass—he marched
to the beat of his own drum.

"Besides, they were all about increasing customers
and revenue." He waved his heavily metaled hand. "I have
plenty of customers. The right ones. Still, I became Frank's
personal mission. Something to conquer." He smiled now
too. "I'd even started to enjoy the game. I thought he was
harmless. And too ambitious."

It fit. From what I could tell about Frank, he liked control. Fixating on someone who blatantly refused to acknowledge him seemed like something he would do. "He
was trying to take my grandpa's house away." I picked at
the fringe on the pillow. "His son wants the property to
build some kind of transportation rental *hub*." I made a
face. "And when Grandpa didn't go for it, he used threats.
Subtle, but still threats. So much for harmless."

Cass raised an eyebrow. "To the chief of police?"

I shrugged sadly. "He's not that, anymore."

"Did you tell the police about that?"

"No. I thought it would make us both look bad, considering I'm the one who had lunch with him—about that
very thing, which I didn't mention to the cops—and then
found him." I swallowed. "Dead."

Cass said nothing for a long time. He just sipped and
watched me. I was used to this. He wanted me to have
some profound epiphany and solve my own problem, but
I didn't have the energy today. I wanted to flop down, curl
up in a ball, and go to sleep with some of Cass's crystals
surrounding me.

"Anyway, I'm sure they heard about our conversation.

I told him to stay away from Grandpa and my family." I looked up, defensive. "I didn't say, *Or I'll kill you,* or anything like that!"

Cass remained silent.

I looked away. "There was more to the conversation, but that was pretty much how I ended it. Then the wine spilled . . . and I left."

"And then someone killed him," Cass said.

"Yeah," I said. "Sure did. And I found him, so I'm sure it's only a matter of time before they show up with handcuffs." I was being a tad dramatic, but I didn't care.

"If he is dead," Cass said slowly, "does that solve your problem?"

I gaped at him. "I—I don't know. Not if his son still wants the property and thinks he can pick up where Frank left off."

"So it doesn't make sense they would think you did it, then."

I hadn't thought of it like that. But that wouldn't necessarily convince the police of my innocence. They didn't even know about the Grandpa/Frank drama. And if they found out, they could easily say it was a heat-of-the-moment thing and I hadn't thought about anything except Frank trying to take something from my family.

"No," I said. "But it still leaves me with at least one problem. Grandpa's house."

"There must be a way for your grandpa to keep his home," Cass said. He sounded so confident.

"I don't know how to do it," I said, feeling tears tickling the back of my throat again. "The house needs work and Grandpa doesn't have the money to fix it. I have to figure out how to help him."

Cass got up to pour more tea. "That sounds like a tall order. When are you going home?"

I sighed. "Soon" had turned into my constant refrain,

but I kept putting off the answer. I felt like I had to make sure Grandpa's house was safe before I could even think of leaving. "Not yet. I don't know when I'll go."

Orange Guy rubbed his head against my leg. Cass reached over and laid a hand on his back. The cat immediately stilled and began to purr. Cass closed his eyes. "He is intuitive. He knows," he said after a minute.

"What does he know?" I asked.

"He knew you immediately," Cass said, opening his eyes. "He found you, right?"

I nodded. "In the cemetery. At my grandmother's funeral. When I went back to visit yesterday he came right over. Like he was asking me to take him with me."

Cass nodded. "A *J* name, then. The soul quality of a *J* is intuitive. Knowing." He gazed at the cat again. "Does he like birds?"

I frowned. "I'm sure he likes them more if he can catch them."

He laughed. "You know John James Audubon was born in Haiti? It was not Haiti then, of course."

"I didn't know that," I said.

"I know a lot of useless trivia about my country," he said with a chuckle. "John James. That should be his name. JJ for short. Double intuition."

"JJ," I repeated, looking at the cat. It fit him well enough. Better than Rusty or Pumpkin or Tigger, typical names of orange cats christened in shelters. "I like it."

JJ looked at me and squeaked. I glanced at Cass. "What's the soul quality of *M*?"

Cass smiled. "Divine grace. At ease in all situations."

I wondered if that included murder.

Chapter 14

I left Cass's place still feeling out of sorts. I wasn't sure if it was the lingering ick of yesterday or realizing that I couldn't justify going home until all this Grandpa drama was sorted out. I missed my juice bar. Heck, I missed juice. For all of Daybreak's high-end, hoity-toity persona-in-progress, we were decades behind in the food arena. The reality of living in a tourist hub: the majority of vacationers wanted to eat buttery, high-calorie lobster rolls, French fries, and ice cream. Salad and drinks made out of kale, not so much. Since tourism drove island revenue, we aimed to please. I thought of Damian Shaw again and his seafood shack. And realized I was hungry.

Since it was too early for a lobster roll, I decided coffee would have to do. I was delighted to see Daybreak Donuts still in the same place I'd left it when I moved. I scooped up JJ and shoved open the door.

The spot behind the counter was conspicuously empty. I frowned. That was strange. Pauline Crosby or someone from her family was always here. But as I moved up closer, a familiar face popped up from below the counter, startling me so I almost dropped the cat.

"Oh! Maddie! Hi, sweetie!" Pauline hurried out from behind the counter and wrapped me in a hug. Her waist had grown softer and her face had more wrinkles, but she still smelled like vanilla extract and apples. Flour spots dotted her black apron.

"You scared the crap out of me." I laughed.

Pauline laughed too. "I'm sorry to pop up like a manic Jack in the Box! I lost my bracelet. My pearls that Penny gave me. My daughter will never speak to me again if I can't find them."

"Bummer," I said. "I'm sure they'll turn up. Maybe in someone's doughnut." I grinned.

Pauline was the quintessential island lifer. Her coffee shop had been around since I could remember, and for years before that. My dad used to take us here on Sundays for homemade apple doughnuts. Pauline had always given me and my sisters extra doughnuts and free juice. Locals and tourists alike loved her place. The charm was in what she *didn't* serve, as much as what she did. She offered coffee, plain and simple. Regular or decaf. No light, medium, or dark roast. No lattes, no espresso. She also offered apple, glazed, and chocolate doughnuts. Pauline was a creature of habit, and right now I wanted habit.

"Lordy, I hope not. I'll have to buy them back. Who's this darling?" she exclaimed, chucking JJ under the chin.

"That's JJ," I said, trying out his new name.

"Well, isn't he a handsome devil." She held me at arm's length. "And you look fabulous. Come. Sit. I have warm doughnuts. I'm trying a new flavor." She winked at me. "Cinnamon."

"A new flavor?" I think that shocked me more than Frank's murder. "But you have three flavors!"

Pauline shrugged. "People are demanding these days. Someone came in here the other day and asked for a gluten-free doughnut. Can you imagine?" She shook her head. "It's because of those fancy new places. Like that Bean place. Have you been?"

I hadn't been to the new fancy coffee shop in town, but I'd heard about it. And it was on my list, though I got the sense it would be a mistake to say that. I shook my head no.

She nodded approvingly. "Glad to hear you're immune to that. They overcharge, like all those places do. Six-dollar lattes and soy milk. Blech. But that's the direction everyone seems to want this island to go." Her voice had a bitter tinge to it. "They want to attract the rich people. They think all those fancy folks will come in and make their lives easier. Delusional, in my opinion. Hey, it's fine. I'll bend a little. Try some new things. But I won't make gluten-free doughnuts, that's for sure. Why bother? The gluten is half the fun. Sit. I just brewed a pot of coffee."

"Okay. And I want an apple doughnut," I said, a little sulkily, dropping into a chair at the nearest table. As much as I loved lattes and the sound of Bean, I didn't like the idea of Pauline and her shop changing. My adult self loved the Beans of the world, but my childhood self wanted Pauline's place to be exactly as it was when I was six. But change was inevitable.

I looked around. The place was nearly empty, with only two people occupying tables. One nursed a cup of coffee, the other a bowl of oatmeal. The other, a young man with earbuds, an iPad, and two glazed doughnuts, tapped his foot in time to whatever beat pounded in his ears, his long legs stretched out from underneath the table.

"You got it, sweetie." She went behind the counter and got my breakfast. "I'll tell you, you come home and the island goes right down the drain! Can you believe what happened to Frank O'Malley?"

I slunk down in my seat, still hugging JJ. "No," I muttered. "I can't."

She glanced around, deemed the shop quiet enough that she could sit for a minute, and plopped down across from me. "What a crazy thing. I'm telling you, this world has really gone downhill. Was it a mugging? Do you think we're all in danger? So many people walking around during the season, it wouldn't surprise me."

"I don't know," I said. An ice pick would be a weird weapon to use in a mugging, but I wasn't about to say that. I didn't even know if the police had released that information, and I don't know that anyone but me actually saw it since he was hidden behind a long tablecloth. "Piper showed up at the crime scene though, screaming that she'd told them—meaning the cops—that this would happen, or something like that. It was really strange."

Pauline's eyes widened. "What on earth? That woman is not quite right." She tapped her temple with her index finger. "I can't believe I missed that whole scene."

"You're lucky," I muttered. "Did you have a tent?"

"I did." She smiled ruefully. "I finally gave in after years of Frank badgering me to participate as a *chamber member.*" She injected just enough sarcasm into the last two words to raise my eyebrows. "Leave it to Frank to screw up all that work we'd put in yesterday."

Chapter 15

Then, horrified, she clapped her hand over her mouth and made the sign of the cross. "I'm sorry. That's terrible to say."

I glanced up, surprised. Pauline usually didn't say bad things about anyone. "Not a fan?"

Pauline shrugged, her face immediately turning red. She took one more cursory glance around to make sure no one had heard her. "We didn't always see eye to eye. On chamber business. But my little shop and I didn't figure that prominently into his business plan. And now it's going to be even worse, with that wackadoodle Piper probably taking over. Everyone knows they were sleeping together and that's the only reason she had that job," she said, a smidgen too loud.

My eyes widened. *"What?"*

"It was the worst kept secret on the island. Everyone just pretended not to know."

"Including his wife?" I asked.

"Honey. She'd have to be blind, deaf, and dumb not to know. But some people choose to stay ignorant. I'm sorry. I'm being very unprofessional today." She sat up straight and leaned forward over the table. "The chamber is an important institution around here. We need to stick together as business owners and with Frank in charge it was difficult. Not that it will be easier with Piper. She's got her own agenda. Heck, maybe that agenda caused Frank's demise," she mused. "Maybe she got sick of waiting for him to retire."

Good grief. It was Motive Central around here just with the women in Frank's life. "Wow," I said. "That's a whole lot of information for the police, don't you think?"

She laughed. "Absolutely. I'm sure they'll be around to ask us." Validated, she changed the subject. "Anyway, I'm so sorry about your grandma. That woman was a regular saint on earth. But I don't have to tell you that. She would come in here every Wednesday for her treat. I would take my break and we would talk and talk. It was my favorite time of the week. Until she got too sick." Pauline's face clouded. "My heart breaks for your grandpa. Everyone could see how much he loved her. I'm sure he's devastated."

"He is," I said, swallowing against the darn tears that kept trying to bubble up. "We all are."

"I know, honey. You let me know if he needs anything, you hear? Your grandpa is a good man. I hate to see him suffer in any way."

"Thanks, Pauline." I swiped at my eyes. It made me happy to know how much people loved him. Grandma would be happy too.

She watched me pick at my doughnut. "How is it?"

"It's just like when I was little. Thanks, Pauline."

"Anytime, sweetie." She squeezed my hand and rose to go back to work, but I called her back.

"Did you see Frank last night?" I asked. Even though my rational brain knew I'd left him alive and well at La Rosetta, I wanted multiple reassurances that he'd been up and about and very much alive after we'd parted ways.

"I did," Pauline said, leaning against the chair she'd just vacated, drumming her fingers against the back. "Only from afar, though. He was busy overseeing the setup activities." She smiled wryly. "Then a bit later I saw him on the street talking to his son. Actually, talking might be the wrong word. Yelling is more appropriate."

His son. The one who wanted to raze my grandfather's house. Just thinking about this faceless man made my heart start to pound in anticipation. "His son?" I asked casually. "Does he only have one son?"

Pauline shook her head. "Two. Aidan's the one who moved back here recently from Florida." She lowered her voice. "Screwup, that one is. The other one's Keeran, I think. He's some big-shot artist in Boston. He helps his mother with her nonprofit. Does art shows for benefits, stuff like that. They're very close." Margaret O'Malley ran a big-deal Massachusetts nonprofit headquartered in Boston called Empowering Women. They worked with a diverse group of women from all walks of life to help them reach their personal best. The group received all kinds of awards every year and raised a lot of funding.

"But the other one has problems?" I asked.

Pauline shrugged. "I heard he couldn't hold a job. That he's been in trouble with the law here and there. Frank bailed him out of money troubles a couple of times. Whenever I've seen him he looks like he's three sheets to the wind, so I'm presuming he has *other troubles*." She waggled her eyebrows to make sure I got her meaning. I did. Loud and clear.

"Is that why he was yelling at him?" I asked.

"I have no idea. I wasn't close enough to hear the conversation." She peered at me curiously. "Why do you ask?"

"Just curious. I . . . didn't know he had any family around. I mean, other than Margaret."

"They're usually not around. I do feel bad for those

kids. I'm sure Frank's the reason the older one was screwed up. At least he tried to help, I guess."

I said nothing. I could respect a guy who wanted to help his kid, but not at the expense of my grandfather.

"Anyway, Margaret's been staying on the mainland more and more, I've heard. None of my business, but they didn't seem too much in love, if you know what I mean." Pauline's eyes sparkled with the gossip telling. But I was still thinking about Aidan O'Malley, the screwed-up son.

The bell jingled, signaling a customer. We both glanced up. I recognized Jade Bennett, proprietor of the doomed tent. She glanced at me and Pauline huddled together, then headed to the counter.

"I better get to work." Pauline reached over and gave me a hug. "Come back and see me soon, okay?"

I promised her I would and finished off my doughnut, sorting through the massive amount of derogatory Frank information I'd just learned. Pauline definitely didn't seem too broken up about his death. How many other chamber members or community figures felt the same way? I watched Jade Bennett exchange a few words with Pauline then leave with her coffee, head down, sunglasses covering her eyes. I'd love to hear what other people thought about Frank. And what about Piper Dawes? Sleeping with him?

I also wondered how many people on the island knew about Frank's plans to help Aidan. What effects would a transportation center have on the broader business base, my grandfather's home aside? Good or bad? Or would anyone who knew Aidan fear he would bring bad juju to the island? I drained my cup and stood, wondering if it would be completely insensitive to go have a chat with Aidan O'Malley before they'd even buried his father. It sounded like the police would have a lot of avenues to cover during this investigation. I wanted to make sure they had all the information they needed to arrest someone other than me.

Chapter 16

Once I got outside, I decided to wait to track down Frank's son. It probably wouldn't look good if I went running over there before his father was even cold to find out if he still intended to try to take my grandpa's house. Plus I didn't know where to run to, so I'd have to do some detective work on that front. Maybe the whole lousy situation had died with Frank. Fingers crossed.

In the meantime, I needed to get some things for JJ. I'd seen the new pet supply store in town while I was out walking. It wasn't far from Pauline's, so JJ and I headed over to check it out. The paw-shaped purple sign read A PAWSITIVE EXPERIENCE and boasted both a dog and a cat.

"I hope they have good cat stuff," I commented to JJ. He looked up at me and blinked.

When we entered, my old classmate Mish Hartmann waved at me from behind the counter where she sat with the latest *People* magazine open in front of her and a tiny Yorkie on her lap.

"Hey, Mish. What are you doing here?" I asked.

She laughed. "I could say the same to you, world traveler. My husband and I just opened this place." She looked around proudly. "What do you think?"

"It's awesome," I said, following her gaze around the shop. And it was. Exactly half the store had cat items, while the other half had dog supplies. Stores like these usually focused on dogs, with a few collars or fuzzy mice as an afterthought for cats.

"My husband adores cats," she said, reading my mind. "I'm a dog girl. I married Stevie Warner. You remember him? He's changed a lot. He's still kind of geeky, but he talks to people now. I've been a good influence on him." She beamed. "And we love our pets. We agreed the store should be equal to both."

"Well, it's fabulous," I said. "Congratulations to you two."

"Thanks. So, you're visiting?"

"I am. My grandma died."

"I'm so sorry!" She put the dog on her chair, came around the counter and gave me a hug. "That stinks. Oh, hi sweetie!" She bent down and petted JJ. "Is this your cat?"

I nodded. "JJ. He was a stray. He needs some stuff."

"How sweet! This is Pebbles." She indicated the Yorkie, who gazed at me and JJ impassively, then put her head back down on the chair. "As you can see, she's impressed."

I laughed.

"So let's get JJ some stuff! What do you need?"

"A harness, a leash, a litter box, and food bowls," I said. "And toys."

"How cute. Is he going to walk around with you and stuff?"

"He is," I said, thinking about him taking off into the barricaded tents last night. "And I don't want him getting away and getting lost or hurt."

"No," she agreed. "My goodness, speaking of getting hurt, did you hear what happened last night?" She shuddered. "No one's been murdered on this island in, like, forever. *So* scary!"

"It is," I agreed. I nodded at JJ. "He actually found Frank's body. He took off and I had to chase him, and that's where he was."

Mish stared at me with morbid fascination. "Oh my goodness. How awful. I'd rather not think about it. Let's get this handsome kitty taken care of and stop talking about bad things." She led me to the back of the store. "Harnesses are there." She pointed to the display on the back wall. "Leashes next to them. Litter boxes in the back—we just got the coolest new designs!—and you'll see the food bowls in that same section. We have outfits too." She winked. "I bet he'd love an outfit."

I wasn't so sure about that, but I smiled. "Thanks. We'll check them out."

Mish left us to it. JJ and I perused the selections. The store offered a brilliant harness collection. All kinds of fun colors and designs. I picked out a skull-and-crossbones design in red and black, and the matching leash. He didn't object when I put it on him. In fact, I think he preened a bit. Then I led JJ in his fancy new getup over to the litter boxes. Mish was right—no plain, boring litter boxes here. I had my hand on a hot-pink and purple plaid one, trying to ignore JJ's evil eye, when a woman stopped in front of me.

"Maddie?" she said, a smile breaking over her pale face. "Hey!"

It took me a second—she looked so different. Then it clicked. "Katrina!" I exclaimed, throwing my arms around her.

I'd known Katrina Denning since I was a kid. She'd babysat me during my preteen years, the worst years on this planet. Since she was only seven years older than me, we'd fallen into a friendship once I was old enough not to annoy her. I hadn't seen her at all since I'd been home, and she looked totally different than when I'd last seen her a few years ago. Older, for one. And exhausted. The bags under her eyes would definitely be charged an over-the-limit fee at the airport. Her dark blond hair, cut in a plain chin-length bob with bangs, looked like she hadn't taken the time to brush it. She'd lost weight. Either that, or the khaki pants and uniform shirt she wore had been made for someone else.

"How are you, sweetie? I'm so sorry I didn't get to your gram's funeral," she said, her eyes darkening. "I had an emergency that day. I feel terrible. I did send your parents a card, and I've been meaning to see if you were still here, but . . ." She sighed. "It's been crazy lately."

"Oh, don't worry," I said. "It was, you know, a funeral." I swallowed against the misery that rose in my throat. "What are you doing these days?" I was embarrassed that I'd lost track of her over the years. Last I knew, Katrina had wanted to be a cop. This uniform was not a police officer's, though, and I couldn't get close enough to see what the patch said.

"I'm the animal control officer now." She turned and held her arm up in front of me so I could see the embroidered title on her sleeve.

"Really?" Katrina had always been an animal person, but in small quantities. And domestic animals, usually. I couldn't really picture her chasing after a rogue raccoon.

"You bet. The shirt doesn't lie." She grinned.

"So you changed your mind about being a cop?" I asked.

"Not exactly. It's still on the bucket list. I'm working for the police, technically, so we'll see what happens. This job is definitely keeping me busy in the meantime."

"I bet," I said. "You have a lot of strays?"

"Tons." Katrina rolled her eyes. "I have no idea where

they all come from. My kennel is always full of dogs, and I hardly have anywhere to put the cats. And people call me daily about cats, from friendlies to the ferals that live down by the docks. It's nuts. It's definitely been worse since the rescue closed."

"Closed?" I asked.

She nodded. "Safe Paws. They ran out of funding last year."

"That's awful," I said.

Katrina shrugged. "Yeah, well, it happens." She looked at JJ. "Your cat?"

"Yeah. Since yesterday." I grinned. "I saved you some work. He was a stray hanging out in the cemetery."

"Terrific! Are you keeping him? You're going to bring him back to California?"

"He seems to have adopted me," I said, avoiding her other question.

"His ear should get checked. He may have mites," Katrina said, bending to examine JJ's slightly bent left ear. "Let me know if you want help with an initial vet visit. I can send him through my office."

"I'll take you up on that," I said. "I had a vet visit on my list."

"Okay, call me," she said, fishing in her pocket and handing me a card. "If you don't get me in the office, try my mobile. I'm usually running around like a lunatic. Speaking of which, I need to grab some leashes and get out of here." She gave me a quick kiss on the cheek and hurried off.

I pocketed the card, watching her go. I thought of Damian and his fondness for cats. Could Katrina be the person he referenced who didn't like when people hung out with the cats? I'd have to find out. But right now, I had more pressing matters. I refocused on the litter boxes. With JJ's guidance, I selected one with tiny race cars on it.

More boyish. I was in the middle of choosing food dishes when I felt something warm trickle down my leg. I whipped around and looked down to find a fluffy white dog with his leg lifted, peeing on me.

Chapter 17

JJ hissed at the dog. I guess he couldn't believe what he was seeing either. The dog ignored him and went right on doing his business.

"Finn! No!" The shout came from the other end of a long leash. I recognized the guy holding it as Lucas Davenport. Becky and I had walked by his new grooming shop on Bicycle Street a week or so ago. She'd told me he was a new addition to the island. He raced over and yanked the dog away from me.

Stunned, I looked down at my damp yoga pants, thankful I hadn't worn shorts.

"I am so, so sorry," he said, looking around for something to wipe my leg. "I'll get you some paper towels. Bad, bad dog!"

I looked at the little white dog who stared at me, wagging his tail, and burst out laughing. "It's fine," I said. "He's adorable."

Lucas blinked, seemingly confused about why I wasn't shouting at him. Secretly, I was glad the dog had peed on me. When I'd seen Lucas at his shop, his attractiveness hadn't been lost on me. He'd smiled at me through the window from his seat at the front desk. Ever since then, he'd

been on my to-do list. Going by looks alone, I was in love.
He had messy dark hair, killer ice-blue eyes, and a nice
smile. I'd also heard he was a musician. A double whammy.
Musicians were my downfall. My favorite mistake, because
they were usually jerks. But a girl could dream. There had
to be one out there who wasn't a total disaster . . . right?
Lucas looked down at the pup, who strained at his leash
trying to reach a tennis ball in a display case. "Yeah, real
adorable," he said with a rueful smile. "He's not my dog.
I'm boarding him at my shop for a couple days. My buddy
just rescued him, but had to go out of town on a business
trip."

I surveyed the ball of fluff. Adorable, but way hyper.
"What kind of dog?" The pooch stood straight up on his
back legs, flapping his front paws at me, begging for attention. JJ retreated behind my legs and peered at the dog
with disdain.

"A mix. Probably bichon and Jack Russell. Kind of a
scary combo." We both looked at the dog. Beside himself
now, he barked at us and ran in small circles, straining at
his collar and choking. Lucas shook his head and motioned
to JJ. "Your cat?"

"Yeah. I don't think he likes dogs too much."

"It's probably this dog," Lucas said wryly.

"I didn't realize you boarded too. I saw your shop the
other day. It looks fun." I reallocated my purchases in my
arms and tried not to look like I was checking him out. I
totally was. But he was kind of checking me out too. I
thought.

"I do. Not a ton of it yet, because I don't have a lot of
room, but it's something I want to get into. Hoping to ex-
pand as my business grows." He gave me an easy smile.
"So are you new here?"

"New?" I grinned. "Not by a long shot. I was born here."

He cocked his head. "Really? I've never seen you around

until the other day when you stopped at my window. Well, I haven't been here that long, I guess. About six months. But I'm sure I would've noticed . . ." He had the good grace to trail off, his cheeks reddening slightly.

I was delighted that he remembered me. "It's all good. I haven't lived here since I graduated from high school. I'm only back for a . . . little while."

"Oh. You're leaving again?"

Did I imagine the disappointment that flashed through his eyes or was it wishful thinking? "I live in San Francisco. I own a business out there."

"Really? Cool. What kind of business?"

"A juice bar."

"Juice? Like green, healthy juice?"

"You got it." I waited for the inevitable blank stare or, worse, the *yuck* face. But he looked impressed. "I wish someone would open one out here." Then he smiled. "Maybe if you ever want to move back you can do that?"

Was he flirting with me? I felt my heart trip a little in my chest. Still, I flirted back. "Maybe," I said. "You never know. What about you?" I changed the subject. "Where are you from?"

"Virginia," he said. "But I came here for summer vacations as a kid and fell in love with it. Always said I'd live here one day."

"That's so cool," I said.

He grinned and stuck his hands in his jeans pockets. An awkward silence descended, during which we watched the little dog run in circles as wide as his leash would offer. Then he squatted and pooped in the aisle.

Lucas sighed. "I guess I should clean that up," he said. "Are you sure you don't want me to find something to clean off your pants?"

"No. I'm fine. Honestly. I'm heading home right now to change," I said.

"Okay. Sorry again." He hesitated. "Hopefully I'll see you around before you leave."

"Yes. Absolutely." I smiled at him. Since I couldn't think of anything else to say, I left him to it and headed to the front of the store with JJ to pay for our purchases.

Chapter 18

I realized too late that it would've been easier to get all JJ's supplies home if I'd driven instead of walked. The harness, collar, and silver ID tag shaped like a paw print were easy—I got JJ all decked out in his new gear as soon as we left the store. But the rest of my purchases weren't so easy. I packed the bag with JJ's new toy mice and jingle balls into my purse, then went back inside and asked Mish if she could hold the ten-pound bag of food, litter box, and cat litter until I could run back with the car. She put them aside for me and told me to come back anytime.

Walking home, I worried that JJ would feel constrained in his harness after being a worldly stray in charge of his own destiny, but instead he pranced down the street proudly, almost like he was showing off. *Look, I have a human!* At least I hoped that's what he would say.

People certainly noticed us—the wacky girl walking down the street with the cat in the harness. Some stared. Others pointed and giggled. A few dogs barked. Some people wanted to stop and pet him, which he loved. JJ didn't acknowledge any of the naysayers. I liked that—something I could learn from him.

When we got back to the house I unlocked the front

door and paused, noticing a white envelope half shoved under the door. I bent to pick it up. It wasn't sealed. Inside was a newspaper clipping.

"Cats, Coffee, Cash Cow?" the headline read. I leaned against the door and scanned the piece, which talked about a café in Taiwan that housed cats and allowed people to come in to visit with them, have coffee, relax. I smiled as I read it. What a cool idea.

I checked the envelope for a note or anything identifying who'd left it, but there was nothing else. I thought of Damian's comment about Rent-a-Center for cats. Maybe him?

I went inside, kicked the door closed, and called for Grandpa, dropped the clipping on the counter. I searched the house for him, but he must not have returned from his walk yet. I looked for my cell phone to call Grandpa but it was nowhere in sight. I must've left it upstairs in my rush to get out of the house this morning. I unclipped JJ's leash and raced upstairs. I hadn't been too upset that Finn the dog peed on me, but it was definitely time to shower.

I went into my bedroom to grab clothes and picked up my phone. A bunch of missed calls and a couple of voice mails. Yikes. I scrolled the caller list. My parents. Four times. My mother's voice mail was short and to the point: "Maddie! Are you all right? Just checking up on you this morning. Call us. Or come over! I'll make you soup."

I tossed the phone back on the bed. I didn't feel like talking about Frank or reliving the murder. I didn't even feel like soup. Plus I had to get ready for this newspaper interview. That made me think of Becky, who'd also called. I suspected she was calling about the interview. I ducked into the bathroom, locked the door, and blasted the hot water in the shower.

With the hot water steaming the windows, I lathered shampoo into my hair and had just started belting out

Taylor Swift's "Bad Blood" when a bang from somewhere over my head startled me. Frowning, I stopped singing. Another crash, then something rolling around. It sounded like it was on the roof. I shut the water, completely forgetting about the shampoo in my hair, and grabbed my big fluffy bath towel. Hastily wrapping it around me, I opened the bathroom door.

"Grandpa?"

No answer. Swiping soap from my face, I stepped into the hall and went back toward my room, the direction I thought I'd heard the noise. Although it sounded like it had come from outside, not in. I paused and listened outside my door. There it was again, not as loud but definitely banging and clanging overhead. Still dripping all over the hardwood floor, I moved into my bedroom and looked out the window.

And screamed when I saw a face looking back at me, nearly dropping my towel.

The man looking back at me looked just as startled as I was. I jumped back, heart pounding. I grabbed my phone off the bed and raced out of the room, frantically dialing 911 with one hand while clutching the towel with the other.

"There's someone on a ladder outside my window," I told the dispatcher when he picked up. I gave Grandpa's address and hung up despite his request for me to stay on the phone. The fear that it was a serial killer took second place to my fear of him taking off. I raced downstairs, flung open the kitchen door, and raced around the side of the house. The man had descended the ladder, probably about to make a run for it.

"Hey!" I shouted, skidding to a stop next to Grandma's flowers, a safe distance from the guy.

He looked at me like I was crazy. Too late I realized I probably *looked* crazy, with my towel and soapy hair. But no matter. I waved my phone at him.

"I just called the cops," I said, holding my phone out like a weapon. "So you may as well wait here for them and make it easy on yourself. But stay right there, you perv."

He rolled his eyes but made no move to run. He looked to be in his fifties, with a reddish-brown beard. He wore a Red Sox baseball cap. I could see a white van parked at the curb. If he was a killer, he needed some lessons on how to be stealthy.

"Lady," he said. "Relax. I'm doing the roof job."

"What roof job? I haven't heard anything about that," I countered.

"And how's that my problem?"

A siren let out a shriek, then a police car careened into the driveway, lights flashing. Craig jumped out of the driver's seat almost before the car rolled to a stop. "Maddie?" he asked, looking me up and down. "What's going on?"

I flushed, yanking my towel tighter around me, digging my toes into the grass. "I was in the shower and heard noises on the roof. I went to the window and this guy was looking in."

"I wasn't!" the guy hollered from his spot near the ladder. "I was climbing down and this crazy woman appeared in the window. I couldn't help but look!"

Craig sighed. "Wait here. No, on second thought. Go inside and get dressed. But wash the soap off first, right?" His eyes lingered on mine a moment too long, causing a small explosion of warmth in my belly.

"Fine," I said, then marched inside. Once I was out of sight, I slammed the door and leaned against it. What was I, crazy? Craig was my ex. Just because we'd had a good time in high school didn't mean we had anything in common now, despite getting thrown into each other's paths over the last few days. Over a dead body, of all things. So why did I feel like he totally would've kissed me just then if he hadn't been on duty, investigating a

Peeping Tom in my window? And why was I kind of wishing he had?

I noticed JJ sitting in the kitchen window, looking at me curiously. "I know, I look ridiculous." I went upstairs, turned the shower back on, and finished rinsing my hair. When I was done I pulled on leggings and a T-shirt, combed the knots out of my hair, then raced back downstairs. Craig and the peeper sat on Grandpa's front steps. They both looked up when I opened the door. Craig got to his feet.

"Hey," he said. "So Maddie, this is Abe Tate. He owns Tate Contracting. I guess they're doing some work on your grandfather's roof."

I folded my arms and shot them both a skeptical look. "On a Sunday?"

Abe Tate shrugged. "It's the busy season. Believe me, I'd rather not work Sundays. But you can't turn the work away. I needed to take a look at the roof so I can get supplies."

"So Grandpa Leo hired you?" I asked. He hadn't mentioned anything to me about starting repairs. I'd been under the impression he'd still been sorting through the nursing home and funeral bills, dealing with life insurance and the like.

Tate pulled a small spiral-bound notebook out of his shirt pocket and unfolded a piece of paper. "I have a contract for a roofing job at 167 Shoreline Avenue."

Craig took the paper and scanned it, then handed it to me. It certainly was a contract, with Grandpa's name and address listed. But the signature wasn't his. It was illegible, in fact, just a few scribbles in varying sizes. I knew Grandpa's handwriting, and this wasn't it.

"What's going on here? Abe? Everything okay?"

We all turned to see Grandpa coming up the driveway, a bakery box from Pauline's in his hand. I guess he really did know Tate—which made sense. He knew everyone, after all.

"Grandpa!" I made a move to go down the steps, but Craig put out a hand, holding me back.

"Leo. Come on up," he said.

Grandpa did, slowly. "What's going on?" he said to Tate.

"This guy was on your roof," I said to Grandpa, ignoring Craig's pointed stare that clearly said *Shut up.* "Did you hire him?"

Grandpa's eyebrows rose, nearly disappearing into his hairline. Grandpa had more hair than most guys my age. Over the years it had gone from almost black to totally white, but it was still full and wavy and thick. "I most certainly did not," he said. "When would I have had time to do that, with everything else going on?"

We all looked at Tate. He raised his hands in defense. "Listen. I'm not climbing around up there for my health. I was hired to do this roof. I guess someone was doing you a favor, Chief."

"Hold on," Craig said. "Are you saying you didn't deal directly with Chief—uh, Mr. Mancini?"

Tate shook his head. "I got a phone call. A guy asked me to take on the job; I told him I needed a deposit and a contract."

"It was a man?" Craig interrupted.

"Yep. So I wrote it up, left it with my receptionist. She never saw the person come get it, musta been out to lunch, but the next day the contract was signed and there was five hundred in cash in an envelope." He shrugged. "Today's the first chance I've had to come look at it."

Grandpa, Craig, and I all looked at each other, the same thought running through our minds: *Who was paying to get Grandpa's roof fixed?* More importantly, why?

Chapter 19

"It has to be my dad." I poured iced tea into three glasses and handed one each to Grandpa and Craig. Abe Tate had left, undoubtedly thinking we were all nuts. "Doing something sweet for Grandpa and Mom. Who else would it be?"

"Do any of your friends know about the roof needing repairs? Anyone who has some connection with Tate?" Craig asked.

Grandpa sat quietly at the table, staring out the window. "Absolutely not," he said. "I don't want people's charity."

"Leo, if someone wants to do a good deed," Craig began, then trailed off when Grandpa shot him The Look.

"I'm not taking favors," Grandpa said tightly, and we both knew better than to push the issue.

"Do you know Tate well?" I asked.

"Well enough. His son had a situation when I was on the force. I helped them out. He always kept in contact after that, Christmas cards and such."

The doorbell rang. I froze. Shoot. I'd forgotten about the reporter. I went out into the hall and pulled the door open.

A woman wearing a navy blue suit with a too short skirt stood on the front steps. She wasn't my reporter, though.

I recognized her—Debbie Renault, one of my high school archenemies. Or to be more accurate, she considered me one of her enemies. I didn't really give a hoot about her. She'd never gotten over our junior prom when that silly football player left her at the dance to go to a party with me.

She peered at me for a second, then turned on the fake wattage. "Oh. My. Gosh. Maddie James! I can't believe it's really you. Are you still Maddie James, or are you married yet?"

I sighed. "Hey, Deb. Nope, not married. You?"

"Three years now. To Jonah." She shot me a self-satisfied smile and waved her left hand at me. I hid my giggle. She'd married the very football player who'd left her at the dance. That was so Daybreak. I made a show of squinting for a glimpse of her diamond. Her smile dimmed and she stuck her hands on her hips.

"What are you doing here? Did you move back? I'm selling real estate now. With my mother. If you need a place, we're the best in town." She winked.

"Thanks," I said. "I'm just visiting."

"Oh." Debbie pouted. "Well. Keep us in mind!" She turned to my grandfather, who'd come out to the hall to see who was here. "Mr. Mancini! Good afternoon." She stepped inside without an invite, beaming a smile. "I'm Debbie Renault. I'm here on behalf of O&M Transportation. They've made you an offer on your house. Let's talk in the kitchen." Smiling, she waved a folder as she sailed past him. "I'm also happy to help you find representation if you need it. Do you have an agent?"

"Wait. What?" I asked, stunned. "What do you mean, an offer?"

Red crept up Grandpa's face as he processed Debbie's words. I started to follow but he motioned for me to stay put. A second later, Craig appeared in the hall, bewildered.

"What's that about?" he asked. "Your grandfather just threw me out of the kitchen."

The doorbell rang again. Cursing, I yanked it open, ready to throw the reporter out. Sergeant Ellory stood there.

He smiled at me. "Maddie."

I felt a rush of fear wash over my body. "Hello. Can I help you?"

"Everything okay out here? There's a police car in your driveway."

"Everything's fine. There was a slight misunderstanding. Craig—Officer Tomlin—came and cleared it up."

Craig nodded at his superior. "Hey, Sarge," he said. "What's up?"

Ellory shot him a curious glance, then spread his palms wide. "Just stopping by to have a word with Leo. Surprised to see you here."

"Maddie thought someone was trespassing. Turns out it was a contractor," Craig explained, leaving out the details.

"What did you want with my grandpa?" I asked, before Ellory could sink his teeth into the details of my 911 call. "He's in the kitchen, but he has, uh, company."

"I can wait." Ellory looked around, noticed Craig's iced tea. "I'll take a cold drink, though."

I gritted my teeth. "I can't go into the kitchen right now or I'd be happy to get you one."

"I think I should go," Craig said.

"Or you can stay while I talk to Leo," Ellory said with a meaningful look.

"What do you need to talk to him about?" I asked.

"With all due respect, Maddie, I'd like to talk to him privately," Ellory said. "If he wants to tell you—"

"No, sir," Grandpa said firmly as he reentered the hall, hearing the last part of our conversation. "Anything you need to say, Maddie can hear."

I saw Debbie over his shoulder. She didn't look happy.

"Mr. Mancini," she persisted, after clearly being dismissed. "If you'd like to take a little time to review the offer, that's absolutely fine. They would like an answer next week."

Grandpa bristled. "Thank you, Ms. Renault. Yes, I would like some time."

"Of course." She smiled brilliantly and stepped forward, nearly jabbing him with the folder so he had to take it. He let it hang limply between two fingers as if it might bite him.

Debbie pretended not to notice and turned to me. "Maddie, remember what I said! I'd love to find you a house on the island when you're ready." She squeezed my arm then slipped past us, giving the police a curious look, and sailed out the door.

Craig looked at me quizzically. "You're buying a house?"

"No! For God's sake." I slammed the front door behind Debbie and followed Ellory and Grandpa into the kitchen, Craig on my heels. JJ leaped off his window perch and raced over to me with a squeak. I scooped him up and nestled him against my chest. He purred like a motorboat.

Ellory sat at the table without being invited and regarded Grandpa with interest. "Selling property?"

Grandpa nearly bared his teeth at him. "No. Is there something I can help you with, Sergeant?"

"Sure hope so," Ellory said. "But first, walk me through the complaint you called in, Ms. James?"

I cut my eyes to Craig. He shrugged, the movement so minuscule I may have imagined it.

"Can't you just read his report later?" I asked.

He shrugged. "I could, but I think it would be much more interesting hearing it from you."

"That's for sure," Craig murmured.

I glared at him, then turned back to Ellory and explained what happened.

Ellory nodded. "I'm glad it wasn't anything threatening. So," he said, turning to Grandpa, "tell me about this real estate proposal."

Oh boy. Craig and I looked at each other, unable to leave but not invited to take part in whatever was playing out next.

Grandpa stared at him. "I already told you—"

"Nothing you and Frank O'Malley were working on together?"

I held my breath.

"Frank O'Malley approached me about a real estate deal," Grandpa said through clenched teeth. "It wasn't his company. He was trying to broker the deal. I wasn't interested. So there is no deal. It was a proposal."

"I see." Ellory toyed with the pepper shaker that sat on the table. "Is that what Ms. Renault was just here about?" He nodded at the folder.

"Sergeant Ellory. With all due respect, why are you asking?" Grandpa asked impatiently.

Ellory returned his gaze. Bad cop in action. "I'm just wondering," he said, "if that might be what you called Frank about yesterday. Before he died."

Chapter 20

I froze. What was Ellory talking about? Grandpa hadn't mentioned calling Frank yesterday, and he surely would've told me. Especially since Frank ended up dead and all.

"Grandpa didn't call Frank yesterday," I said. "He was busy helping out with the Food Stroll. Right, Grandpa? Besides, I was with Frank and he didn't take any phone calls." My smugness dissipated after a minute when I remembered Frank's phone vibrating on the table during our lunch. He hadn't answered, but could that have been Grandpa?

Ellory remembered it too. "Maybe so, but you did tell me last night that Frank received a call while you were at lunch." He watched me like a hawk. "Right?"

"I also said I don't know who it was," I reminded him.

"Correct. That's why I'm asking your grandfather if it was him."

All eyes swiveled to Grandpa Leo.

"Leo?" Ellory asked.

Grandpa met Ellory's eyes without flinching. Grandpa's were exhausted. Not the same eyes of the former police chief. My mother's worries bubbled up to the surface again and I felt a stab of fear in my belly. What if it was true? What if he was getting old, losing his ability to be . . . Grandpa? The thought nearly stopped me from breathing.

"Leo?" Ellory repeated. "I can just pull the records to find out for sure, but I'd recommend you tell me now."

"I called him," Grandpa said, his tone defiant. "I was working the Food Stroll and I had some questions."

That made me feel better. A perfectly rational reason to call Frank. Except that Frank probably didn't have any clue where the boxes of tickets were, or the volunteer contact list.

"So it wasn't about this real estate deal?"

Grandpa bristled. "I told you, there is no real estate deal."

Ellory pointed to the door where Debbie Renault had been a few minutes ago. "That sounded like someone thought there was still a deal."

I held my breath. I could see Craig holding his too.

"Well," Grandpa said, "clearly it wasn't Frank's, since he's gone."

Oh, boy.

"I told you there was a proposal," Grandpa said. "It's not going anywhere."

"Tell me about the proposal," Ellory pressed.

Grandpa sighed. "Frank wanted me to sell my house."

Ellory's brow arched. "This house?"

"Yes."

"He wanted to buy it for himself?"

"No. He was trying to help a company who wanted the property. To rent bikes, cars, kayaks, whatever." Grandpa couldn't conceal the disgust from his face. I cringed inwardly. Did he get what Ellory was doing here?

"And you didn't like that idea."

Grandpa said nothing.

"Hey, I don't blame you. I wouldn't like it either," Ellory said, one pal to another.

I gritted my teeth. "Grandpa. You don't have to answer these questions," I said, throwing his words from last night back at him.

He waved me away like he would a black fly buzzing around his head at the beach. "You're damn right I didn't like it," he said to Ellory. "I had no intention of selling. Still don't."

The two men had a stare-off.

"Did you tell Frank no?" Ellory asked.

"I told him I'd think about it." Grandpa didn't mention anything else, like Frank telling him his property values would go right down the tubes and how he could easily get the land rezoned. Which was probably a good idea.

Ellory arched an eyebrow. "If you were so dead set against selling, why didn't you just tell him no? Why string him along?"

"I told him no a few times, but he kept at it," Grandpa said. "So I let him believe I was considering it. I had other things on my mind."

"Did you send your granddaughter to talk to him about it?"

"Nobody *sends* me anywhere," I cut in, offended. "I wanted to talk to Frank as one businessperson to another."

Ellory shot me a skeptical look. "So you didn't go talk to him on behalf of your grandfather?"

"I went to talk to him on behalf of me," I said. "Because I thought his idea was lousy and wanted to tell him so." I wanted to take the words back as soon as I spoke them. At this point, I think he pegged me and Grandpa as perpetrators of some twisted criminal partnership.

Ellory nodded. "So you didn't want your grandfather to sell his house."

"Because Grandpa didn't want to," I said, trying to keep the annoyance out of my voice. "I was merely reiterating his wishes."

"Leo," Ellory said slowly. "What time did you go to the Food Stroll yesterday?"

"Around three, with the rest of the volunteers," Grandpa said.

"Did you see Frank?"

"I didn't," Grandpa said. "Too busy."

"What about the question you needed answered?"

"I found Piper Dawes," Grandpa said. "She took care of it."

Ellory watched Grandpa for a long minute. I could see him doing the calculations again—*how far can I push him?*—then he shifted his gaze to me.

I felt compelled to say something. "Besides," I added for good measure. "Grandpa was with a whole crowd of people the whole time. Right, Grandpa?"

"Right, doll," he said. "I was wrangling volunteers. Oh, and Sergeant, if you're looking to pin a crime on me, you should talk to Colin Hardy. I'll confess—I stole some fudge off the table while he was setting up." He fixed an innocent look on Ellory, but I could see his eyes twinkling.

I don't think Ellory appreciated the joke, but he let it go as the doorbell rang again. Definitely the reporter this time. And I'm sure she'd be full of questions about why the cops were here.

"Okay," Ellory said. "If I have any other questions, I'll give you a call. And I'm sure I will." He followed me to the front door where a young woman with a pixie haircut and a yellow sundress waited. A man stood behind her carrying a camera around his neck.

Jenna's eyes brightened. "Sergeant. Can I ask you a quick question?" She followed him off the porch, conferred briefly, then came back.

"Maddie?"

"That's me."

"Oh, good, and here's the cat." She beamed at JJ, still in

my arms, then looked at me. "I'm Jenna. This is Syd. Sorry about that." She waved after Ellory. "I never waste an opportunity when the police are standing in front of me."

"No problem. Come on in." I held the door for them. They trooped inside as Craig stepped out of the kitchen. He looked from them to me and raised an eyebrow.

"Can you give me a second?" I asked Jenna, and followed him out the door.

"What was that about?" I demanded once we were out of earshot.

Craig looked grim. "I don't know, Maddie."

I sniffed. "Sure. Just say you can't tell me. But why on earth would you guys question the former police chief? Your former *boss*?"

I could tell the question bothered him. His jaw clenched. "Ellory's just covering his bases. This is his first murder on the island. Why is a reporter here? Are you doing an interview?" he asked.

"Sort of. They mostly want to take pictures of JJ. They tell me he's a hero."

"Be careful engaging with the press on this," he said.

I rolled my eyes. "I know, I know. My best friend's the editor, remember? I get it. Maybe Ellory should be careful accusing innocent people."

Craig sighed. "I'll call you," he said quietly. "I'm sorry about . . . all this." He turned and strode back to his police car. I watched him go, then pasted on a smile and headed back inside for JJ's and my five minutes of fame.

Chapter 21

Grandpa's booming voice jolted me out of a deep sleep early Monday morning, startling JJ so that he jumped across my face, leaving a scratch down my cheek. Cursing, I sat up, disoriented, my hand flying to my cheek. I looked around, bleary-eyed. I must've fallen asleep on the living room couch, because I was still here. Wearing yesterday's clothes. A blanket had been tucked over me.

"Jeez," I said, blinking at Grandpa Leo. "What's wrong?"

He held up the newspaper. "You're doing interviews about finding Frank?"

I squinted blurry eyes at the paper. JJ's picture took up about two-thirds of above-the-fold space. I could see it from across the room. More real estate than Frank had gotten as a murder victim. "They wanted to do a piece on the cat, mostly," I said. He could be cranky all he wanted. By the time I'd come inside after Craig left he'd already been gone, out the back door, not even bothering to see who else had showed up. "Besides, I hardly said anything."

Grandpa came closer and peered at my cheek. "You're bleeding."

"That's what happens when you startle the cat sleeping on my head." I snatched the paper and scanned it for any grievous misquotes that would've gotten Grandpa so riled and didn't see anything too disturbing. She'd written about me heading to the Food Stroll after rescuing a stray cat, which I thought was a nice plug. She'd exaggerated a little bit when it came to JJ finding the body:

As if the cat could sense death, he bolted toward the scene of the crime, making the grisly discovery and possibly saving other lives by alerting people to the tragedy.

I glanced at JJ, amused. He sat in the window, cleaning his paw. There were probably traces of blood from my face on it. "Wow, JJ. You're really big news."

Grandpa didn't look as amused. "She talked about how the police were here."

I skimmed the rest of the article. She hadn't mentioned the murder weapon, which meant the police weren't talking about it. She'd included my answer to her question about the safety of the island and the frequency with which murders happened, to which I'd responded with a nice plug for the police:

"They're working really hard and they'll figure it out. I still believe Daybreak Island is a safe community."

I'd also told her how I still felt comfortable here:

"I grew up here. I know things change, but I don't believe the heart of a community ever changes that much when people believe in it and are dedicated to it."

Wow, I'd even impressed myself. That was a pretty good quote. But then at the end, she'd managed to get in how the police had been at our house:

"At the time of this interview James, who's currently staying at the home of her grandfather, former Daybreak Harbor Police Chief Leopold Mancini, is continuing to cooperate with police, according to Sergeant Mick Ellory as he left Mancini's house Sunday afternoon."

Great. Thanks, Jenna. If the killer wants to find out what I know, he can just stop by and join the conversation.

Still, it wasn't terrible. I tossed the paper aside. "It's not that bad, Grandpa. Why are you so upset?"

"I don't like them talking about our family," he muttered. "I'll have to talk to Becky about this."

"Becky didn't know about the Frank thing," I said. "I hadn't told her."

"It's still not appropriate. I'm going out." And he stomped out of the room. I heard the front door slam minutes later.

I frowned at the door and looked at JJ. "Grandpa's being sensitive about this." I'd better give Becky a heads-up. I glanced at the clock on my phone. Eight-thirty. She might not be in the office yet. I called her cell.

"Hey," she answered on the first ring. "So what'd you think?"

"About the story?" I sighed. "It was fine. Grandpa didn't like the part about the cops being here."

"Yeah, I figured. Sorry, I had to use it. You know how it is. Good color."

"I know, I know. He might say something to you, just be forewarned. Anyway, we never got to catch up after the cops came Saturday night," I said pointedly.

"I know. Craig and one of the state cops kept me late. I think they were trying to stop us from getting something up on the Web. Then I got stuck at work all day yesterday. This is big news."

"Did they question you?"

"Sure did. They sequestered me in the Arts Center building across the street. It was open for a private event. I think they wanted to make sure I didn't start tweeting."

"Well, you probably would have," I pointed out.

"Of course," she said. "That's not the point. Hold on."

I heard a lot of wind, then a door slamming.

"Sorry, just getting in the car," she said.

"What did they ask you?" I asked.

"After they left me there for an hour or more? They wanted to know what time we'd arrived, who we saw, who was around, if I'd been with you when you found the body. The usual stuff." She hesitated. "And what time we met up. Which I told them, but why would they ask me that, Maddie?"

"Because I had lunch with Frank and we had a . . . disagreement. I didn't get to tell you about it."

Silence. "Is that the story you were going to tell me after the stroll?" she asked finally.

"Yep."

"You going to tell me what it was about?"

"I planned on it. Want to get together later? It's kind of a long story."

"Of course it is," she muttered. "I wonder if this is why we can't get anything out of the cops. Okay, let's grab a drink tonight. I'll call you later when I have a better idea what time."

I hung up and flopped back down on the couch, pulling the blanket over my head. I wondered if Frank hovered on the edge of the afterlife, laughing at all these shenanigans.

My mother certainly wasn't laughing, as was evident by her phone call a few minutes later. "Madalyn. I tried calling you all day and night yesterday," she said when I answered.

It was true. She had. I'd finally put my phone on do-not-disturb.

"I'm sorry," I said. "I had a long day."

She sniffed. "You had time to talk to a reporter!"

"That was more about JJ than me. He's a hero, you know."

"That's nice," she said. "Odd, but nice."

"Yeah. Hey, did you and Dad hire Abe Tate to work on Grandpa's roof?" I asked.

My mother paused. "I didn't. I don't think I know that name. I can call your dad and ask him, but why would we do that? Is there something wrong with the roof?"

"Just curious," I said. "He was here yesterday and said he'd been hired to do work, but Grandpa didn't hire him. We thought some good Samaritan sent him."

"Really? That's wonderful!" my mother exclaimed.

"Is it?" I tended to be a bit more cynical, but something was weird about Abe Tate's story.

"Why not?" my mother wanted to know.

"I don't know. It seemed weird."

"I think it's nice. I hope nothing serious is wrong with the roof. So when are you coming over? I want to hear what happened the other night."

Sheesh. My incredibly creative mom, who'd had many artistic jobs in her lifetime, had recently decided to write a mystery novel. This was after she passed the baton as director of the community theater group after a wildly successful Daybreak Island rendition of *Wicked!* and needed a new project. So far she's run an online, gluten-free bakery; managed a flower shop; done freelance writing work for national publications; and opened an Etsy shop, where she sold handmade scarves, hats, and jewelry. She still had the shop, but she'd wanted to sink her teeth into "something meatier." According to my sister Val, she'd ripped a murder headline from the national news and was fictionalizing it, but she wouldn't tell anyone the story line yet.

"Soon," I said. "Tomorrow?"

"I can't wait that long," she protested. "I'm getting all my news from the newspaper."

"I don't have any news, Mom," I said, exasperated. "I don't know anything other than Frank's dead."

"Goodness, Maddie. You don't have to be vulgar." She

paused. "If you come for an early dinner I'll buy you sushi," she said slyly.

My mom had always been good at bribery. "I'll be over later on," I said.

Chapter 22

I went back to the kitchen and poured myself a cup of coffee. I carried it to the sitting room on the second floor, the one with the view of the ocean, and sat in Grandpa's favorite chair, a recliner that had seen better days. Next to the chair was a little table that held his selection of pipes. He rarely smoked them anymore, but he still had the setup I remembered from my childhood. Every night he and Grandma would retire up here. Grandma would knit, Grandpa would pack his pipe, and they would either watch the news or listen to a radio program. I'd happily sack out on the couch and enjoy whatever they chose.

Now I watched boats gliding silently by, sailboats and fishing boats, one of the high-speed ferries. For many people, a house like this was a thing of dreams. Well, aside from the flood insurance costs. Property like this had gotten harder to come by as the island became more and more built up, as houses got bigger and builders got greedy, cramming them onto every available square foot. The number of houses with real history like this one was dwindling, as people tore them down to build newer, more modern places.

The thought made me sad. I tipped Grandpa's chair

back and closed my eyes, intending to just rest for a few minutes. When I woke up it was almost ten, and JJ sat on the back of the couch scratching his ears. Feeling guilty, I tried calling Katrina so she could set up an appointment with her vet and got her voice mail. I left her a message, then got JJ suited up in his harness for a walk. I needed to drive downtown and pick up his supplies—I'd completely forgotten in the mayhem of yesterday afternoon—but figured he wanted to get some fresh air first. I poured some coffee into a travel mug and we stepped outside.

Another beautiful island day. The sun shone against a cloudless, baby-blue sky, already heating up the street. No breeze today to add a chill to the air. My kind of weather. I tilted my head back and closed my eyes, letting my face warm. Even Frank's dead body taunting me couldn't take away from the beauty of the day.

JJ seemed to feel the same way. We started walking down Grandpa's street toward the ferry area, him trotting along with a purpose all his own. A jogger slowed to pet him. "Is this the cat from the paper?" she asked.

I nodded.

"What a doll! And so brave!" She blew him a kiss and ran on. JJ squeaked after her, like he was saying *Thank you*.

Too cute. I kept walking. By the time we'd reached Damian's Lobstah Shack, he'd been stopped three more times by people who recognized him from the paper. It was kind of hilarious. We'd paused at the Lobstah Shack, where he lingered a bit to sniff in case anyone felt like giving him scraps, when a little girl came racing over to us. She looked about five, her long brown hair weaved into two perfect braids. Her mother hollered after her. "Amanda!"

"I want to pet the kitty!" she shouted back, pointing insistently at JJ. She looked up at me with wide eyes.

"You can pet him," I said, smiling at the mother to show I didn't mind. "His name is JJ."

She dropped to her knees right on the side of the road, leaving a dirt stain on the knee of her white tights. Her mother grimaced as she reached me. "I'm sorry," she said. "We had to board our cat while we're on vacation and she's angry at me. Her grandmother doesn't like cats."

I looked at the little girl, who hugged JJ while she sang a One Direction song to him. "It's okay," I said. "I don't blame her."

The mother gave me a funny look. I knelt down. "What's your kitty's name?" I asked her.

"Sadie," she replied. "My mummy won't let me have her all summer." She glared daggers at her mother.

"It's not all summer, Amanda," her mother said with exaggerated patience. "It's just for a few weeks."

Amanda dropped her head back down to whisper something to JJ. I felt bad for her.

"Hey, Amanda. Tell you what," I said.

She looked up at me suspiciously, hugging JJ like she thought I would take him away.

"I live right there." I pointed to Grandpa's house. It was only a teensy white lie, because I did live there for the moment. "Anytime you want to visit JJ while you're on the island, you just come by. If we're home, he'll be happy to play with you. Okay?"

She stared at me for so long I wondered if I'd said something that seemed insane to a five-year-old. Then she broke into a thousand-watt smile. "Mummy, can we?" she begged. "Please?"

I smiled at the girl's mom, all innocence.

Her mother sighed. "I'll never get away with saying no," she said with a small laugh. "Of course, Amanda. As long as this lady is home, okay?"

I got up and brushed off my jeans. "I'm Maddie," I said. "JJ and I will see you soon, okay, Amanda?"

Amanda kissed JJ's head then got up, still beaming. "Okay!"

"Thank you," Amanda's mother called after us as we walked away.

I glanced down at JJ. "You're a hit, dude," I said. "I bet I could charge for admission."

From inside the shack, Damian waved at us. "I have a plate set aside for him," he called out.

I led JJ over. "That's really nice of you."

"It's no trouble." He came out of the side door and set a plate of shrimp, cod, and a few pieces of lobster in front of JJ, who launched himself at it with a vengeance. We both watched, fascinated, as the food disappeared.

"I saw him in the paper." Damian glanced at me. "I guess he's a star?"

"Sure is," I said.

"That's so weird, that he found the body," Damian said. "Do you think he knew?"

"I have no idea. I've read about cats who know when people are about to die, but I've never heard of a cat sniffing out a dead person before. Maybe JJ has some kind of supernatural power."

We both considered this.

"He definitely has the power to make fish disappear fast," Damian said. "So, you want a sandwich?"

What the heck. I'd skipped breakfast. "Sure," I said.

He brightened. "A lobsTAH roll? Or fried clams?"

"I'll have the lobster," I said. "Light on the mayo."

"You got it. Have a seat." Damian waved at the picnic tables. "I just finished wiping them down."

I perched on the edge of a wooden bench and scooped JJ into my lap. He licked his lips and washed his face. I wasn't totally starving, which made me feel bad for Damian, who was putting together a sandwich fit for a food critic. "Homemade potato chips too," he said proudly, presenting me the food with a flourish.

I studied the plate. It looked delicious. Truth be told, it looked way better than the previous owners' sandwiches, which I remembered as kind of soggy and built on cheap bread. This roll had been toasted with evenly distributed butter to give it a golden glow. The lobster had just enough mayo, not enough to leave the sandwich drippy, but enough to give it the right amount of moisture. Green flecks of celery and what looked like chive were sprinkled throughout, along with pepper. "It looks great," I said, picking it up to take a bite. To my surprise, it tasted awesome. Damian's own lack of self-confidence in his ability to make "authentic" New England fare had colored my view of his food without even tasting it.

He watched me anxiously as I took another, bigger bite. My eyes widened. It was really good. Like, *really* good. The lobster tasted like he'd swum out and caught it while I waited. "Delish," I said. "Better than the Rices' version. I'm serious," I said at his skeptical look. "You really shouldn't tell people that you don't make real lobstah rolls because you're not from here." I wagged a potato chip at him. "You need to get better at marketing."

Relieved, he sat down next to me. "Really?"

This guy needed some self-esteem lessons. "Really," I said. "I wouldn't waste my time lying to you. I don't even live here anymore. Is business still slow?"

He shrugged. "A little. But yesterday I sold out of fried shrimp."

"That's a good start," I said. "What do you do for marketing?"

At his blank stare, I sighed. "You need a marketing plan. Social media. Better signage. A spot on those tourist maps."

"I don't have a marketing person," he said.

"You can learn. I do all the marketing for my juice bar. Look." I shoved the last bite of sandwich in my mouth. JJ pawed at my plate indignantly. I hadn't left any for him, that's how good it was. "I can show you some stuff. Help you with a marketing plan. What do you think?"

"Would you really do that?"

"Sure." Why not? Ethan and I had had help when we started our business. I believed in paying it forward. And I knew what the poor guy was up against.

"Thank you so much." He gazed at me with puppy-dog eyes. "I tried to get help through the chamber but they never had time for me. And when I looked up a public relations person online it was way too much money."

Through the chamber. "Like through Frank?" I asked. "What kind of help?"

"They were running ads about a program where people could get basic marketing help, social media training, that sort of thing. Every time I called they blew me off. I don't know who was in charge."

Interesting. I was getting the sense that smaller businesses were the redheaded stepchildren of the chamber overlords. "No worries. We'll get you going." I ate the last of my potato chips and stood, brushing the crumbs from the front of my clothes. "Remember—no more telling people your food isn't authentic because you're from out of town."

"You don't think they'll figure it out?" he asked, doubtful.

"Just keep dropping those *r*'s." I patted him on the back. "We have to run. How much do I owe you?"

He waved me off. "On the house. Thanks for your help, Maddie. I really appreciate it."

As he walked away I realized I should've asked him if he'd left the cat café article for me. Maybe next time.

Chapter 23

JJ and I walked up by the ferry just in time to see the second one of the day docking. We stopped to watch while the passengers disembarked. Some were clearly tourists; others headed to the parking area to retrieve their cars. JJ and I took the long way back to the house so I could walk off some of my lobster roll and chips. Grandpa still hadn't returned. Where on earth did he go for so long? I grabbed Grandma's keys off the rack near the door and loaded JJ into the car. I needed to pick up his stuff from the pet store or he'd have no food tonight. He probably preferred Damian's leftovers, but still.

As we drove the short distance through high-volume traffic into town, my mind inevitably drifted back to Frank and the bits and pieces I'd heard about him and the chamber. I ticked them off on mental fingers: there was no big love lost for Frank in town and he was scamming at least one person (Grandpa). Some people, including Pauline Crosby and Damian Shaw, felt he didn't treat some of the smaller businesses fairly. Frank could be cheating on his wife with Piper Dawes. (Ew.) I thought of her frizzy hair and shrill voice and shuddered. Cass thought Frank was fixated on getting every business on board as a member, and he took it personally when that didn't happen. It sounded to me like Frank wanted to create a fiefdom and have all the businesses in town dependent on him. And perhaps push to eliminate the ones that didn't fit in with his new idea of what would make Daybreak Island great.

I blew out a frustrated breath as I drove around the block for the sixth time without finding a parking space. Finally I pulled to the curb on a side street that was more like an alley. At this rate it would've been easier to walk. I helped JJ out. Hurrying around the corner, I almost slammed into Officer Craig.

He reached out to steady me. "Hey. Slow down," he said automatically, as if patrolling a school hallway.

"Sorry," I said and went to move around him, but he still held my arm.

I raised my eyes to his. He stared at me and I couldn't quite read his expression, but it was thoughtful.

"On patrol?" I asked, since I had no idea what to say.

"Maddie."

"Yeah?"

"What happened to your cheek?" He reached out, his finger light against the scratch.

I lifted my own hand self-consciously. "The cat. Grandpa startled him."

Craig raised an eyebrow but didn't question it further. "I'm sorry about what happened yesterday. Ellory was hard on your grandfather."

I shrugged. "Not your fault." I didn't think so, anyway.

"I know. But it sucks. How are you doing? With everything. What happened the other night." He shuffled from foot to foot, a physical demonstration of his attempt to dance around the reality of the murder.

"You mean finding Frank's body?" I said.

He flinched. "You always were direct."

I acknowledged that with a nod. "You're a cop, Craig. If you can't talk about a dead guy . . ."

"Of course I can. Jeez, Maddie. I was trying to be respectful of you."

"Oh." Now I felt bad. "Sorry. I'm fine. I just wish you guys would figure out who did it, you know? I feel like there's some weird fixation on Grandpa right now."

Craig tugged me around the corner, back into the alley. "Look. You know I can't talk about this, so I won't remind you." His eyes pierced mine as if he could see inside my brain. He'd already started to get that intense look, the one I'd seen on so many cops over my lifetime. I wondered if crime on the island had gotten worse while I'd been gone.

"Let's be honest," I said. "This wasn't random. Someone wanted Frank O'Malley dead, not just to kill some guy on the street for the fun of it."

Chapter 24

Craig lifted his chin, a teensy bit of acknowledgment. He leaned against the brick wall of the pizza shop, his body shielding me from view of the street. "I know your grandfather didn't kill anyone. But since there was some trouble with him and Frank lately, they're going to look into it."

"We never said he was having trouble," I pointed out. "We only said he was approached—repeatedly—for a real estate deal he didn't wish to do. Besides, I'm sure a lot of people had trouble with Frank. I would never wish anyone harm, but that guy was a sketch."

"Why do you say that?" he asked.

I hesitated. Grandpa would kill me if he found out I told Craig about Frank's threats—it definitely added to the motive bucket Ellory wanted to fill with Grandpa's name. But maybe Craig could do some work behind the scenes to figure out what Frank was doing—and to whom. Maybe there was something illegal. Maybe he'd ticked off someone who really had authority over zoning and property disputes. Or another property owner in town. Who's to say his son wasn't looking to build an empire? Looking for more than one location? There could be a whole slew of suspects out there that the cops simply didn't know about, just because Johnny Citizen was too afraid of Frank O'Malley to open his mouth.

I looked around to be sure no one listened. We were alone in the alley. Craig stood so close to me I could smell his aftershave. It reminded me of the air just after a rainstorm—earthy, kind of woodsy, but with a hint of spice.

"Maddie?" He waited for me to answer him. I forced my mind away from how good he smelled and focused. I had to tell him. Someone had to know.

"You can't tell anyone," I said.

"That's not realistic," he said. "Once I hear what you have to say, I'll likely have to bring the information to Ellory. He's the investigating officer."

I figured that was the case, but it was worth a shot. "Frank wanted my grandfather's house, but it wasn't as simple as asking and being told no. He threatened him."

"Threatened him?" Craig repeated, standing up straighter. "What kind of threat?"

"That he could mess with his property values. That there was a new law that permitted lots in certain areas to be rezoned as commercial lots and his was one of them. I think he made it sound like it could eventually become an eminent domain thing. So if he didn't sell to Frank now, his values would go down and when the time came he'd get nothing. Which is scary when you're already in the red, I would imagine."

"Wait. What do you mean, in the red?"

I explained Grandpa's repair dilemmas and financial challenges of late. "So the roof thing was part of a bigger issue, but he doesn't want to broadcast it."

Craig's lips set in a line. "I wish I'd known that," he said. "I would've tried to help."

I don't know what Craig would've done, but the thought was lovely. "That's sweet," I said softly. Our eyes lingered probably a minute longer than necessary before he broke the contact.

"I'm confused, though," he said. "Your grandpa is one of the smartest guys on this island. And obviously knows a lot about town government and how things work. Why was he giving Frank's story the time of day?"

I shrugged miserably. "No idea. I think he's been struggling, honestly. He still hasn't gotten over retirement." Grandpa had been off the job for five years now, and I was convinced he still missed it every day. "And watching my grandmother die hasn't been great for his well-being either. Maybe he just figured things had changed so much since he'd left the job that guys like Frank O'Malley could get the town officials in his pocket, and he had no control over it anymore."

We both digested that thought. Disgust filled Craig's features. "Slimeball," he muttered.

"Agreed. But Grandpa didn't kill him. And neither did I," I added, just in case that was the next question.

He smiled. "I don't think I'd ever peg you as a murderer."

We fell into that silence again. Behind us, crowds of people milled around Bicycle Street, shopping and eating and exploring. This tiny side road didn't exist in that world. We were the only ones on it.

"But I think you're right," he said after a minute. "This wasn't random. Whoever killed Frank didn't mistake him for someone else, or rob him. It screams heat of the moment, to me at least. The murder weapon was handy." He cringed. "I shouldn't be telling you this. If you repeat it, I'll hunt you down."

"Have you talked with his wife yet? They say it's usually the spouse. Or Piper? They seemed . . . close."

"Who's they? TV?" He shook his head. "Ellory's talked to them both."

"And?"

He shrugged. "His wife wasn't even on the island that night. She's been spending most of her time up in Boston, near her son. She came over Sunday morning. It was too late for her to catch the ferry by the time we called Saturday night. And Piper was in the area all day, but during the window Frank was killed she was over at town Hall arguing with the department of public works staff about lighting. It's documented."

"Oh." I tried not to feel deflated about Frank's wife having an alibi. "Well, I heard he was cheating on her." I watched his face carefully. It barely changed, but there was a flicker. He hadn't known that.

"We're looking into every angle," he said.

"Wow, you've got all the cop lines memorized already," I said, softening my sarcasm with a tiny smile. He didn't bite.

"What about Jade Bennett?" I asked. "He was found in her tent." I thought about Frank's dirty-old-man vibe. Jade was pretty. Maybe Frank tried something with her and she flew into a rage and stabbed him.

Craig frowned. "You're reaching. Jade's a nice girl."

"I'm sure she is, but if he tried to grope her or something . . ."

"Grope her? Jeez, Maddie . . ."

"Have you been around him when young women are around?" I asked.

"No. What are you saying?"

I shrugged. "He was a dirty old man, Craig. I'm surprised no one's mentioned that."

Craig's eyes darkened. "You know this firsthand?"

"I've seen it, sure. If you're asking me if I let Frank grab me and didn't deck him, I think you know me better than that. One more thing. I've been hearing that Frank's chamber wasn't really a friend to small businesses. Some, but not all."

"Meaning?"

"Look, I'm just telling you what I've heard. Shouldn't you go out and investigate?"

His gaze drifted behind me, watching people walk by on the main street. "I guess people would have resented that if they thought it was true."

"Yeah. And I get the sense that he didn't like when people resisted his charms," I said, remembering Cass's comments about how it had become Frank's mission to get him on board as a member. "He wanted everyone as a member, but didn't seem to care about certain businesses."

Craig gave me a funny look. "How do you know all this? You haven't lived here in almost ten years."

I shrugged. "People talk to me. Plus my best friend is the editor of the paper."

"Touché."

We both looked down at JJ, who'd flopped onto his side to nap. He looked like a seal.

"How can he just sleep like that?" Craig asked.

"I have no idea. But I should probably go get his stuff."

"When are you going back to California?" he asked abruptly.

"I'm not sure. Why?"

"Just curious," he said.

"Are you going to tell me I can't leave or something?" I asked, crossing my arms over my chest.

He stared at me, then shook his head. "No, Maddie. We don't actually do that," he said, the ghost of a grin touching his lips. "But . . ." He hesitated. "This probably isn't the best idea, given the situation," he said, almost to himself.

I tapped my foot. "Craig, for the love of Pete, spit it out."

"Do you want to have dinner some night before you leave?"

"Dinner?" I repeated, caught off guard.

"Yeah. You know, food." He grinned. "Or don't you guys eat out West?"

I flushed a little. "Yes. We eat. I eat. Sure. Dinner sounds nice."

"Yeah?" Craig looked surprised.

"Yeah," I said.

"Okay. So. I'll, um, let you know when I have a night off." He smiled apologetically. "I'm putting in a lot of OT this week, I think."

"I get it." I scooped up JJ and started to walk away, but turned back. "Hey, Craig?"

"Yeah?"

"You're not going to stop looking for the real killer, are you? Because it's not my grandpa."

He sighed. "Of course we won't stop looking, Maddie."

"Thanks." I blew him a kiss and walked around the corner to the pet store, leaving Craig standing by my car.

Chapter 25

I spent the drive home lecturing myself on the wisdom of agreeing to a date with my ex-boyfriend. Luckily it was a short ride, because I didn't really want to talk myself out of it. Plus, I argued with myself, we hadn't even set a true *date* for the date. It may never happen. This whole mess could be cleaned up tomorrow and I'd be on the first flight back to California. But if I was honest with myself, I kind of hoped that wouldn't happen. Well, the first-flight-out part. Not the cleaned-up-mess part.

I wasn't sure what had prompted this sudden reattraction to Craig. Aside from the hotness. Maybe it was the cop thing—the complete antithesis of the musicians I usually went after.

"Why am I spending so much time thinking about this?" I asked JJ, who stood with his paws against the windowsill looking out at the town. "We're heading back to California soon anyway. I'll forget about him in five minutes. I think you'll like it there. It's pretty warm most of the time. And when it gets cold, it's nothing like here."

He ignored me in favor of glaring at a big fluffy dog walking down the street on a leash.

When I got back to Grandpa's there seemed to be a

party going on. Four cars were parked outside. Thankfully none were police cars. But apparently my grandfather had a much more fulfilling social life than I did. I'd hoped for some alone time with him, figuring he'd had most of the day to cool off from being mad about the newspaper article. I wanted to ask about Abe Tate, and tell him about Pauline's commentary on Frank. I definitely didn't want to tell him about my conversation with Craig. He'd probably hit the roof again if he knew I'd told the cops about the threats. I wasn't sure when a line had gone up between Grandpa and his beloved police department, but it was unsettling.

I brought JJ inside, then returned to unload the car. I could hear laughter and mens' voices from the basement. I didn't head down there until I'd filled up JJ's food bowl and fixed his litter box. Then I descended the stairs into what looked suspiciously like a man cave. I hadn't been down here in a long time. Grandpa had done some remodeling, if the room with the sixty-inch TV and round table clearly set up for cards was a clue. Pipe smoke wafted at me, through the voices. Frank Sinatra played in the background.

The voices trailed off as they noticed me. "Maddie," Grandpa said, getting up. "What are you doing?"

"I heard voices. Came down to see what you're up to." I surveyed the four other men sitting around the table, holding cards. "Poker?"

"Forty-fives," one of them said helpfully. I'd heard of the game, though I didn't know how to play it. It was very specific to a certain area of Massachusetts, up north of Boston.

"Do you all remember my granddaughter?" Grandpa asked.

"Hi, Maddie. Sure do." One of them rose and shook my hand. "I worked with your grandpa. Lester Hayes."

They each reminded me of who they were. Three of the four, including Lester, had been on the force. One ran the Daybreak Island Historical Society. They all looked vaguely familiar.

"Nice to meet you all," I said. "I didn't mean to interrupt. Grandpa, I'll see you later."

"Okay, doll," he said, already refocused on his card game.

I climbed the stairs slowly and looked for JJ. I found him in the kitchen, snacking on his dry food. "Come on, then," I said to him. "I guess I'll do some investigating on my own, if Grandpa's too busy. At least you're an engaged sidekick."

Ten minutes later I drove away from Grandpa's house in the direction of Duck Cove. As long as I was going to my mother's later, I might as well not waste a trip. And I'd happened to find out that Tate Contracting, Abe Tate's office, was also in Duck Cove. I had a feeling he knew more about this mysterious good Samaritan than he'd let on in front of the cops. I mean, everyone liked stories like that, but most people—especially the self-employed—tended to be more skeptical. I wanted to know why he'd taken the job. Maybe he'd be more inclined to talk if it was just the two of us. I'd called ahead to make sure he was in the office and, according to his receptionist, he would be there for another hour.

The Tate Contracting offices were housed in a bright yellow two-family home near the center of town, tucked between a pizza shop and a day spa. If you didn't notice the sign with the business name, you could mistake this place for a regular house. He kept his property maintained well, with a flower bed and lawn ornaments out front and hanging plants on the porch. I guessed he had to. No one would want to hire a contractor whose own offices didn't look good. The driveway extended around the house. Two white vans with ladders on the roofs were parked at the back of the driveway.

I parked on the street in front and walked to the front door, opened wide to let in the summer air. I pushed the screen door open and walked in. A woman sitting behind a high, round counter looked up expectantly. She wore glasses and had shoulder-length hair that looked like it had been the victim of a bad perm. Frosted pink lipstick dressed her lips.

"May I help you?" she asked, looking from me to JJ, whom I held.

JJ squeaked.

"Hi. Don't mind him," I said with a smile. She didn't return it. "Um, I just called. I'm looking for Abe."

"And you are?"

"Maddie James. I wanted to talk to him about the job at my grandfather's house. Shoreline Avenue."

"One minute." She rose and walked to the back of the office. While I waited, I perused the photos lining the walls. One showed the stages of a new home, from foundation all the way through to finished product. The house was gorgeous.

"Ms. James?" I turned. Abe Tate waited next to the front desk. His admin brushed by him and took her seat, busying herself with something on the computer.

"Hi," I said. "I was hoping you had a minute?"

Tate motioned for me to follow him. We walked down the hall to the room in back, which he'd transformed into an office. I presumed it had been a master bedroom in a past life, given its size and placement. I took the seat in front of his desk while he sat behind it. He looked just as much at home there as he had on the ladder the other day.

"Nice cat," he said, gaze falling to JJ. At least he didn't

make a snide comment about me dressing better for this visit.

"Thanks. This is JJ." I stroked his head. He curled up in my lap and went to sleep.

Tate returned his gaze to me. "What can I help you with?"

"First, I'm sorry about the whole police thing," I said. "With the murder the other night, well, you can never be too careful."

A shadow flitted across his face and then was gone. "Yeah. That's scary stuff. Of course I don't blame ya. I would've done the same thing in your shoes," he said.

I smiled. "Thank you. Are you a chamber member, Mr. Tate?"

He nodded. "Not that I ever go to the events. I'm always workin'."

"I hear you. It's a lot of work owning your own business," I said, trying to establish a connection that would put him at ease with me.

"Yup." Then he looked at me curiously. "You own a business?"

"I do. Out in California. A juice shop."

He frowned. "What kind of juice? Like, you sell apple juice? Orange juice?"

I couldn't stop the giggle but covered it with a coughing fit. "Excuse me. No, we make juice out of vegetables and fruits. Like kale, and apples, and cucumbers."

He looked like he couldn't comprehend what that meant. Before we got lost down that rabbit hole I hurried to the next subject. "Speaking of the other night. Did you know Frank O'Malley well? I figure you must've, with both of you being prominent in the business community and all."

Abe's expression didn't change. " 'Course I knew him," he said. No affect, good or bad. This guy had a good poker face. Grandpa should invite him over.

"Were you friendly?" I asked.

Now Abe snorted. "Friendly? That depends. We got a lot friendlier when I called him every day to try and get paid for the work I did at his house."

Chapter 26

I tried to hide my surprise. "Really? He stiffed you?"

He crossed his arms. "He tried. And that ain't me bad-mouthing the dead. He tried to say I didn't finish the work, but I did. His wife knew it too. She finally paid me."

I absorbed that information and found it didn't really surprise me. If Frank could try to scam a prominent senior citizen through his business status, why wouldn't he try to cheat someone in his own business dealings?

"That certainly goes against chamber principles of helping local business," I said.

Tate snorted. "You ain't kiddin'. I almost canceled my membership, but Ms. Piper asked me to reconsider."

Ms. Piper? I wouldn't have guessed she'd be good at PR. "When was this?" I asked.

He narrowed his eyes at me. "Right before his wife paid up last month. You writing his biography or something?"

I hated when condescending men got flip with me. "No," I said smoothly. "But the police are looking for the killer, and you don't want to look like you were hiding information. Right?"

Abe Tate thought about this. "It ain't no secret," he said, but with less conviction. "But it got settled. Nothin' more to talk about. I don't hold grudges. Bad for the heart. And the ulcer."

"Fair enough," I said. "Anyway, I did come by for another reason. Since yesterday was a little crazy, I didn't get to talk to you as much as I would've liked. I'm really interested in finding out who wants to help my grandfather fix his roof. I'd like to personally thank them."

He smiled, relaxing a bit. "It's refreshin' in times like these, isn't it? I wish I could tell you more, Ms. James. But what I told you and the police yesterday is all I know."

I'd already pegged Abe Tate as a classic contractor—cocky, patronizing, willing to say anything to your face and then flipping you off behind your back. And right now, Tate wasn't telling me the whole truth.

I smiled sweetly. "As a businesswoman myself, I'd want to be certain before I completed a job that these payments would continue to come. Might there be some due diligence you did to get a flavor for that before committing?"

Tate's expression had morphed into poker face. "Look," he said finally. "I've been in business a long time. I don't usually take on anonymous-caller projects. Believe me, I have plenty of other work to do. But this person insisted."

"Insisted," I repeated. "Did you get a sense of why?"

Tate shrugged. "Who knows. Maybe they just love your grandfather. Maybe it's a rich lady with a secret crush on him." He winked. "Or maybe your granddad's got the goods on someone and they're trying to even things up."

I hated to think any of this was true. "Those are interesting reasons," I said. "Do you know if any of them are true?"

I think Abe Tate thought I'd accept the good Samaritan explanation and walk away. Since I wasn't, I could see him reconsidering how to handle this. After a minute he rose, went to his office door and shut it. Now I was interested. Top secret stuff, apparently.

"Look," he said. "I'm only telling you this because it's your grandfather. I respect him. Truth is, I'da probably done the work for free anyway, had I known he needed it."

Was he really being sincere?

"Your grandpa was a good cop," Tate said. "He helped me out once with my kid, and I always remembered that." He blew out a breath and raked a hand through his hair, leaving a few spikes sticking up. He pulled a key out of his desk drawer, then went to the filing cabinet behind him. He pulled out an entire drawer jammed full of rumpled manila folders, set it on the floor, then reached in and extracted a large lockbox while I watched.

He came back to the desk, took out another key and opened the case, then spun it around so I could see inside it. My eyes widened. Cash. A lot of it. I counted fifteen small bundles of hundreds. I raised my eyes to his, a silent question.

"I sorta fibbed. There was more than $500. I got a phone call asking if I could take the job, and the guy said if I agreed he'd leave me a payment, but I had to have a safe place for it. I thought it was someone messing around, so I said they could leave it in the van. I keep my crappy old van out back and don't lock it 'cause I never leave tools inside. Anyway, I near forgot about it. He called back two days later to ask if I was all set. Had to admit I'd forgotten; so I went out and looked. Sure enough . . ." He motioned to the case.

I frowned. "So it definitely was a man."

"Yep."

"And you have no idea who. The voice didn't sound familiar?"

He shook his head. "I swear," he added, seeing the skepticism on my face. "Look. I didn't wanna tell the cops I got a cash payment. I'm sure they got an inside line to the IRS, you know what I mean? Being a business lady and all?" He winked, looking for camaraderie.

I felt no camaraderie. This turn of events puzzled me. Who on the island carried a wad of cash like this around and used it to perform anonymous good deeds? "Are you going to talk to this person again? Will they owe you more money?" I asked.

"More money?" He barked out a laugh. "Sweetheart, there's enough here to fix more than the roof. He told me to take a look around, see what else was urgent and take care of it, no questions asked. That he'd check in again to see if I needed more once this part was done. I have no idea how he's gonna know it's done, but I guess we'll cross that bridge when we come to it."

This was too wild. Who on earth would be handing over fistfuls of cash to fix my grandfather's house? Now I knew for sure it wasn't my father. He wouldn't have the slightest clue how to operate stealthily like this. Plus, he was big on paper trails, being a hospital CEO and all.

"What did his voice sound like?"

"Like a guy. How do I know? I'm not a voice expert!"

I managed to not roll my eyes. "Have you found any other things to fix?" I asked. "Did the person give you specifics?"

Tate shook his head. "Nah. Just told me to check it out. First chance I got to go over was yesterday, and we all know how that turned out."

I nodded. "You better get that to the bank. Aren't you nervous about people breaking in and having that much cash around?"

"The bank?" Tate snorted. "I'm better off stuffing it in my mattress. I'm sure they'll find a way to tax me on it anyway if I take it to the bank. Don't you worry, miss. I know how to keep my money safe."

Chapter 27

My mother didn't live far from Tate, but I took the long way to her house since I was still early for our early dinner. I cranked open the sunroof and let the salty air circulate. I concentrated on breathing and letting the ocean fill all my senses. It really is the best remedy for any ailment, emotional or physical.

My mind worked overtime as I drove, trying to think this through. I'd left Tate's office with more questions than when I'd gone inside. There were three major events happening simultaneously: Frank's murder, the bid for Grandpa's house, and the mysterious gift of home improvement. Could the last two be related? That would mean someone knew about Frank's intent to take my grandfather's house by using the looming repairs as leverage and wanted to thwart it. Grandpa thought he'd kept it quiet, but who knew? If a town gossip like Lilah Gilmore heard even a glimmer of that story, it would reach all four corners of the island within hours. So someone knowing wasn't that hard to believe.

Or was I projecting? Being a crazy conspiracy theorist? Someone could have simply heard that Grandpa needed work done on his house. Someone who knew what he was going through with Grandma and wanted to do something kind. It wasn't that far-fetched.

But someone having that kind of cash was. Anyone in Grandpa's regular circle, anyway. He'd always surrounded himself with like souls—those who wanted to do good in the world. Their bank accounts usually weren't overflowing. Certainly none of them that I could think of would have thousands hanging around in their mattresses.

Outsiders didn't understand the reality of a place like Daybreak Island. They saw the beauty and prosperity of the summer months, when celebs and politicians and other millionaire types arrived by boat and plane and threw cash around like it was going out of style. They didn't see the long, cold winter days that stretched to infinity, when most shops were closed and people like Pauline had to live off what they'd saved from the prolific summer crowds or find part-time jobs at the local liquor stores because those never shut down. A typical islander's life could be difficult. My family had always been lucky—between my father's hospital career, my mother's creativity, and my grandpa's public service career, our lives had never been dictated by the seasons. Others weren't so lucky.

Tate's confession bothered me. I thought of calling Craig to tell him, but decided against it. If Tate got in trouble for anything he'd take the money and run without touching Grandpa's house. Not that Craig would call the IRS, but still.

"I'm being stupid, right, JJ?" I asked my traveling companion. "I should just be thankful someone's trying to help. If anything it will buy Grandpa time."

JJ didn't answer. He was sound asleep in a ball on the front seat with his tail curled around his face. I sighed. Even he was bored with this conversation.

When I got to my parents' my mother's little red convertible sat in the driveway blocked in by a silver Volvo that I'd never seen before. A landscaping truck sat at the curb behind my sister Sam's old green VW Bug. Sam stood in the yard, engaged in a serious conversation with two men. One held a weed whacker. I waved at her as I pulled to the curb behind the truck. My father's car was absent, but I hadn't expected him to be home. He left for the hospital around seven every morning and didn't get home until five or later, depending on the day's events. Since my mother wanted to have an early dinner, I guessed Dad had a hospital thing tonight.

I got out of the car, let JJ jump down and led him in through the open garage. I saw the landscapers stop and stare at the cat on his leash. Grinning, I climbed the short flight of steps into the house when I heard voices from inside. My mother's and another woman's, quiet murmurs that I couldn't completely discern. But I did hear the word "Frank." I eased the door open a crack and pressed my ear to it. JJ sat at my feet, waiting expectantly.

"I'm so sorry, Margaret," my mother was saying. "I had no idea things were that dire between you two."

Margaret. O'Malley? Had to be. What other Margaret would be talking about Frank? I couldn't wait to hear what had been so dire between them. I leaned forward eagerly.

"It was a long time coming," Margaret said, her voice thick with tears. "He had been . . . living his own life for some time now. It should've happened long ago."

I froze. *A long time coming . . . Should've happened long ago.* Was she talking about divorcing him? Had they been split up when he died?

But before I could hear anything else, my sister's voice said in my ear, "What the heck are you doing?"

Startled, I stumbled forward. When I grabbed the door to steady myself I forgot I'd cracked it open. I fell right through it, sprawling on the floor a few feet from the kitchen table where my mother sat.

Chapter 28

JJ raced in behind me. I managed to keep hold of his leash
as I crashed down. Shocked, my mother and Margaret
stared at me; then my mother jumped up.

"Maddie! Are you okay?" She reached for me and
helped pull me to my feet. "What on earth are you doing?
You brought the cat? Is this the one from the paper?"

Sam stood behind me, her hand over her mouth. "Sorry,"
she said. "I didn't mean to startle you."

"I'm fine," I said, my cheeks pinking with embarrass-
ment. I brushed my pants off and smiled at Margaret, trying desperately to look normal. "So sorry to interrupt. I . . .
tripped. Such a klutz. Yes, this is JJ."

My mother looked confused about why I had a cat in a
harness, but she refocused on the issue at hand, trying to
move past my embarrassing entrance. "Maddie, do you remember Margaret O'Malley? She's . . . she was . . . Frank's
wife." She cleared her throat, clearly uncomfortable. With
what? Reminding us all that Margaret was newly wid-
owed, or because Margaret had just told her something
that freaked her out? Or maybe because I was the one who
found her dead husband?

"I do. Hello. How are you?" I wanted to kick myself as soon as the stupid question came out of my mouth. "I mean, um, nice to see you again." But Margaret, as was her style, handled my awkwardness with aplomb.

I hadn't seen her for years. She looked largely the same—graceful, elegant, well dressed—if not a few years older. And right now, distraught. Bloodshot eyes, a grim set to her jaw.

Still, she forced a smile. "Nice to see you too, Maddie. Although not necessary to fall at my feet." She winked, then rose before I could say anything. "Thank you for the coffee, Sophie. I should go. Lovely to see you girls again," she said to me and Sam. She got to her feet and gave my mother a kiss on the cheek.

My mother followed her to the door. "Please let me know what's going on," she said, squeezing Margaret's hand. "And if you need anything."

"I'll walk you out." Sam offered to Margaret.

Once they'd left, my mother turned to me. "You really should be more careful, Maddie. You can break something falling like that. And you're early. I thought we said four? I haven't even gotten the sushi yet."

"I had an errand to run nearby and it went faster than I thought. Don't worry about me. Go do your thing. JJ and I will just hang out. Or I can go get the sushi for you."

My mother looked uncertain. "Margaret's visit was unexpected, and I'm getting to a really good chapter in my book." She rubbed her hands together. "Elise—that's my main character—has to figure out if her doctor kidnapped and tortured the natural healer. But that can wait," she decided. "I want to hear about this botched Food Stroll." She led me into the living room and steered me to the couch. "Sit. I'll get us some lemonade."

I sat, arranging JJ on the couch next to me.

"Did you find out more about this Secret Santa person who wants to help with Grandpa's repairs?" she called from the kitchen. "It wasn't your father."

"Yeah, I figured it wasn't him." I sighed. I gave her bare-bones details about Abe Tate's story as she came in with a tray and two glasses. I left out the part about the clandestine cash stashed in the back of the van.

But she didn't seem to think the story sounded odd. "What a miracle! I'm so happy," she said. "Did you find out what's actually wrong with the roof?"

"I don't know," I admitted.

"I'll have to ask him. Oh! You two need to come for dinner tomorrow," she said. "I want to start getting Grandpa into a routine. It's nice that you're there, but when you leave he'll need somewhere to go for dinners a few times a week, don't you think?"

"I hope you already had him pencil you in," I said dryly. "He's got a pretty active social calendar."

She tsked at me. "It's good for him."

"I guess." I didn't tell her I had no idea where he went when he vanished, or that his basement had been full of smoking men playing cards.

"Anyway. Before I forget, will you bring dessert? That's the only thing I'm not making."

"Sure."

"It should be vegan," she added. "And gluten-free if possible."

I frowned at her. "Is there such a place on the island?"

"I have no idea," she admitted. "But there should be. Now. Tell me about Saturday night."

"Not much to tell." I reiterated what I'd told the reporter.

"How'd Frank die?"

"I . . . don't think the police have said."

"Oh." She frowned. "You couldn't tell?"

"Jeez, Mom."

"Fine, fine. So who do they think did it?"

Besides me and Grandpa? I shrugged. "I'm not at the top of the police confidant list. What have you heard? Any suspects?" I asked casually. *Like his wife?*

"I haven't heard much. I've been home yesterday and today. Writing," she added. "I only talked to Lilah."

"Margaret too," I pointed out.

"Well, yes, of course," she said, her eyes sliding away a bit.

"Does she have any thoughts on who would want to kill her husband? I mean, if anyone should know," I said.

"Obviously I didn't ask, Maddie," my mother said. "That would've been quite intrusive of me."

Sometimes I wished my mother was nosier. "She must be devastated," I said, trying a different tack.

My mother became intensely interested in her lemonade.

"What was she talking about?" I asked.

She paused. "What do you mean?"

"When I fell, uh, came in. I heard her saying something about Frank and how something was a long time coming."

Frowning, she set her glass down. "It's really none of your business, Maddie. We were having a private conversation. That poor woman has been through enough without being the center of a gossip circle. Now. What do you want to eat? I'll get the menu." My mother sailed out of the room, leaving me wondering why that simple question had hit such a nerve.

Chapter 29

My mother had a night of murder ahead of her—on the computer of course—so after we pigged out on spicy tuna and shrimp tempura rolls, I collected JJ and headed back to Grandpa's. I'd gotten halfway there when Becky called.

"Let's meet at Jade Moon at seven," she said without preamble. "I'll be in the office until then, eating cold pizza and waiting to hear if the police are ever going to get back to me with a *No comment*."

"About Frank?" I asked.

"Yeah. They're playing this one close to the vest."

I swallowed hard, hoping it was for a reason other than that they wanted to arrest Grandpa.

"So does that work?" she asked.

"What?"

"Jade's. Seven. Are you paying attention?"

"Yes. Sorry. That works. I'll see you then."

I took JJ home. Grandpa's truck was gone. I wondered why exactly it was that my mother thought he'd be sitting home alone every night lonely and listless. Clearly she didn't have a clue about his social life. I got JJ set up with some wet food and fresh water, then got back in Grandma's car. I hoped I could find a place to park near Jade's. Her bar, though not located right on the main drag, sat in a prime location on the corner of Bicycle and Ocean Avenue. She had her own parking lot, but it was tiny. If it was full, you had to take your chances on the street. But since it wasn't yet prime drinking hour, I rolled right into a spot and hurried inside.

I'd beaten Becky there so I grabbed two bar stools and surveyed the place. I hadn't been in here yet, but I liked the vibe. Everything was purple—the walls, the bar stools, the images of the moon on the ceiling. Each table in the lounge area had a sleek silver vase with one purple flower. She had cool art on the walls—paintings of clocks that said NOW across the faces, moonscapes, star constellations, the sea under a full moon. It was kind of enchanting.

I recognized Jade Bennett behind the bar, mixing a vodka and tonic. I'd seen her around a couple of times since I'd been home, most recently standing outside her tent at the Food Stroll after I'd discovered Frank's body in it. She was purple too, sort of. Her shoulder-length hair was equal parts black and purple, and she wore—you guessed it—a purple Jade Moon shirt.

I caught her eye and smiled. She held up a finger, finished making her drink, handed it to a guy standing at the end of the bar then came over to me.

"What can I get you?"

"I'll have a glass of merlot," I said.

Jade nodded and went to turn away, but I reached over the bar and stuck out my hand.

"I'm Maddie James."

The look she gave me asked why I thought she cared, but politeness won out and she shook. "Jade Bennett."

"How are you doing after . . . the other night?" I asked. I had no idea how she'd react to talking about Frank's murder, but heck, the guy had been killed in her tent. She had to have some thoughts on it.

Jade's jaw set. "I would've been better if Frank'd picked someone else's tent to get offed in," she said.

I didn't know if I should laugh or be shocked at that, so I simply nodded. "Crazy town, right? Did you know him?"

"Sure I knew him. Everyone knew him. Look. I've told everyone and their brother that I had nothing to do with it—" she began, but I jumped in.

"Hey, listen. I hear you," I said. "I'm the one who found him. How do you think I feel?"

At that, her demeanor changed. She leaned onto the bar. "That's right. I knew you looked familiar. How are *you* doing?"

I shrugged. "Fine. I'd be better if they caught the killer, though. It's kind of unnerving, you know?"

"You're telling me." Jade shook her head. "Of all the tents, right?"

I couldn't have finagled a better opening if I'd tried. "What *was* he doing in your tent?" I asked.

She wrinkled her nose. "Probably drinking my wine."

I laughed, until I realized she wasn't kidding. "What do you mean? The stroll wasn't open yet."

"Oh, I know. He thinks—thought—he had carte blanche with my booze." She smiled wryly. "I told him I couldn't join the chamber this year because I was watching my finances. I just opened last year. He's been after me ever since. He told me he'd waive my dues if I gave him a drink when he came in to the bar. Of course, I agreed." She rolled her eyes. "I just didn't realize he meant like every five minutes. So I presumed he was helping himself to my wine. What happened from there, who knows?" She stopped talking as Becky hurried up behind me.

"Sorry, I got delayed," she said. "Hi, Jade."

"Hey. What're you drinking?"

"Martini?" Becky asked.

"You got it." She turned away to get our drinks.

Becky slid onto the stool. "Investigating?" she asked with a smirk.

I shrugged. "I had to ask."

"Find out anything good?"

I watched Jade mix Becky's drink. I wanted to ask her more questions, like if she'd seen Frank alive that evening and if he'd been with anyone, but if I asked too much she might wonder why. "Just that Frank thought he was entitled to booze whenever he wanted because he waived Jade's chamber dues."

Becky frowned. "Sheesh."

"Yeah. Did *anyone* like this guy?"

Jade put our drinks down in front of us. "My guess would be not many," Becky said, answering my question after she'd moved on.

"Seems to be a trend," I said.

Becky nodded thoughtfully. "It does. There's definitely an undertone to the comments about him. I asked Jenna about it and she said people are polite but almost robotic, like they're saying something people expect them to say. Anyway—how are you holding up?"

"I'm fine. Do the cops have any leads?"

"I don't know. My crime guy can't pin them down. They're totally not commenting at all, which makes me think they might have something they're following. Of course, it could mean they have absolutely nothing. So I've been dying to hear your story. Go."

No comment at all? I didn't like the sound of that. Trying to tuck my worry away for later, I sipped my wine and launched into the narrative, spilling everything I hadn't gotten to tell her after I'd stumbled over Frank's body. Becky's eyes were wide when I finished, and there was a look I didn't quite recognize on her face.

"Yikes," she said when I paused.

"Tell me about it." But I could see the journalistic

wheels turning in her head. I bet she wished she had a notebook right about now. Speaking of—she'd know better than anyone if Frank was lying. "Do you know if there've been any zoning-law changes?"

"Absolutely not," she said immediately. "There've been some proposals—and now maybe we know who's behind it—but nothing official. I'll talk to my city reporter to see if there've been any developments."

Ha. Validated, I felt better for about five seconds before I realized it didn't really matter. If they were going to make Grandpa's life miserable anyway, or keep dragging proposals before the zoning board, he'd still feel pressured.

But Becky was more worried about the murder. "So you had lunch with Frank like, hours before he died?"

I nodded. "I was going to tell you the whole thing at the Food Stroll, but we never got that far. And then I went to my mother's today." I told her about the cryptic conversation my mother and Margaret had been having. Becky's eyebrows almost shot out of her forehead.

"What do you think she meant? Divorce?"

"I guess so." I glanced around to make sure no one was listening.

Becky took out her phone and tapped in a note. "I'm going to make sure Jenna circles back with her. She hasn't been able to track her down for comment."

"And then there's the roof guy," I went on.

"The roof guy? There's more to this? I think I need another drink." She caught Jade's eye and nodded enthusiastically at the unspoken question. "She'll have another too," she called, pointing to me.

"Do you know Abe Tate? Tate Contracting?"

"Yeah," she said immediately. "He did some work for my landlord on my house last summer." Becky lived in one of the adorable pastel-colored duplexes not far from Grandpa's. There was a whole street of them, and they were in huge demand every summer.

"What's his deal? He on the up-and up?" I asked.

"I don't know," she said. "I didn't deal with him except when he came to my door to tell me he'd be working there that day. Why?"

I told her about him showing up on my grandfather's roof. She burst out laughing when I described my confrontation wearing a towel and sporting dripping, soapy hair. Once again I left out the suitcase full of money left in the van like a ransom payment. "But it's still weird," I finished. "Who else would it be? And why?"

"Maybe it really is some person trying to pay it forward," Becky said.

"I guess." I took a sip from my fresh wineglass. "I thought you were supposed to be the cynical one."

Becky shrugged. "I am. But people love your grandpa. Sounds like he did him a favor once. Maybe a big one."

"Yeah," I said. "Maybe. Craig asked me to go to dinner."

Becky paused, olive halfway to her mouth. "Craig your ex?"

"The one and only."

"Are you going?"

"We didn't make official plans. Just sort of said if we had a chance before I left, we'd go out. I figured, why not? He's pretty cute," I said.

"Yeah, he did grow up well. Although he's a cop." Becky wrinkled her nose.

I grinned. "You have something against cops?"

"Nothing against them. I just think sometimes they get a little brainwashed. And they need to get the chip off their shoulder about the media. Especially this department. Trust me, we treat them fairly."

I thought about that. "So who's your spokesperson?"

"They have a PR guy. A corporal."

"And he's had no updates on Frank? No suspects, no person of interest?"

"No," Becky said. "Not that they've told me."

That was good news, at least. "Well, you'll give me a heads-up if you think they're going to arrest me, right?" I was only half kidding. Really, I wanted her to promise me she'd let me know if they were going to arrest Grandpa, but didn't want to say that out loud.

Becky didn't laugh. "Only if you'll give me the exclusive interview," she said.

Chapter 30

When the bar stools started filling up, Becky and I stopped talking about murder. We'd just started on our third drink, reliving some high-school story, when I felt a hand on my arm. I turned to find Lucas the dog groomer grinning inches from my face.

I blushed—I hadn't had two and half glasses of wine in a while—and I tried to look normal.

"Hey," I said.

"Hey," he said. "Did you ever end up taking that shower?" Then his face turned beet red also.

I knew what he was talking about—the dog peeing on my leg—but Becky watched with interest.

"I did," I said with a smile. "Lucas's friend's dog peed on me," I explained to her. "Lucas, do you know Becky Walsh? She works at the *Chronicle*."

"I don't. Nice to meet you," Lucas said, shaking her hand, then his eyes widened. He dropped Becky's hand and turned to me. "The *Chronicle*. I saw the story today. I hadn't realized you found Frank." He dropped his voice. "That must've been horrible. I'm so sorry."

If there was any positive in finding a dead guy, this had to be it.

"Thanks," I said. "It was . . . kind of crazy."

"Well, on the bright side, her cat's a hero now," Becky said.

Lucas cocked his head at her, trying to figure out if she was serious.

But her brain had moved on. She leaned forward, excited. "Hey, while you're here. We're going to be doing a Sunday series about island transplants who've opened businesses. Do you want to be featured?"

"I would love to. That would be amazing," Lucas said, grinning.

"Terrific." Becky made another note in her phone.

"Always working," I said, shaking my head. "I have another guy you should talk to for the series. Damian Shaw. He took over the Rice family's lobster shack by the ferry."

"Oh, good one. I'd forgotten about him." She bent over her phone again, then looked up at Lucas. "So are you playing tonight?"

Lucas shook his head. "Thursday nights are live music. We'll be here then. My band," he explained to me. "The Scurvy Elephants. You should come see us," he said, then blushed again.

I thought he was adorable. Better yet, he totally wasn't full of himself. I could see Becky's smirk out of the corner of my eye and knew she knew exactly what I was thinking.

I opened my mouth to tell him I'd love to when a man staggered up to the bar behind us. I'd never actually seen anyone who could qualify as something the cat dragged in, but today was, apparently, my lucky day. Glazed eyes surveyed the booze selection from underneath a face caked with dirt and, quite possibly, blood—I couldn't tell. He had dirty-blond hair, and I couldn't tell if the "dirty" part was his hair color or actual dirt. Same with his scraggly beard.

His jeans looked like they hadn't been washed in a week, and his shirt had a hole in the sleeve. He stood way too close to me. I could smell the booze wafting off him in waves.

Jade's other bartender, a woman about my age with two hoops in her nose and a sleeve of tats up her arm noticed him first. She didn't look so thrilled as he staggered up to the counter. She glanced around for Jade, but Jade was at the other end of the bar talking to someone and hadn't seen her new patron. I looked at Becky and raised an eyebrow. She shrugged, but I could see the reporter's gleam in her eye as she gauged the potential for a drunk-and-disorderly arrest story.

I fully intended to ignore him and hope he went away, but in his drunken stupor he stumbled and nearly fell into Lucas. Lucas automatically held up an arm to both block himself and keep the guy upright, but in the process his beer dumped down my back. The shock of the cold liquid infiltrated my T-shirt, causing me to jump up. Lucas muttered a curse and tried to step out of the drunk's immediate path. "Are you okay?" he asked me, grabbing some napkins. "I'm sorry."

The drunk, meanwhile, showed no gratitude at all. He grabbed my bar stool to keep from falling the rest of the way, almost tipping it with his off-balance weight, jamming the stool into my leg. Annoyed now, I shoved the stool back into place, knocking him off kilter as I did so.

He looked around, confused. "Keep your hands off me," he slurred, trying to focus on Lucas.

Lucas slammed his now nearly empty beer bottle down on the bar and drew himself up to his full height. The drunk stood almost to his chest, and he had a heck of a lot fewer muscles. "Take it easy, pal. You're the one falling all over everyone."

"Maybe if you *moved*." The guy sneered, and shoved

past him. "Hey," he yelled to the bartender, who still stood frozen, watching this play out. "Gimme a drink."

Lucas put his hand on the guy's arm. "I don't think you need—"

The guy turned, fist raised, and tried to clock Lucas. Luckily his inebriated state hindered his ability to do that. His arm rose in slow motion, the fingers awkwardly trying to close into a fist. Lucas responded with little effort, grabbing his arm and twisting it behind him. The guy started bucking like a wild horse at a rodeo, sending the other people sitting nearby scattering. I heard glass hitting the floor as someone lost a drink and I dove out of the way, pulling Becky with me. A couple of guys rushed over, trying to help Lucas hold on to him. They finally got a good grip on him and started hauling him toward the front door when I heard a familiar shrill voice reaching higher than any of the noise from the drunken brawl.

"Stop! Leave him alone."

I peered over the flurry of arms and heads to see a head of frizzy black hair rushing into the fray. Piper Dawes reached past two men and yanked the drunk guy's arm away from Lucas.

"Lady, be careful. This guy's not in great shape," one of the men warned, still holding on to the guy's other arm.

Piper glared at him. "I said, leave him alone."

The guy stepped away, hands raised. "Your choice."

But at the sight of Piper, the drunk stopped struggling, standing almost meekly. Piper gipped his arm and turned around to Jade, who'd come out from behind the bar looking like she was about to take his head off.

"I'm very sorry," she said stiffly.

"Great. You can tell it to the cops," Jade said. "They're on their way."

"Look." Piper tried to relax her face into a friendly

expression but it didn't look natural on her. Must be the lack of practice. "Can we just drop it? I'll take him home."

Jade folded her arms. "He just caused a ruckus in my bar. Again. No."

I watched, fascinated. Who the heck was this guy? Didn't seem like Piper's type; she usually went for the old, rich, and successful ones. This guy couldn't even stand up straight.

Piper's eyes went to slits. She moved closer to Jade, still dragging the guy with her. I saw him wince as her nails dug into his arm. "It's not bad enough that Frank is dead, but after everything he did for you this is how you show your gratitude?"

At Frank's name, my ears perked up. What did Frank have to do with this?

Jade, to her credit, stood her ground. "I'm not the one causing a problem in someone else's place of business. If this was the first time, maybe. But it's not."

If looks could kill, Jade would be dead on the floor a few times over. Piper gripped the guy's arm and started propelling him to the door, but she wasn't quick enough. Or the cops were too quick, because before she could get across the bar I saw flashing lights in front of the door, then Craig strode in, followed by another cop. The crowd parted to let them through.

Jade went over to meet him. She leaned close and said something, then pointed to the culprit.

Craig's resigned expression said he'd been down this road before. "Was anyone hurt?"

Jade pointed to the corner where Becky, Lucas, and I stood. "He was throwing punches but you'll have to ask them."

"Let's go, bud." Craig took the drunk's arm and handed him off to his fellow officer. "You can sober up at the station while we see if Ms. Bennett or any of her patrons will be pressing charges."

"Craig." Piper stepped up to him and tried to look seductive. "Isn't there something we can do?"

I nearly burst out laughing. Craig's expression of horror said it all, and he took a step back.

"Yeah," he said. "Arrest him for drunk and disorderly and possibly assault. Hanson, take him while I talk to the other folks?"

The other cop led the drunk out. Craig brushed past Piper, earning his own nasty look, and headed our way. He did a double take when he saw me, and then his eyes traveled to Lucas and back. "You guys were involved?"

"We were just sitting here," I said. "He came up behind us and started demanding a drink. Then he got belligerent and fell over and it all went south from there."

Craig's eyes lingered on mine for a minute, then he looked at Lucas. "Who got in a fistfight with him?"

"He tried to hit me. He didn't make it very far. Too drunk." Lucas shook his head. "But then he got really crazy. It took four of us to restrain him until Piper showed up."

"Anyone pressing assault charges?" Craig asked.

Lucas shook his head. "Nah, man. Seems like he's got enough problems."

Craig nodded. "You can say that again." He melted away into the crowd to talk to some other folks, and I turned to Becky.

"Do you know who that was?"

Becky shook her head.

"Did you hear what Piper said to Jade about Frank?"

Becky frowned. "No. I was too far away trying not to get hit."

I searched the room for Piper's awful hair but didn't see it. Maybe she'd followed the cops to post bail for the drunken fool. I saw Jade, though, and veered off in her direction. She'd stopped on her way back to the bar to talk to someone. I went up behind her and tapped her on the shoulder. "Sorry. Can I talk to you for a second?"

She looked like she wanted to say no, but followed me to a quiet spot in the back.

"Who was that guy?" I asked. "What's he have to do with Frank?"

Jade snorted. "You really don't know?"

"I wouldn't be asking," I said.

She shrugged. "That's his loser son, Aidan."

Chapter 31

I stared at Jade in disbelief. "I'm sorry?"

"Frank O'Malley's son Aidan," Jade repeated, a little more slowly, in case I had trouble understanding English. "The one who just moved back here. You would've thought it was the second coming, the way Frank talked about him and how much he was going to do for the island. He's doing something for it, all right." She paused and gave me a long look. "Why?"

"Why is right," I muttered to myself. "Why does Piper care?" I asked Jade.

Jade made a dismissive gesture with her hand. "She's self-appointed as babysitter, I guess. I really don't know, Maddie. I have to get back to work, now that this joker interrupted my night. Again."

I resisted the urge to keep peppering her with questions. Like, what did Frank do for her that Piper referenced? Was she talking about the waived membership dues, or was there more? And why would a couple hundred bucks that he probably drank off the other end of her balance sheet stop her from throwing some degenerate out of her bar? But her expression told me she was done talking. I watched her walk away, my head still spinning from her initial bombshell. That hot mess was Aidan O'Malley. This is the guy who wanted to tear my grandpa's house down?

Becky and Lucas made their way over to me. "Hey," Becky said urgently, grabbing my arm. "I just found out who that was."

"Aidan O'Malley," I said. "Frank's son."

Lucas's eyes widened. "Get out."

Becky grinned. "Jeez. You want a job as a reporter? Anyway, I think this could be newsworthy. I'm going to run over to the police station and follow up. I think my night reporter is out at a council meeting and my cops reporter is sick. Do you mind?"

"Of course not. Go." I waved her away.

"Thanks. I'm also going to check up on some of that other stuff we talked about." She waggled her eyebrows in a meaningful way. I guessed she meant the zoning stuff. At least, I hoped so. She gave me a hug and zoomed out, leaving me with Lucas.

I looked up at him. "Are you okay?"

"I'm fine. He didn't even hit me. Too messed up to even land a punch. Are *you* okay?"

I plucked my wet shirt away from my skin, thankful the air-conditioning wasn't on full blast in here. "I'm fine."

He shook his head. "That's really Frank's kid? What the heck happened? I never would've guessed."

"Did you know Frank?" I asked, then smacked my forehead. "Of course. The chamber. Duh."

He gave me a funny look. "Yeah. I was shocked when I heard he'd . . . been killed."

I felt stupid. My brain hadn't made the jump to connect Lucas's business with the chamber. "You're a member, then."

Lucas nodded. "Yup. First thing I did after I opened.

Frank personally came to talk to me about joining. I didn't know him well, but he ran a lot of good events. I hope Piper will keep it up. I'm guessing she'll take over."

Someone jostled me, trying to get to the bar. People had forgotten about Aidan's scene and were getting back to the business of having a drink. Lucas noticed. "You want to get out of here?" he asked. "Go down to the beach?"

The beach. My heart swelled a little. If I were ever to write a dating profile for myself, it would be at least part cliché: *Loves books, coffee, long walks on the beach. And hot musicians.*

"Yes, let's," I said impulsively.

He smiled. "Yeah? Cool. Oh. But your shirt—you're going to be cold. Oh, hang on. I have a sweatshirt in my car."

Thoughtful too. The nights did get chilly around this time of year. I followed him outside. He'd parked on the street. He drove a Subaru. I nodded approvingly. Especially in New England. He took a Virginia Tech sweatshirt out and tossed it to me. I hesitated before tugging it on.

"Do you care that it will smell like beer? I'll take it home and wash it for you," I decided.

He offered me a wry smile. "Not really worried about it."

We left Jade's and strolled down the street toward the water. I wanted to enjoy the night and the company, but my mind drifted. Mostly I was trying to connect Aidan O'Malley to his father. Frank hadn't been a stand-up guy, but at least he'd presented well and made *some* contributions to society. So why would he try to install this kid as the head of a business on the island that could potentially hurt tourism instead of help it, if the idiot was too drunk to figure out what he was doing?

I didn't realize Lucas had been asking me a question until he waved his hand in front of my face. "Earth to Maddie." He laughed. "What's got your attention?"

"Oh. I'm sorry." Flustered, I focused on him. "What was that?"

"I said, Jade's place is pretty nice, right? Have you been there before?"

"Yeah, it's great. No, that was my first time."

"Yeah, so like I was telling you guys when that bozo crashed into us, we're playing Thursday night." He glanced over at me. Thanks to the nearly full moon I could see the hopeful look in his eyes. "Want to go?"

That was enough to jolt me out of my Aidan O'Malley reverie. What on earth was going on here? Two guys asking me out in the span of two days on a tiny island like this. In San Fran, I hadn't had a date in months. But I'd just said yes to Craig. Sort of. We hadn't made official plans. Would that make it wrong to say yes to Lucas? And was I jumping the gun? He'd just asked me to see his band play. Would that count as an official date?

"I mean, if you like rock music. That's what we play," he added. "If you don't it's cool."

"No, I love rock music," I said quickly. "Sure, I'd love to come."

He grinned. "Yeah? Cool."

I grinned back. "Cool."

I watched him as we walked. He and Craig couldn't be more opposite. Not just Craig's short blond cop hair, sandy eyes, and pale skin versus Lucas's dark, shaggy, smoldering look. Lucas seemed laid-back, calm, down-to-earth. Craig had already started to develop a cop's persona—wound tight, on edge, and hell-bent on rules.

Aw, hell. Why was I making this so complicated? Lucas was adorable. And hanging out with anyone while I was here meant nothing, because I was going home. Soon.

Still, I hoped Craig wasn't planning to take in a show Thursday night. Hopefully, he'd be working overtime finding Frank's killer.

Chapter 32

We walked out of the crush of downtown, heading to the small beach area by the tip of the island. Around the bend from the ferry dock was a stretch of sand that reached all the way in front of the expansive town green. Perfect to walk and dip your toes.

Lucas held out his hand. I took it and we hopped the rocks, landing on the sand. I immediately kicked off my shoes, happy I'd worn flip-flops. I always felt like I could think more clearly with the ocean stretching out before me, miles of blue tranquility accentuated by the soundtrack of crashing waves. I let out a contented sigh.

"It's so beautiful here," Lucas said, as if reading my mind.

"Sure is," I agreed. "Despite the murder."

"Yeah." He sighed. "I have to admit, I was floored. I mean, there's plenty of crime where I grew up. But I figured here it was less. Maybe that was naïve of me, but . . ." He trailed off.

"I get it. There usually isn't that kind of crime here. We get a lot of domestics. A lot of DUIs, which sometimes end up with people getting killed. And drugs. You know, things people do when they're bored. Which they totally are out here in the winter." I looked at him. "You lived through a winter already, right?"

He nodded.

"And?"

"Not what I expected," he admitted. "It's a ghost town."

"Yup. Which is why so many people have to depend on the tourist months to make their living. It's a crazy way to live."

"Is that why you left?"

"I left because I thought the island would be too small for me after I conquered NYU." I grinned. "Turns out I like city life."

"Yeah." He gazed out into the water. "I don't."

I sensed a story there. "Let's sit," I suggested.

We did. Lucas immediately buried his toes in the sand. I thought it was cute.

"Where are you from in Virginia?" I asked.

"Newport News."

I'd never been. I'd heard it was nice, though. "Do you still have family there?"

"No."

Another story, or maybe the same one? He didn't seem to want to say, so I didn't push it. Instead, I turned the conversation back to Frank. "I don't think Frank's murder was a random thing, though. I don't think the island's changed *that* much."

He glanced at me. "So you think he knew his killer."

I shrugged. "I do, but I don't know why. I always suspect the worst. I have one of those imaginations. You know, conspiracy theories, creepy stuff." I tapped my finger against my temple.

"Conspiracy theorist? Let me guess. You watched the *X-Files*."

"Totally," I said, grinning. "I have all the seasons on DVD."

"Why am I not surprised?" Lucas said.

I laughed. "You can tell already I'm kind of weird."

"Not at all."

Then we descended into that awkward silence that occurs when two people are just getting to know each other and figuring out what's next. Lucas broke the silence first. "So did you know Frank?"

I hesitated. How much should I tell him? I thought he was cute, sure, but that didn't mean he was trustworthy.

"I knew him a little. He's not a lifer, but he's been here since before I was born. He . . . knew my grandpa."

"I'm sorry," Lucas said.

I acknowledged that with a nod. Not much to say there. "Did you ever notice Frank having problems with anyone?"

"Problems?" He thought about that, eyes trained on the ocean waves in front of us as they lapped gently at the sand. Other people were out taking advantage of the beautiful night. I could see fishermen out in the distance near the docks and people walking along the surf, mostly couples. "I didn't really notice. I mean, we were always in groups of people."

I picked up some sand and watched it run through my fingers as I let it fall back to the beach. "Did you ever meet his wife?"

"Margaret? Once. She came to a breakfast event with a senator. But she didn't even sit at Frank's table."

"No?"

He shook his head. "I only knew it was her because Frank gave her a shout-out during his opening remarks and she stood up. But she barely talked to him."

That fit what I'd heard. Especially if she knew he was screwing around. "Did you ever hear of him treating the smaller shops badly?"

At that, Lucas frowned. I could see his eyebrows draw

together when I looked at his profile. "I'm a small shop, and they were supportive of me," he said. "But I can't speak for other people. I mean, there were a few who definitely weren't satisfied with their membership. I felt lucky, actually. The other guy who's super new to the island, he's gotten the shaft a few times. The one you mentioned to Becky."

Damian. "He told you?" I asked.

"Didn't have to. He had a blowup with Piper once at an event. She wouldn't let him in, even though someone had put him on the guest list. Told him he'd been a guest already and needed to become a paying member. I thought it was just her being neurotic because of finances or whatever." He shrugged. "But I never saw Frank and him speak, so I have no idea."

Interesting.

"And Jade, she's pretty new here too," Lucas said. "I know she's not in love with the chamber. But it's almost like political suicide to not belong."

A strong statement. Belonging to a business association shouldn't feel so . . . mandatory.

"So are you trying out for a job on the police force or something?" His tone was light, but I caught his point: *Do you want to talk about Frank, or did you want to get to know each other?*

"I'm sorry," I said. "This whole thing has me kind of freaked out. And being friends with Becky has me trained to ask a lot of questions."

He laughed. "I get that."

My phone vibrated in my bag. I pulled it out and read the text message from Becky.

At the police station. Piper is here having a meltdown. Craig told me they called Margaret. Fireworks??

From the sounds of it, things were going to get all kinds of interesting. I was torn between wanting to hang out with

Lucas and wanting to get home so I could try calling Craig
for dirt. Nosiness won out. I tossed my phone back in my
bag and stood up. "I should get back. I have to check in
with Grandpa," I said.

Lucas rose too, brushing off his jeans, and we left the
beach. I reluctantly slipped my shoes on once we reached
the end of the sand. Our walk back was quiet, me still lost
in my thoughts, him probably wondering why he'd asked
me sort-of out in the first place.

I felt bad. I'd been kind of a crappy sort-of date.

"Hey. Maybe we could grab lunch sometime before
your gig on Thursday?" I suggested as we reached Jade's.

I hadn't realized I held my breath until he nodded. "I'd
like that. I'm usually at the shop, but I can sneak out for
lunch. Tomorrow? Wednesday?"

Maybe I hadn't wrecked my chances after all. "Let's say
Wednesday," I said. Tomorrow would more than likely be
busy. A visit to Margaret O'Malley and her wayward son,
if he could avoid being jailed tonight, was at the top of my
list. That and a vet visit for JJ. I needed to follow up with
Katrina on that. Maybe by Wednesday I'd actually be able
to concentrate on Lucas.

"Sounds good." He took out his cell. "Give me your
number and we can touch base before then."

I recited it.

He saved it with a flourish and smiled at me. "Looking
forward to it," he said.

"Me too. I'll bring your sweatshirt back too." I waggled
my fingers at him. "See ya." I headed for Grandma's car. I
could feel his eyes on me as I walked away.

Grandpa's truck still wasn't back when I got home. I felt like
a worried parent. It was almost eleven. Where on Daybreak
Island did a seventy-four-year-old hang out all day and
night? I found JJ tucked into my book nook, though, which

was too cute for words. When he saw me he squeaked and raced over, head-butting and looking for pats. I stroked his back. He arched, tail raised, and squinted at me.

"Where's Grandpa?" I asked him. "Have you seen him?"

JJ hadn't. I sighed. Maybe the card game had moved to his friend's house. I knew I shouldn't be frustrated—Grandpa needed a life too, and he hadn't had much of one since Grandma got sick, but the selfish part of me wondered why he wasn't spending more time with me while I was home.

Oh, Maddie, grow up, I chided myself. *You weren't home either. And the world doesn't revolve around you.*

Scolding myself didn't make me feel much better. I poured a glass of ice water and realized I'd never texted Becky back. I fired off a quick note.

Just got back from a walk on the beach with Lucas. What's going on?

It was a full ten minutes later when she wrote back.

Trying to figure it out. I think they're trying to get the charges dropped. And hoo boy! Two guys fighting over you?

She'd added a winking emoticon to her words, but I was more focused on the potential dropped charges for Aidan O'Malley. If Frank's influence could make that happen—even dead—it was no wonder he thought he could use whatever means he could dream up to try and take Grandpa's house.

I wished Grandpa was here so I could talk to him about it. My head spun with questions. Did Craig know about this? Did he agree with it? I texted him to please call me, but my phone remained quiet. Finally JJ and I went up to bed.

Chapter 33

I didn't mean to sleep so late the next morning. When I woke, JJ wasn't wrapped around my head anymore. The house remained quiet, and I started to wonder if Grandpa had already moved out and forgot to tell me. I didn't even smell coffee this morning.

I flung the covers off and threw open my window, breathing in the ocean air floating toward me. Sometimes that had almost the same effect as coffee. Yawning, I tied my hair back and made my way down the stairs.

"JJ!"

Nothing. I peeked into the living room, but he wasn't there. Not in the kitchen waiting for food either. I hadn't checked the sitting room on the second floor. He was probably there, watching the boats or the seagulls. He'd come when I opened his wet food.

I went downstairs and peered out into the driveway. Grandpa's truck was still parked in the driveway. There was no note, no sign that he'd even been home. I wondered if I should be worried. I made coffee, then grabbed the kitchen phone and called my mother.

She answered, sounding distracted.

"Have you heard from Grandpa?"

She paused, and I could hear her shifting from creative mode to focus-on-Maddie mode. I wondered if she was having as much trouble unraveling her fictional mystery as everyone was unraveling our real-life one. "Not this morning. Or last night, now that you mention it. Why?"

"I don't know if he came home last night and there's no sign that he's been here this morning." I hesitated. "Mom, is this what you mean when you asked me to keep an eye on him? I feel like . . . this is troublesome."

My mother took a deep breath. "I really didn't know what to expect when I asked you to do that," she admitted. "No, that's not true. I wanted you to reassure me that he was fine. That everything was fine. But I guess it isn't."

We were both silent for a minute. My coffee burbled and sputtered and finally started its slow drip into the pot. Thank God.

"It might be," I said. "I'm probably overreacting. He had a bunch of his friends here yesterday, so maybe he went back to one of their houses. It's probably fine." I hesitated. "Or do you think I should call someone?" But something didn't seem right about that. My gut told me Grandpa hadn't wandered off, that there was some other reason for his absence. "Maybe he really did just go for a walk. He does that in the mornings."

I could tell my mother was deciding whether or not she should freak out. But before she could make the command decision to call out the National Guard, Grandpa walked through the front door.

I breathed a huge sigh of relief. "Never mind, Mom. He just walked in."

"Oh, thank God!" she exclaimed. Then she said in a much more stern tone, "Put him on."

"Uh, I think we'll just see you tonight for dinner," I said. "Okay. Love you." I hung up before she could go off on both of us, then swiveled to face Grandpa, hands on hips. "Where have you been?"

He stared at me, then went for the coffee. "Did I miss a curfew or something?"

What was this, Freaky Friday on a Tuesday? Had we reversed roles? "Grandpa. Seriously. Did you even come home last night?"

"Of course I came home. I can't help it if you were sleeping when I got here and still sleeping when I left." He poured coffee, then went to the fridge for cream. "What's wrong with your mother?"

"Nothing. I called to tell her I hadn't seen you."

He sagged against the fridge. "Oh, Madalyn. Why? And we're supposed to go there for dinner?" He shook his head and sipped. "I'll never hear the end of it. She'll be moving me into her over-the-garage apartment before we know it."

"Well, I'm sorry, but I didn't know what else to do. Grandpa. Be straight with me. Are you feeling okay? Is something wrong?"

Grandpa Leo stared at me, and the hurt in his eyes took my breath away. "Are you going to start asking me those questions too? I thought you, of all people, wouldn't fall into that trap." He turned away, fetched his cream and busied himself making his coffee.

Now I felt like crap. "Grandpa," I said.

He didn't answer. I went over and pulled on his arm like I used to do when I was five and wanted something. He turned to me but kept stirring his cream into his mug.

"I'm sorry. I was just worried." I threw up my hands. "You're hardly ever here. I wanted to spend time with you. I have a million things to tell you. Mom's always asking where you are. Plus you got mad at me yesterday about the paper and then I didn't see you again. What am I supposed to think?"

He sighed, abandoning his spoon and pulling me into a bear hug. "I know. I'm a grumpy old man these days, doll. I'm sorry. And for the record, I'm feeling fine. Under the circumstances."

"I know." I hugged him back, relieved that he wasn't going to stay mad this time.

He kissed the top of my head, then grabbed his mug. "Come, sit. What are these million things?"

"Wait," I said, indignant. "Aren't you going to tell me where you've been?"

"Relentless, just like her granddad. Depends," Grandpa said, narrowing his eyes. "Are you going to tell your mother?"

"Not if you don't want me to."

"I don't. I've picked up a couple odd jobs," he said.

"Odd jobs? Like what?" I hated this. Grandpa shouldn't have to feel like he had to work now, at his age, after working all his life at a job he loved, just to keep a house that's rightfully his.

"Some security work," he said evasively.

It was my turn to narrow my eyes. "Where?"

He waved his hand. "Now, Maddie. I can't tell you everything. That wouldn't leave me any air of mystery." He winked, but I could tell he wasn't budging. "Plus, I was trying to pretty up your gran's grave. You know how she loved flowers." His face fell a little.

I knew he wanted me to drop the security job thing, which made me want to know even more, but mentioning my grandma had sufficiently halted me. For the moment. I grabbed a mug and poured my own coffee. "Fine. You get a reprieve. So back to my million things. First of all, I checked with Becky. There haven't been official changes to zoning laws in town, Grandpa. Frank was lying to you."

He didn't look too excited. "I'm sure it's just a matter of waiting for the check to clear, Maddie," he said.

"What do you mean?" I asked, indignant. "She would know. She said there've been proposals—"

"Of course there have. There are more meetings scheduled, and open-comment sessions, and different ways they're attacking this. And I'm sure Frank's been standing in the sidelines with his wallet, waiting to see if it would happen the so-called legal way, ready to pay up if it didn't. So it may not have happened yet, but it's only a matter of time." He smiled wryly. "Frank was just trying to expedite things."

Not entirely unexpected, but it took the wind a little bit out of my sails. "Fine," I said. "Guess who may have gotten arrested last night?"

"Who?"

"Aidan O'Malley." I waited for his shock. I didn't get it.

"What else is new?" he said.

I stared at him. "You knew he's a loser too? Jeez, Grandpa. You're raining on my parade here."

"Of course I did. You only have to meet him once to know that. And it's pretty obvious even if he isn't drunk. Which is barely ever."

I sat down at the table. "So why does—did—Frank want him running a business? If nothing else, Frank took the tourism stuff seriously, right?"

"Sure he did." Grandpa sat too. "But I don't think he had a choice in this matter."

"What do you mean?"

Grandpa shrugged. "I think his inability to be there for his family caught up with him. Your grandmother told me Margaret used to cry about Aidan all the time. She tried to help him on many occasions. It was one of the reasons she spent so much time in Boston. I think it was less about her charity and more about Aidan, because he was living up there. His brother helped him out too, when he could."

"So she's behind this," I said slowly. "How could she do that to you guys?" My blood boiled at the thought. But Grandpa was quick to correct me.

"No. I didn't say that. I think she told Frank to get the boy here and do whatever it took. She holds the power in that house, you know. All their money is really her money. Old money," he added. "Frank was at her mercy."

I sat back, surprised. That put another spin on the whole mess. "Then why would Aiden risk upsetting her by getting drunk and causing scenes?"

Grandpa shrugged. "Who knows. Anyway, I'm speculating, Maddie. All I know for sure is that boy can't run his own life, never mind a business. Which I assumed Frank knew as well. I'm sure he's got someone trustworthy in charge. Aidan will just have a respectable bio on paper."

That sounded like a backwards way to help someone, but what did I know. I didn't even know if it was the true story. "Do you think we should find out?" I asked.

He smiled a little. "Who's we?"

"Me and you, of course. I want to go see Aidan. You in?"

His face turned from relaxed to intense so fast it caught me off guard. In an instant he was out of his chair and in my face. "You stay away from Aidan O'Malley. You hear me?"

What the . . . ? "But Grandpa," I protested, but he cut me off.

"I'll ship you back to California tomorrow unless you promise me, Madalyn. Do you understand? That kid is bad news. This isn't going to be a falsely civil lunch at a fancy restaurant."

"Do you think he killed his father?" I asked breathlessly.

"I don't know anything about that. That's the police department's job. Leave it be, Maddie."

"Grandpa. Who do you think sent Abe Tate?"

Grandpa's eyes darkened even further. "Abe Tate is part of this whole thing," he said. "And if you bought into his story you're being naïve, my dear."

I frowned. "Part of what whole thing?"

"This Frank thing. This whole bloody mess." He waved his arm around the kitchen. "He's not doing anything to be nice. Trust me."

"It sounded like he wanted to help you," I said, playing devil's advocate.

"Abe Tate has a motive, just like everyone else," Grandpa said. "I don't believe a word of it."

Chapter 34

"What motive could he have?" I'd been cynical about Tate and his story, true, but I didn't so much believe there was an ulterior motive. Unless Tate had fabricated the whole thing and filled a case with money to drive his point home. But it wasn't like Grandpa to be so unyielding, especially with no good reason. I opened my mouth to tell him about Abe's bad experience with Frank to illustrate my point, then closed it again. Better that Grandpa doesn't know right now that I'd been to see him. Especially after his reaction to my suggestion about visiting Aidan.

"There's no such thing as a free lunch, Madalyn," he said, repeating a phrase I'd heard him use often as a kid. And one I'd come to disagree with. "I don't buy Tate's story, and if I see him on my property again, we're gonna have some words."

I thought he sounded a little paranoid, but thought better of saying it out loud. I rose and grabbed JJ's wet food out of the cabinet, and spooned it into his dish.

"JJ," I called. "Breakfast."

Nothing. I shook his treats. Still nothing. I glanced at my grandfather, who stared into his coffee. "Have you seen the cat?"

"Hmmm?" He raised his head. "No. I don't think so."

I went from room to room on the main floor, then climbed to the second floor. He wasn't in any of his usual haunts. I started to get a bad feeling. Was he sick? I thought of his itchy ears, the one folded over. I'd only had him for a couple of days, but I felt neglectful. I should've taken him to the vet right away.

"I'm sorry I've been a bad mom. I'll take you to the vet today to get your ears looked at," I called. "Well, if I can get Katrina to get me an appointment."

Still no answer. Where could he be? I searched inside cabinets, inside closets, and behind shower curtains. Nothing. I finished checking upstairs and went down to the basement. I can't imagine he'd come down here, but maybe he'd followed Grandpa to check out the man cave.

Grandpa. I gritted my teeth. He must've let him out when he left for his walk. Grandpa wasn't used to watching out for cats trying to escape. He probably hadn't noticed, or if he had, thought nothing of it. I'd never specifically said *Don't let the cat out*. And he'd seen me take him out before.

I did a halfhearted sweep of the basement just to be sure, then went back upstairs. "Are you sure you didn't let him out?" I demanded.

Grandpa jumped up. "You still can't find him? I don't think so, but . . . I don't know." Now he looked upset. "I'll go look for him." He hurried upstairs.

I forced myself to take a few deep breaths. He was fine, I assured myself. If he did get out he wouldn't go far.

The doorbell rang. I walked over and peered through the side glass. Damian Shaw from the Lobstah Shack stood there with JJ in his arms. With a gasp, I threw open the door.

"JJ!" I reached for him. "I've been looking everywhere for you!"

Damian smiled apologetically and handed him over. "He was going through my trash."

"Oh, no. Bad cat!" I scolded, but kissed JJ's head. Now that he was safe, I allowed myself to really feel the rush of fear when I'd thought he was gone. I focused on Damian. "I'm so sorry. Did he cause any damage?"

"Of course not. Please don't be sorry. I feel like it's my fault for tempting him with all that fish."

"I think Grandpa let him out accidentally when he left this morning." I cast an accusatory glance over my shoulder at Grandpa, who'd come into the hallway.

"I'm sure he didn't mean it," Damian offered, glancing at Grandpa.

"I didn't," Grandpa said. "I'm sorry, Maddie."

I sighed, still hugging JJ. "No harm done," I said. "But please be careful, Grandpa. He's not a free-range cat anymore."

Grandpa nodded and disappeared into the kitchen. Damian frowned a little. "I think he feels bad."

"I know, I know." I sighed. "I've been cranky this morning and I took it out on him. He wasn't here when I got up and I was worried. Then JJ vanished too."

"Oh. Wow." Damian leaned against the door frame. "That's not a good way to start the day."

"Nope. But I guess it's all fine now."

Damian nodded. "Glad I could help." He turned to leave, but I followed him onto the porch.

"Hey. Wanted to let you know I volunteered you for something yesterday. My best friend, Becky Walsh, is the editor of the *Chronicle* and she's doing a series on people who moved here and started businesses. I told her she should talk to you. I hope that's okay."

"Me?" He brightened. "Sure! Wow. A newspaper feature." He got kind of a dreamy look. "Thanks, Maddie. That means a lot."

"It's no problem," I said. "But before you go, quick question." I glanced behind me and closed the door so Grandpa didn't hear me. "Has Grandpa mentioned anything to you about needing work done on the house?"

Damian thought about that. "I remember him putting in a new water heater recently," he said. "Is that what you mean?"

"Sure. Anything else? Maybe more major, like the roof?"

"I don't think so. Not that I can remember. I'm sorry."

"Don't be. It was just a question."

"Is there something I can help him with? I mean, I don't do roofs, but I can do other stuff. I know he mentioned a friend who's a plumber," Damian said.

"Yeah? Do you know who?"

He sighed. "I don't. Sorry. I'm not very helpful."

"Don't worry about it. That was very helpful," I assured him.

He shrugged, as if he didn't believe he could be. "Thanks. I'll see you soon," he said. He started to turn, then looked back. "Actually, not sure if this is helpful, but I did see someone here yesterday. I try to take a walk once a day when I have extra help in the kitchen, and I like to come this way because it's quiet. Looked like it might have been a town guy or something, but he was walking around the property line taking measurements."

I frowned. "You sure it was this property? Not next door?" Grandpa didn't have a fence, so the lines weren't clear. To me, anyway.

"Nope. He was on your side. Not sure if that has anything to do with repairs."

"What'd he look like?" I asked.

Damian grimaced. "I'm so bad at describing people. Taller than me. Baseball cap." He shrugged. "I didn't get real close. Sorry. Hope that helps."

"Yeah," I murmured as he walked back to his shack. "It helps." It had helped get my blood boiling, anyway. I'd been kidding myself that this house dilemma would go away with Frank. Time to call out the big guns. I needed to go back to my original plan A and call the first select-man, Gil Smith.

I went inside, kicked the door shut behind me, and set JJ down on the floor. He wandered over to his bowl of cat food, sniffed, then turned and went into the living room. He jumped lightly onto the windowsill, curled into a ball and went to sleep, apparently stuffed from his big lunch out.

And here I was feeling bad for him. I still needed to get him to the vet, of course. And I fully intended to do that. I'd stop by the Humane Society later. But first, I needed to talk to Gil. And Margaret. And Aidan, if he'd managed to keep out of the clink. I'd ask Becky the status of that. And hopefully Grandpa wouldn't find out.

Chapter 35

Grandpa had disappeared into the basement. I figured I'd let him be for now. After firing off a quick text to Becky on Aidan's status, I went upstairs to shower. I brought JJ with me and locked him in the bathroom. Instead of singing my wake-up song, I lectured JJ about the dangers of finding himself back on the street.

"There are cars out there, and mean people," I went on. "You just got out of that situation. Why on earth would you want to go back?" I pulled the shower curtain back to see what he was doing, wiping water from my eyes. JJ sat in front of the shower, watching intently, as if he understood everything I said.

That made me smile. "See, I always said cats were better than kids. You actually listen, and you don't really talk back. Unless you count the squeaks," I said.

He made a different noise this time. Almost like a chirp. I laughed and pulled the curtain shut, finished my shower and dried off. I checked my phone. A triumphant text from Becky that the drunk-and-disorderly charges had stuck for Aidan but he'd been released on meager bail this morning. Which meant he might be home with Mommy, licking his wounds. I grabbed my iPad and googled Frank and Margaret O'Malley. Score—they were listed. I sent their address in Turtle Point to my mobile, pulled on a pair of white cropped jeans and a T-shirt, and got JJ suited up in his harness.

I yelled down to Grandpa that I'd be back to pick him up before dinner. He called a distracted "That's fine" up the stairs. I hesitated. He'd been so adamant about me not going to try to talk to Aidan. But my desire to find out more about these people, and possibly who killed Frank, won out. Telling myself it was all for his benefit, I slipped out the front door.

Ten minutes later I'd shifted my focus to Margaret and a game plan since I hadn't really thought through my approach other than, *Talk to Aidan.* I needed a good reason for showing up at her front door randomly at two in the afternoon. I mentally listed my options. Condolence call would probably be my best bet. Also it was the only one I could come up with on the fly—the O'Malleys only lived about fifteen minutes from my parents' house, out in Turtle Point. I figured Margaret wouldn't question that too much. Maybe she'd be grateful someone cared enough to come visit.

Quashing the guilt about that, I slowed in front of number 12 Sea Glass Lane and gaped. I remembered hearing that Frank and Margaret had moved to a different part of town in an upgrade. Upgrade was putting it mildly. The house resembled a castle, with a stone front and two turret-shaped balconies on both ends of the upper floor. The perfectly manicured lawn looked like someone paid attention to it daily. It also looked like no one lived here. Curtains were drawn, and no windows were open. I swung into the driveway, wondering if anyone was even home. I saw no sign of Margaret or Aidan. Of course, their cars could be in the three-car garage right in front of me. If Aidan even had a car.

"JJ, stay here," I said, cranking the sunroof open and rolling the windows down just enough so he couldn't jump out. It was breezy and still cool today, so I didn't feel horrible leaving him in the car for a few minutes. "I'd venture a guess you're not allowed inside."

He squeaked, then settled back on the passenger seat and rested his chin on his paws. So obedient. I locked the car and walked up the front steps, pressing the doorbell. Margaret O'Malley opened it almost immediately.

She looked like she'd had a sleepless night. Her fancy outfits were nowhere in sight. Instead, she wore simple khakis and a white T-shirt with a pair of flats. She wore no makeup, and exhaustion carved out extra lines around her eyes.

I pasted on a sympathetic smile. "Hi, Margaret."

"Maddie. What a lovely surprise." She swung the door wider, her eyes scanning the driveway. "Come on in, dear. What can I do for you?"

"I wanted to stop by and . . . offer my condolences again." I raised my hands in front of me and let them fall, hoping I sounded sincere. "I've been thinking about you."

She gazed at me, her eyes growing moist. "Aren't you sweet. Please join me for a glass of lemonade."

I followed her into a kitchen that looked exactly as I'd imagined it—marble floors, the latest in fancy countertops, gleaming copper pots hanging from a rack over the stove—and just as unused. She motioned to a bar stool at the island. "Sit. Can I get you anything to eat?"

"Oh, no, thank you," I said, accepting the glass of lemonade she set down in front of me. "This is lovely. So how are you doing?" I asked when she sat too.

She sighed. "I'm still adjusting. And it's difficult because we can't get the services set up quite yet, so it's weighing on us all."

I nodded sympathetically. "That's terrible. Any idea

when they'll . . . let you do that?" I'd been about to say "release the body" but that sounded too much like cop speak.

"No, I'm afraid not. They had to do an autopsy, given the circumstances. So it's going to take a bit longer. I hope to have services late this week."

Cool as a cucumber. Either she had perfected New England–private, or she was just going through the motions. "Margaret." I laid a hand over hers, silently apologizing to my mother. "Do you have any idea who would've done this to Frank?"

She raised her eyes to mine. "No," she said evenly, and I didn't believe her at all.

"How are your kids taking the news?" I feigned ignorance. "Don't you have two sons?"

"I do. They're upset, naturally. Aidan, my oldest, just moved back to the island a few months ago to work with his father." Margaret sipped her lemonade, then lapsed into silence. She wasn't big on elaboration.

Work with his father. Is that what she called it? Aidan's drunk, enraged face swam in front of my eyes. I couldn't see that guy succeeding at serving pizza if all he had to do was take a tray and put it on a table. I pasted a smile back on my face and tried to figure out what else to ask her.

But I didn't get a chance. We were interrupted by the doorbell, followed by a rapid knock, systematic as gunfire. Margaret gritted her teeth, then excused herself, leaving me to indulge my curiosity. From my vantage point at the island, I could see into a dining room that looked like no one ever ate in it. Then there was the front hall, where Margaret had gone, and another, smaller room off the back of the kitchen, its door partially ajar. I could see luggage. Maybe she hadn't unpacked yet after arriving Sunday and having to deal with her husband's death. I rose, listening intently. I could hear the murmur of voices from the general direction of the front door. It sounded like she'd gone out on the porch with whoever had showed up. Satisfied that she was busy, I crept over to the little room, which seemed to serve as a small mudroom, with an another door leading into the garage. I pushed the door all the way open.

Piles of clothes, crumpled and carelessly tossed, were strewn all over the floor. The set of luggage sat in the middle of the mess—beat-up luggage, not luggage I would ever envision Margaret O'Malley carrying around. I pictured her with elegant, hard-shell suitcases carried by some bellman. These were clearly old, covered in half-ripped-off stickers boasting old heavy metal bands: Metallica, Anthrax, Megadeath. Someone needed anger management, and I had a sneaking suspicion I knew who. Guess I was right about his crashing with his parents, at least until Frank helped him get his transportation business off the ground. From the looks of the guy, it would've been in their best interest to get him up and running and self-sufficient sooner rather than later. But now Frank was gone. Maybe Margaret was kicking him out? Had she had enough of him too?

If he was here, he'd probably be upstairs somewhere sleeping off his bender. I probably couldn't get much out of him in that condition anyway.

The voices from the foyer had gotten louder. I froze. Were they coming this way? I edged back into the kitchen and strained, trying to hear, catching Margaret's voice, an angry hiss: "You'll have to go outside and wait. I have someone here right now."

I couldn't make out the other voice, but it was female. I slunk back to my seat and slid into it just as Margaret appeared, alone. I sipped my lemonade and tried to look innocent.

"Maddie. I'm so sorry, but I have to attend to something," she said. Her expression was still pleasant, but underneath I could see the hard lines of anger.

"Oh, sure." I jumped up, downing the rest of my lemonade—which was quite good—and thanking her. "You'll let my mother know about the services?"

"Of course." She glanced at her watch. "Thank you very much for coming by and paying your respects. It's very kind of you."

But don't let the door hit you. She followed me into the foyer and let me out. I saw the black Lexus parked on the street with a figure inside it. Dying of curiosity, I shoved my sunglasses on, trying to hide the furtive glances I cast over at the car. Whoever was visiting, Margaret didn't want our paths to cross.

Chapter 36

Even though I typically would've taken a right out of her driveway, I took a left so I could drive by the car in hopes of identifying the visitor. I snuck a sideways glance as I passed it and saw Piper Dawes's profile. Her head was bent, her hand shading her face, but there was no mistaking the hair.

My imagination kicked into overdrive. What were Piper Dawes and Margaret O'Malley doing together? Wouldn't they be mortal enemies, if what Pauline said was true about Frank's affair? There had to be a story here. I wondered, What if it *was* a conspiracy? What if they had worked together to get rid of Frank? Maybe both of them got tired of being "other women."

I drove down the street and around the corner, then swerved to the side of the road, jamming the car into park. "Let's go, JJ," I said, picking up his leash. "Something tells me we want to hear this." He followed me out of the car. I locked it and we hurried back to Margaret's street.

I paused when I got to the house next to Margaret's. It didn't look like anyone was home, so I took my chances. Praying for no vicious guard dogs, I scooped up JJ, detoured into their yard, and crouched behind a dense shrub, peering around the side in time to see Piper Dawes standing on Margaret's front porch, dressed in a flouncy yellow sundress and tapping one red high-heeled foot expectantly.

Then the door opened, and a handful of clothes came flying out, almost knocking Piper's wispy frame off the step.

"You. Have. Some. Nerve." Margaret's voice, loud enough to carry even though I couldn't see her. "This is still my house, and your belongings don't belong in it!" More items went flying through the air. I peered out from behind my shrub, hand clapped over my mouth to keep from laughing out loud. This was better than *Real Housewives*.

"You're lucky I didn't have you arrested," Margaret continued, even though now Piper's shrill voice had joined hers in her own defense, though I couldn't make out what she said. "And if you set one more foot on this property after today, I *will* have you arrested!"

"I don't need to take this abuse," Piper shrieked, her voice reaching eardrum-shatter level. "Frank was helping me out. And I was helping *you* out with your son!"

A few seconds of angry silence. I risked another moment of rubbernecking to see what was going on. Then I heard Margaret, clear as day. "Helping you? Frank *helped* you after your poor sap of a husband figured out what was going on and threw you out. And don't tell me how you're helping my son. He's in worse shape now after spending all that time with you and Frank."

"Well, if you weren't spending all your time with your golden-boy son or that boyfriend of yours!" Piper yelled back.

Boyfriend? Margaret had a boyfriend too? Please say who . . . please say who, I chanted to myself. I was so engrossed in the drama unfolding in front of me that I never saw the man come up behind me until he cleared his throat.

"Excuse me, miss?"

Startled, I lost my footing and toppled over into the bush with a yelp. Unfortunately, the yelp came just as both Piper and Margaret stopped shouting at each other. Both their heads swiveled in our direction.

Crap. I stayed in the bush, hoping they couldn't see me, and tried to smile at the man. "I'm sorry," I said, almost whispering. "My cat got loose and I . . . just caught up with him." I motioned to JJ, who'd moved from my lap to a nice grassy spot.

"I'm glad you found him," the man said. "I like cats." He reached a hand down to help me up. I waved him off.

"I'm fine," I said. "I need to fix my shoe." I busied myself fiddling with my flip-flop, praying desperately for the catfight to continue so I could slip away unnoticed. Still silence from the next house. I willed Piper to start shouting again. Lord knew she always had plenty to say. Why did today have to be different?

"Young lady, are you sure you're all right?" the man finally asked, after watching me tug at each part of my flip-flop. JJ rolled over and squeaked. The man's eyes widened.

"That's him!"

I stared at him, grabbing JJ close as I got to my feet, certain the guy was nuts. "What's him? Who?"

"That cat! That's the hero cat. I can't believe the hero cat is here." He reached into his pocket. I prayed he wasn't going for a weapon. Instead, he pulled out an iPhone. "May I . . ." He hesitated, his voice quivering with excitement. "May I take a selfie with him?"

I wasn't sure whether to oblige or run screaming. This dude had to be sixty-five if he was a day, and he wanted a selfie with my cat?

Behind me, I heard Margaret say to Piper, "You get off my property now or I'm calling the police."

"Uh. Sure," I said, reluctantly handing JJ over, praying

he wouldn't scratch or bite his fan. I kept a firm grip on his leash in case the guy tried to run off with him, while trying to keep an ear on what Piper and Margaret were up to. I heard a door slam and tried to contain my impatience as the man arranged JJ in his arms, trying different poses before holding his phone at arm's length and snapping a few pictures. I heard the Lexus roar to life. It blew past us, going in the same direction I'd driven on my way out. I hoped she wouldn't notice my car parked on the side of the road. I glanced in her direction as she zoomed away. The whole front of the driver's side was caved in. I cringed. Was that what happened when Piper got mad—bumper cars? I hoped her husband hadn't been the recipient of that dent. I hoped she wasn't angry enough to hit Grandpa's car too if she noticed it.

Finally, the dude handed JJ back with a huge smile. "Thank you very much, miss. Say, is he available for visits?"

"Visits?" I repeated.

"Yes. I volunteer at the senior center, and he's a hot topic in town," the man explained. "I was talking about it with some of the staff and we thought we could organize a bus trip."

"A bus trip." I sounded like a parrot. "Currently, no. But maybe I can bring him to you. At the senior center." I glanced at JJ. "Want to go visit some people?"

He squeaked.

The man beamed. "Excellent. I'm Stewart, by the way. Stewart Payne."

"Maddie James." We shook.

He reached into his wallet and handed me a card.

"Thanks," I said. "I'll be in touch."

"Excellent. Are you finished in my shrubs?"

I flushed, even though he seemed sincere and no longer annoyed that a strange woman had been caught crawling through his shrubs. "Of course. Yes. Sorry about that." I made a big show of brushing off my pants and straightening my hair. A quick glance next door told me Margaret had gone back inside. Phew. She wouldn't see me snooping.

Still, I kept my head down as I hurried back toward Grandpa's car. Once JJ and I were safely inside, I let out a huge breath, my head spinning with information.

Frank was cheating on Margaret with Piper. Piper was staying at Frank and Margaret's house while Margaret was away. Margaret knew this, which meant she knew he was cheating. How long had she known? And did she really have a boyfriend? And then there was Piper. Maybe she was mad too—mad that Frank was still married. If her husband had thrown her out because she was sleeping with Frank, and Frank still wouldn't ditch Margaret for financial reasons, that could be enough to drive her to murder.

From the tone of their conversation, they weren't working together on anything so I crossed that off my list. That left both of them as possible suspects. I just couldn't decide which one I would put my money on yet. Even though Margaret hadn't been on island the night of Frank's murder, she could've enlisted some help. Which would go along with my gut feeling that she wouldn't do the ice-picking herself.

Chapter 37

I turned the engine on and called Becky. "Oh. My. God," I said when she answered.

"What?" she demanded.

"I have to tell you about my morning. Can you meet me?"

"I missed lunch," she said immediately. "I can sneak out for a bit. And I'm starving."

Typical Becky. She lived to eat. And she still weighed about a hundred pounds soaking wet. "Sure, wherever you want," I said, pulling away from the curb.

"Let's go to La Rosetta."

I froze. Was she joking? I never wanted to set foot in that place again. Before I could ask her what was wrong with her, she burst out laughing. "Gotcha. Never mind, let's get Mexican. Oh, and do I have some news for you."

"Really? About Frank? What?" In my excitement I almost sideswiped a bike driving in the bike lane next to me.

"I'll tell you when I see you," she singsonged. "Meet you at Tequila."

"Get a table outside. JJ's with me."

* * *

Becky waited with waters, chips, and homemade guacamole while she perused the drink menu at an outside table when I arrived. I passed JJ to her over the railing. I had to go inside and out an inner door to get to the patio.

"I wish I had the day off," she said. "Today's special margarita is key lime pie."

The aptly named Tequila, nestled in the heart of Bicycle Street, was famous for its giant happy hour margaritas. The restaurant rarely had an empty seat. Becky always managed to get a table, though. The power of the pen was mighty.

"That sounds yummy, but I'm happy with the guac." I used a chip to spoon up a glob while JJ settled himself under my chair. I wrapped his leash tight around my wrist. "Okay. Can I tell you about my morning? I'm dying here."

"Go." Becky listened to my story. I filled her in on this morning's drama, only pausing when the waitress arrived so we could order—an extra serving of guac since we'd already mostly demolished what was in front of us, a taco salad for me, and cheese quesadillas for Becky. When I finished, she exhaled and sat back in her chair. "Wow."

"Right?" I scraped the guacamole bowl clean as the waitress approached with a bowl of avocados. She whipped up the guacamole then presented it with a flourish. Another waiter swooped over and deposited a new bowl of chips. "And," I continued. "Grandpa has some mysterious job now. He won't tell me what he's doing. I'm worried it's illegal or something."

At that, Becky burst out laughing. "If your grandfather is doing something illegal, I'll never drink a margarita again."

That was serious. "So you don't think so?"

"Nah. If he's trying to make extra money, he probably found some sweet little security gig."

"You think? He made it sound more . . . sinister." I picked at the chips.

"I do think. Your grandpa would never do anything bad. He's good at heart," she said.

That made me feel better. "So what about the rest of it? Who do you think Margaret's boyfriend is? If that's true. That was right about the time the guy found me in the shrubs."

Becky arched an eyebrow. "Explain?"

Laughing, I filled her in on my recon skills. "JJ has a new gig too. He's going to the senior center to visit. The guy forgot all about me trespassing in his shrubbery when he recognized the cat. Go figure."

"Wow. See? That story got way more hits than Frank's murder story. A cult hit, I'm telling you. Anyway, I don't even know what to think about all this." Becky ate some chips. "So maybe Margaret has a beau. And Frank and Piper were having an affair." She shook her head. "What was it with that guy? She's got to be thirty years younger."

"She's no prize," I pointed out. "And maybe she didn't know Margaret held the purse strings. Grandpa told me that. Maybe Frank never had an intention to leave, she thought he did, then when she tried to pin him down he blew her off. Bam, ice pick in the back. Seems a very Piper thing to do."

"I could see that more than I could see Margaret doing it," Becky said. "I'm sure she'd have found a classier way than stabbing him in broad daylight with a million people nearby. I mean, really. Who does that? Not someone very smart. And you're right, Piper's not very smart."

"Yeah. I heard Margaret wasn't even on the island that night, but she could've hired someone," I said, offering a new theory. "You know what else," I said, remembering my conversation with Tate yesterday. "That contractor who's helping my grandpa? Tate? He told me he and Frank had a problem. Frank didn't want to pay him for something. Margaret finally settled the bill just last month." I hesitated, thinking about the rest of that conversation. Should I tell her about the cash? In the end, I decided to keep it quiet. If Tate was on the up-and-up, I didn't want to subject him to the gossip that would surely circulate if word started getting around about clandestine cash deals done out of a broken-down van in the dead of night.

Becky waited until the waitress had set the food down. "I've never heard anything sketchy about Tate," she said. "I asked my mother too and she's used him. And my mother is *very* picky about her contractors. Most of them try to take single women for a ride."

"Anyway, what was the big news you found out?" I asked.

"Well." Becky's blue eyes flashed with the spark of a story. "There's a couple. But the one I'm most interested in is a nugget one of my reporters remembered after our initial conversation about Frank." She dropped her voice almost to a whisper and looked around. "He was planning to run against Gil Smith in next year's election."

Chapter 38

My eyes widened. *"What?"*

Gil had been first selectman of Daybreak Harbor for, like, ever. Everyone loved Gil. He was middle-of-the-road enough that he didn't seem to make anyone too angry. He volunteered his time with different organizations around the island. He marched in parades and cooked food for the hungry at Thanksgiving. Daybreak Harbor seemed to run pretty well with him around. I don't know that he'd even been contested at the last few elections. Gil's wife had died a few years back, and they had no children. After that he'd devoted himself even more fully to the town. My dad said every member of the community was part of his family. "Why would Frank do that?"

Becky shrugged. "Guess he wanted to shake things up a bit."

I thought about that as I sipped my water. Frank had been in politics earlier in his career. Maybe he missed it. Or maybe he had another motive. Being the head of a group of business owners was one thing. You advocated for them—hopefully—and helped to drive positive change in the community. But as first selectman, you had more control over how much things actually changed. As long as you could get the rest of your council on board.

And Frank seemed to have very definite ideas about what the new face of tourism should look like, at least given his plans for a new transportation center. Not to mention how he'd get there. What had he been planning? Had Gil known? And if he'd known—how angry had he been? Angry enough to kill Frank? Another thought crossed my mind, leaving me cold. What if he'd found out the night of the Food Stroll? What if they'd gotten into an argument about it and Gil stabbed Frank in the heat of the moment? I'd seen Gil in the general vicinity of Frank's body that afternoon, before JJ ran off and I'd made my gruesome discovery. Why had he been there so early? Was he volunteering? Overseeing? Or did his presence indicate something more sinister?

Good Lord, what on earth was *wrong* with me? I needed to go back to California. Suddenly everyone I looked at had the potential to be a murderer.

I rubbed my arms, which had sprouted goose bumps to go along with my thoughts. "Now I really have to talk to Gil," I said, picking up my fork.

"Talk to Gil about what?"

Becky and I both looked up at Gil Smith, standing next to our table.

He smiled at us. "I hope it's good news. Or something fun."

"Uh," I managed. "Hey, Gil."

He winked at me, then looked at Becky. "Rebecca," he said. Gil believed in being formal with the press. "I really enjoyed the paper's coverage of the art show at the Cove Gallery. I think it's so important to nurture new artists, especially locally."

"Thanks, Gil," Becky said, beaming.

"Well. I don't want to interrupt your lunch. I'll be at

your parents' house for dinner tonight, Maddie. They said you'd be there. We can talk then? I heard you were bringing dessert. Chocolate, I hope?"

Dessert. Shoot. My to-do list had gone out the window after my visit to Margaret's. "Sure," I said, smiling weakly. "Chocolate. And we can definitely talk then."

"Terrific." He checked his watch, then patted me on the back. "Looking forward to it."

Becky and I watched him walk away, then she looked at me. "You gonna tell him?"

I sighed. "I don't know. In front of my parents? That'll be a fun conversation."

She chuckled, then covered her mouth with her hand. "I was just thinking an awful thought."

"That if he didn't know about Frank's plans, maybe he won't get so mad because Frank's dead?"

Eyes wide, she nodded. Ashamed, I glanced at my plate. "I was thinking the same thing."

"There's a reason we're still besties," she said, forking up her last quesadilla. "Oh, and one other thing I heard about Frank. My city reporter told me that earlier in the year a petition circulated among some local businesses, trying to get signatures to bring to the chamber board. Apparently this group of business owners wanted Frank to resign. Claimed unfair business practices."

Wow. All roads led to possible Frank-killers. I leaned forward. "Who were the business owners?"

"I don't know all of them. The reporter couldn't remember, and he never actually saw the petition." Becky sipped her water. "He never wrote about it because it died on the vine. But he did tell me who tipped him off to the potential story."

I nearly danced in my seat with impatience. "Who?"

"Damain Shaw."

I sat back. "The lobster guy."

"You got it."

I whistled softly. Apparently he'd really been upset with Frank and the way he operated. I knew the chamber was influential, but apparently I hadn't realized exactly how influential. "Why did it die?" I asked.

Becky shrugged. "I don't know that either."

I knew we were both thinking the same thing—Frank caught wind of it and it got quashed. Or someone else had it quashed for him. If Frank's connections had helped make that happen, would that have made Damian—or another petitioner—angry enough to take matters into their own hands to try and remove him?

Chapter 39

After I left Becky, I walked a few hundred feet up Bicycle Street to the chamber offices. Leave it to Frank to get an office smack-dab in the center of the action. He'd probably kicked out some poor defenseless shop owner for the space.

I went to the door and yanked the handle. Locked. I frowned and peered inside. It was—I checked my phone— nearly three-thirty. Why wouldn't they be open? Unless they'd closed for the week to honor Frank. Cupping my hands around my eyes to keep out the sun glare, I peered inside. And saw a shadow of a movement from within.

Someone was in there. Piper? I hoped not. I'd been hoping for another staffer—someone who would be easier to ply for information. But I was here now. Might as well see if I could find anything out. Readying my second condolence-call script of the day, I rapped on the door.

Piper didn't appear for almost a minute. When she did, she didn't look happy to see me but she unlocked the door anyway. The fancy outfit she'd had on at Margaret's a few hours ago was gone, replaced by a pair of jeans, a long-sleeved T-shirt, and not-very-trendy tennis shoes. A slim headband held her hair back, causing it to stand up in an electric halo around her head.

She cracked the door and gazed at me and JJ impassively. "Can I help you?"

Maybe she didn't recognize me. All the better. "Hi," I said. "Sorry, I didn't realize you guys were closed."

She shot me a look. "I'm sure you heard we lost our president."

I nodded.

"Given the circumstances, I thought it best to give everyone the week off. But if someone needs something I like to be available. Come on in." She turned and walked back inside, not looking to see if I followed.

Already taking the leadership role. I supposed it was the thing to do—as the vice president she'd naturally step in, at least in the interim. I followed her into a small sitting area with a reception desk, currently empty. I could see a few offices, also all empty. Same with the cubicles. I wondered exactly how many people worked here. Aside from her and Frank, who must account for two of the offices, I counted four more, and six cubicles. That seemed like a lot of personnel for an outfit on such a small island.

Piper flared up a Keurig machine and chose a coffee. "Would you like something?" she asked without turning around.

"No, thank you. I just went to Bean." I held my cup up.

"Ah. They have delicious coffee, don't they?" Piper waited for her coffee to brew then sat in one of the comfy chairs and motioned for me to do the same. I did, pulling JJ onto my lap. She squinted at him. "Is that the cat . . ."

Shoot. I nodded slowly.

Her eyes moved from JJ to me then she jumped up, almost sloshing her coffee all over her. "You're Mancini's granddaughter," she said, her voice dangerously soft.

I tried for a smile. "That's me."

"*And* you were at her house today. Frank's wife's. What are you doing here?"

My smile faded. I wasn't sure why she was annoyed with me when they were the ones trying to scam my grandfather. I dropped my pretense. "I wanted to talk to you. See if you were involved in this scheme to buy my grandfather's house."

"*Scheme?* I beg your pardon. We're trying to conduct business here. Improve this island so we're not all doomed to this summer insanity every year and living in a ghost town for the rest of the time. Frank had *ideas.* He had a *vision.*" She was nearly shouting now, using me as the punching bag for all her pent-up anger and frustration. "Your grandfather is just being difficult. He doesn't want to live in that house anymore. That's what Frank told me!"

I stood up too, so angry my voice shook. "Then Frank lied to you," I said. "That house has been in our family forever. He's not selling it, Piper. And I don't know why you're involved, if it's his son's business venture."

"This chamber is the most successful in the state," she said, biting the words off. "We didn't get that way by sitting around waiting for things to happen. We make things happen. And bringing in the right business will help make those things happen. The people who can't seem to let go of the past, well, they have no place here." She sounded insane.

"You can't dictate who and what thrives here, Piper. This is a living and breathing community. If there wasn't a mix of old and new it wouldn't have balance. Look. All I'm asking is that you look somewhere else for land for this venture. We don't want any trouble. My grandpa just wants to be left alone. He deserves that, don't you think, after serving this community for so many years?"

My words didn't sway her. Either that or she had no capacity for rational conversation. She was just getting started. "You had lunch with Frank that day. He told me all about it. How convenient that he ends up dead a few

hours after you didn't get your way." She smiled trium-
phantly. "And I'm not the only one who thinks that. I
heard the cops were asking about you too."

I resisted taking the bait. "I'd like to find out just
as much as you would who killed Frank," I said. "Believe me. This whole thing has been a nightmare."

She laughed, a harsh, unfriendly sound. "Ask his wife.
You should've asked her today, while you guys were
having tea."

"Why would I ask his wife?" I asked innocently, ignoring
her snarky comment.

"Because I would think she would be their other top
suspect. She was terrible to him. And when he helped me
out with a place to stay, she was terrible to me too." Piper
nodded, getting into her story. "Hateful woman who lords
her money over everyone. She wanted him gone. She
wanted to move on with her new fella, and she knew she'd
have to give him half of everything if she did."

The boyfriend thing again. I was dying to know if it was
true. The good news was that she seemed angry enough to
spill it if I asked.

"A boyfriend? That seems out of character for her," I
said. "Do you have proof?"

"*Proof?* This is a small place. I'm not the only one who
knows it. Go ask around."

"Well, who is it?" I asked.

We hovered for a moment, eyes locked, Piper's mind
trying to work through the pros and cons of spilling the
gossip. She must've figured a name would give her more
credibility. And when she said it, I'm sure I gasped out
loud.

"Gil Smith."

I didn't even realize I'd let go of JJ's leash until I heard
a squeaking sound, and saw a blur of orange fur as he took
off into the depths of the office.

Shoot. Bad timing. I dashed after him.

"Hey!" Piper followed me. "You can't go back there!"

"JJ!" I peeked into the first office. Nothing. "JJ?" I followed the squeaks to the back office—the largest of the group. Must've been Frank's. It didn't look like an office today, though. It looked like a makeshift apartment, with clothing piled on the desk and chair. Blankets, a pillow, and more clothing covered the small couch. Toiletries, a hair dryer, a bunch of shoes, all of it scattered around like a messy teenager's bedroom.

Piper must be sleeping here.

JJ nosed through the piles of clothing. I prayed there wasn't a dead body somewhere in here. I stepped over and scooped him up. "Bad boy," I murmured.

She appeared behind me, looking furious. "Excuse me. This is a private office," she spat, icicles in her voice. "And you need to leave now."

"I'm sorry. The cat took off and I didn't want him getting into anything." I guess this killed my chance to ask more about Gil and Aidan.

"You can leave this way," she said, shoving open an exit door in the back next to Frank's office. Next thing I knew, I was out in the alley behind the chamber, wondering what the heck had just happened.

Chapter 40

I still needed to get dessert, and I was going to be late for dinner. I half ran down the street back to Grandpa's car, trying to digest this new information. This entire thing was starting to sound like a bad soap opera. And Piper had to be lying about Margaret and Gil. Didn't she? Good grief. And here I wanted to talk to him about Frank. That was probably the last thing he wanted to do, politics aside.

But if Piper was telling the truth, that was another motive. Now Gil had two—the election, and his girlfriend.

The thought left me cold. I loaded JJ into the car, made a quick pit stop at the bakery, and zoomed back to Grandpa's to pick him up. His truck wasn't there. Cursing, I called his cell. No answer again. Maybe he was working at his mysterious job. Or maybe he'd gotten tired of waiting for me and headed to my parents' house already. Fingers crossed the latter was the case, I drove there.

Alas, it wasn't. The driveway was full, but his truck was missing. Both my mom's red convertible and my dad's dark blue sedan were in the driveway. He'd left work early tonight. My sisters' cars were parked out front. My heart swelled a little at the sight of my family's home, all of us present. I hadn't been terribly homesick after my first year away, but now, after spending so much time here, I realized how much I'd missed them.

No sign of Gil yet, which gave me more time to figure that situation out. I pulled in behind my mom, grabbed my purse and the cupcakes I'd picked up, and hurried to the front door, peering in through the screen. I could hear music—Italian. My mother loved music from all over the world.

"Hey," I called, letting myself inside, JJ straining at his leash to reach the food smells wafting out the door. Sam and Val argued over something at the counter. Val went on about how much red pepper was appropriate to add to the chili. My mother was nowhere in sight.

They both turned to me. "Hey, Maddie." Sam waved with her wooden spoon. My sister looked like a pixie. She'd lopped off all her hair into a short, messy style. Her sheer, flowy dress and bare feet completed the look.

Val didn't bother with pleasantries. "Do you know how much red pepper she just dumped into the chili? Mom asked her to do one thing, and she screwed it up."

Sam rolled her eyes at me, then spotted JJ. "Awww!" She dropped to her knees and petted him. He nuzzled her hand.

I dropped the bakery boxes on the counter and went over to give Val a hug. "It's only chili," I reminded her. Now it was Val's turn to roll her eyes, but I could feel her smile. My middle sister was the practical one. I had a bit of both their personalities, which I always told my mother made me the perfect child. She usually rolled her eyes at that. Must be where Val and Sam got the habit.

"Where is everyone?" I asked.

"Mom's writing," Sam said. "She had to finish a chapter. That's why she asked me to make sure the chili was perfect." She preened at Val.

"You may want to order pizza," Val said to me.

"Who's ordering pizza?" my dad asked, walking in from the back door. "Hi, honey," he said to me. "How are you holding up?" He hugged me. I rested my head on his shoulder, wishing I were five again and all my troubles could melt away if my dad just hugged me tight enough.

But it wasn't so, unfortunately. I sighed and pulled back. "I'm fine, Dad."

He studied me for a minute, and I could tell he didn't quite believe me. Then again, there were times when he didn't know what to make of any of the women in his life. As if my mom's quirkiness wasn't enough, he'd also been cursed with three quirky daughters. He noticed JJ sprawled on the floor, went to ask, then closed his mouth.

"No one's ordering pizza," Sam said. "Wait'll you taste this chili. It rocks."

"At the very least, we have cupcakes," I offered.

"Is that Maddie?" My mom swept into the room. She wore her trademark writer look—a multicolored maxidress with a scarf tied around her unruly dark blond curls, bare feet, and a beat-up sweatshirt from their trip to Hawaii twenty years ago. She had a pen stuck behind her ear. "Oh, and the lovely kitty. But where's your grandpa?" She swooped over and kissed my cheek, then headed over to test the chili.

"I don't know," I admitted. "He wasn't home."

My mother frowned, the wooden spoon halfway to her mouth. "Did he forget we were having dinner?"

"I don't know. I'll try calling him again." I found my cell phone in my purse and walked to a quieter spot to make the call.

Straight to voice mail. I disconnected and tapped the phone against my thigh. Then, impulsively, I texted Craig.

Seen Grandpa today?

Maybe Craig had an idea about Grandpa's new "security job." Pocketing the phone, I went back to the kitchen in time to see my mother take a huge bite of chili. I held my breath, silently rooting for Sam.

She closed her eyes, chewed and swallowed, then burst into a brilliant smile. "Delightful!" she declared. "This is nice and hot, so everyone be warned!"

"What?" Val yelped.

My mother ignored her and looked at me. "Well?"

I shook my head. "No answer."

"Really. Maybe he doesn't want to come to dinner," Val said, looking at my mother. "Maybe he just wants to be alone."

"Maybe," she said. Her tone made it clear she didn't want to discuss it.

I heard a muted ding, signaling a text message in my pocket. I resisted the urge to pull it out. "Is Gil still coming for dinner?" I asked.

My dad looked at me, surprised. "He said it would probably be more like dessert. How'd you know that? I just invited him this morning during our racquetball game."

"I saw him today when I was having lunch with Becky. He mentioned he'd see me tonight," I said. *Maybe he's having dinner with Margaret first.* I pushed the thought aside.

My mother motioned for Sam to bring bowls over and started filling them with chili. "Did you bring dessert, Maddie?"

"Sure did. Cupcakes. Fun for everyone." I grabbed silverware and delivered it to the table. "Vegan and gluten-free options too."

"Lovely." She smiled as she set bowls down on the table. "Though I'm afraid I don't have food for the kitty."

"That's okay. He can eat when he goes home. He's been out running errands with me."

"He's a nice-looking cat," my father said. "I saw his front-page story."

"Yeah. People are a little obsessed with him. Would you

believe I had some old guy taking selfies with him on the street? And he wanted to know if the seniors from the senior center could visit him."

"That's nice. People love to make a big deal out of hero animals," Sam said. She pulled JJ into her arms and nuzzled his head. "Come on, let's sit down and eat."

"Did you know Katrina's in charge of the animal shelter now?" I asked as we took our places at the table. "You'd think people could go there and visit animals?"

My mother shrugged. "It's not really that type of place. I think poor Katrina is overwhelmed, to be honest. She's just trying to keep up and get them adopted out quickly."

"Which is why it makes sense that people would go in there and spend time," I said. "That's what a shelter is for."

"It's not really a shelter, though," my dad pointed out. "The only true shelter we had closed last year."

I would have to stop by and see Katrina. Maybe she just needed a few volunteers to organize adoptions or something. Maybe I could find her someone before I left.

"So what's going on with that dead guy? Anyone heard?" Val asked, changing the subject.

Everyone looked at me.

"Why are you looking at me?" I asked.

"Oh, no reason." My mother sent a sly look in my direction as she ate a spoonful of chili. "I just thought Craig might share information with you."

I swallowed guiltily, thinking of the text messages burning a hole in my pocket. The gossip mill was already hard at work on the possibility of me and Craig rekindling our high-school romance. "Did you forget the cop's code already? I have a better chance of getting an early scoop from Becky than from Craig. What have you guys heard?"

My mother sighed. "I haven't heard much," she admitted. "Your dad and I may go out for a drink later at Tootsie's. Perhaps we'll hear some news there."

Tootsie's was a high-end piano bar that Lilah Gilmore frequented. I hadn't known my parents to hang out there. I suspected my mother was looking for intel. By the look my dad sent her, I knew I was right.

"The whole situation's quite disturbing for Daybreak Island," Dad said. "Certainly not the kind of image we want to project. It could hurt tourism." He dug into his chili and immediately started to cough. I handed over a glass of water. "Wow," he said, waving at his mouth. "Hot."

Val sent Sam a look.

"That's true," my mother said. "Although everyone knows it wasn't random."

Chapter 41

The doorbell rang.

"I'll get it," my father said, still waving at his mouth as he went to the door.

My mother turned a brilliant smile toward the doorway when Gil walked into the dining room and rose to give him a hug. "Hi, there, Gil. Please sit! Do you want some chili?"

"It's spicy," I heard my father murmur as he sat down again.

I studied Gil from behind my water glass. He didn't look like a killer, or a guy keeping a deep, dark secret. He just looked like Gil, a guy who was practically part of the family.

"Thanks, Sophie, but I think I'll save room for dessert," he said with a wink. "Hello, girls." He nodded to me and my sisters. "I thought Leo was coming?"

"So did we," my mother said, sitting again.

Gil chuckled and pulled out a chair. "Poker game running long?"

I ate a few more bites of chili, listening to the small talk swirl around me. My cell phone dinged again in my pocket and I excused myself and slipped into the bathroom. The

texts were from Craig, as I'd figured. The first was short
and to the point:

Haven't seen him.

The next seemed more urgent:

Found him yet? It's important.

I frowned and texted back.

No. Why?

I took a long time washing my hands, waiting for his
return text. Why was Craig looking for my grandfather?

Craig had stopped texting, so I returned to the table
before anyone started to wonder what I was doing. My
mother had arranged the cupcakes on a platter. I smiled,
hoping it looked normal.

"These look delicious, Maddie!" she exclaimed, passing the plate around. "What are the flavors?"

I pointed each one out. Everyone chose. Gil settled back
with his mocha fudge cupcake, then he noticed JJ, who'd
been under the table the whole time and had just emerged.
"Look at that," he said. "Isn't that the hero cat?"

"Yep, that's him," I said.

"How's he taking his newfound celebrity?"

"He's loving it. He gets stopped on the street and everything," I said.

Gil nodded approvingly. "He did a service to the community. I expect he'll get a citation."

A citation? I was all about animals being treated like
people, but this seemed a little over the top. I refrained
from comment. "So Gil," I said instead. "Do you have any
theories on who killed Frank?"

The entire table went silent. I avoided my parents'
gazes. They wouldn't be pleased. I, however, didn't think
the question was that odd. My dad said this sort of thing
happened to Gil all the time. Hazard of the job, but he always seemed to have an answer to whatever question a

citizen threw at him. Often the correct one. Which was probably why he'd been the longest-running selectman in Daybreak Harbor. Was it my imagination, though, or did Gil's face shift ever so slightly?

"This is yummy!" my mother exclaimed around a mouthful of cake. She sounded manic. Too bad. I was on a mission. I heard my phone buzz in my pocket again.

"I mean," I went on, "it sounded like he wasn't going to win Daybreak's Person of the Year award anytime soon."

"Honey. Isn't there a better dinner topic than murder?" my mother asked, shooting daggers at me.

But Gil waved her off. "It's fine, Sophie. People are concerned. It's my job to help them feel better about the investigation." He smiled tightly. "I know how hard the police are working on this. They have assured me there's no danger to the public."

"You think it was business or personal?" I couldn't help myself.

"Now, Maddie, that's for the police to figure out. I couldn't possibly say." I watched as he methodically ripped his cupcake into pieces, but didn't put any of it in his mouth.

"Some of the business people in town didn't think much of the chamber," I said.

Gil nodded. "That's true."

"Did they have legitimate gripes?"

"Well now, to them I'm sure it was legitimate," Gil said. "I can't speak for what other people feel."

"Did anyone ever complain about him to his board?"

"Maddie, these cupcakes are very good," my father said.

"Better than the chili," Val added.

Sam wasn't paying attention at all. She'd set JJ on the floor and was feeding him something. I hoped it wasn't a chocolate cupcake.

"They are very good," Gil agreed. "And something like a board complaint wouldn't be public information. The chamber isn't a state organization."

That was a very diplomatic way to answer that question.

"I *also* heard," I said, seeing my parents cringe, "a rumor that Frank had been contemplating a run for first selectman." I batted innocent eyes at Gil. "Had you heard that? I mean, of course it's a crazy thought, but interesting."

Gil's hand tightened around his fork, just a tad. If I hadn't been looking for it, I wouldn't have seen it.

"I had heard that," he said. "The competition would've definitely made for an exciting race, don't you think so?"

"I have no idea," I said. "I haven't been part of an election here. What was his platform?"

"I'm not really sure, since he didn't announce a campaign," Gil said. "But I suspect it would've been tourism. That is—was—his forte."

"Yeah, he had plans for the island, didn't he," I said. "I've been hearing that a lot. How were his relationships with the business owners?"

"It varied." This topic seemed to relax Gil a bit, enough to eat a few more bites of his mocha fudge cupcake. "He wanted more flash and flair on the island. New people, more hip—his word, not mine—stores."

Which was why Lucas and Cass were on his good list, I thought. They both brought new things to town—things that rich people would use.

"Interesting," my father said. He'd been listening intently to the exchange. I couldn't tell if he was surprised about the campaign or not, but my dad was used to keeping things close to the vest. "Do you think that's where the island is trending? A hipster transformation?"

Gil thought about that for a long minute before answering. "I think that was Frank's intent," he said finally. "Frank was convinced that Daybreak was due for a metamorphosis, given the uptick in celebrity clientele over the years. He thought we could turn the island into a better version of the Hamptons and attract even more people. I think ultimately his intention was good. But what he failed sometimes to understand is the old-timers don't know any other way. They don't see all this change as a good thing. And it will take a while to change their minds on that, if it happens at all."

I desperately wanted to ask him about Margaret, but this wasn't the forum. Instead, I turned this latest information over in my mind as my mother swooped in and started asking Gil about the plans for the elementary school renovations.

Frank's personal life was a mess, clearly. That scene this morning had clinched that for me. But if his views on changing the island had angered enough people, that was a whole other motive. Throw in the fact that he was killed in a very public place where pretty much everyone on the island had reason to be on that street the night he died, and the police really didn't have an easy job. Now it was three days into the investigation. The more time that passed, the harder it would be to narrow it down.

My phone vibrated again. I set my cupcake down and glanced down at the readout. They were both from Craig.

Call me please.

And the next one, more urgent: *Maddie. We need to talk.*

I excused myself and went out to the front porch, hitting Craig's name in my contact list. "What's up?" I asked when he answered.

He sounded like he was outside with lots of people around. He also sounded very grim. "Nothing from your grandfather?"

I laughed nervously. "Craig, I appreciate your concern about Grandpa. Gil thinks he's playing poker—"

"Maddie," he interrupted. "I have to tell you something. You'll read about it on the newspaper's Web site any minute anyway, the Duck Cove police are giving a reporter the statement now."

My heart did a slow flip. "What happened?"

"I'm at Abe Tate's office. Maddie, he's dead. Hit-and-run."

Chapter 42

I thought I might pass out. I slid onto the porch right where I stood and commanded myself to hold it together, at least until I found out why Craig felt the urgent need to share this breaking news. In the same breath as him asking, for the twentieth time tonight, where Grandpa was.

"Maddie?" he asked. "Did you hear me?"

"Yes. Crap. I heard you. How did you . . ." Tate's office was in Duck Cove. A few minutes from my parents' house, to be exact. But why was Craig involved in a different police force's investigation?

"I have a buddy on the force. He called me," Craig said, as if reading my mind.

"Oh." I wanted to ask if they called because they thought it was linked to Frank, but part of me didn't want to know. "Do they think . . . was it an accident?" I asked instead.

"Not sure." His flat voice told me he suspected otherwise.

"So someone may have done this on purpose?" I heard the note of hysteria in my voice. "What does that have to do with Grandpa?" I heard Grandpa's angry voice again from this morning, telling me that Abe Tate was . . . what had he said? Part of "this whole thing," meaning Frank's scheme?

"I can't get into it, but I really need to talk to him," Craig said. "If you hear from him, please have him call me. Immediately. And Maddie, don't say anything about this to your family, if you're at their house."

He hung up. I shot the dead phone a dirty look. Sure, that was easier said than done. Especially if I walked in there looking like I'd just seen a ghost. I buried my face in my hands. Why was everyone dying? And why did they have to be connected to my grandfather?

I sat in the same spot for a few more minutes, trying to calm down. Okay, I told myself. Maybe Craig and the rest of the cops are just paranoid, with Frank's death looming over them. Maybe he did get hit by someone accidentally, some teenager texting or a mother looking behind her to see what her toddler was up to.

Then why didn't they come forward, if they were innocent?

Easy, I argued with myself. Fear. Reckless driving, even without intent, could earn you jail time. But that was a pretty big secret for the average Joe or Jane to keep.

The door swung open, almost whacking me in the head. "Oops." Val stared down at me. "Sorry. What are you doing?"

"Nothing." I jumped up, probably a little too fast to look innocent.

Val raised an eyebrow. "Mom's looking for you. Gil wanted to ask you about your business and stuff." She turned to walk back into the house.

"I'll be right there," I called after her. Once she'd gone all the way inside I hit Grandpa's number on my cell. This time, it rang four times before going to voice mail. So the phone was on, but he still wasn't answering. Trying to hide my frustration—and fear—I left him a terse message that he'd missed dinner and needed to call me. Then I went back into the kitchen. My mother gave me an odd look, but didn't say anything.

"Oh, there you are." Gil smiled. He'd finally finished his cupcake and sipped from a mug of coffee. "I wanted to ask you about California, and your business. Your parents say it's quite successful."

"Yes, it's doing really well, thanks." Desperate, I looked around. My mother pointed to the kitchen, where the freshly brewed pot sat. Gratefully, I filled up a mug and returned to the table, sipping with jerky hands. Of course, I slopped it onto the table. My mother jumped up to get paper towels.

"Sorry," I muttered, swabbing at the stain.

"So you serve drinks?" Gil asked.

"Juice. Green juice. Well, some of the juices are pink, or orange, depending on if you use beets, or carrots or whatever." I babbled, feeling like I was going to explode.

Gil nodded. "I've never had green juice. Is it . . . tasty?"

"It's delicious," I said automatically. "And really good for you."

"Who's minding the shop while you're here?"

"My partner. Ethan. He's an awesome juicer. And he's really smart about blending healthy ingredients and coming up with campaigns for each drink. People who are into wellness eat it up. Literally."

"Now see," Gil said to my parents. "That's the kind of thing Frank would've championed for the island. I know those juices are all the rage these days, and we haven't one place that makes them. Or if we do, it's off the side of their menu, so to speak."

I wanted to scream. This mindless conversation was so hard to get through right now, but I couldn't tell anyone what happened yet. And I certainly couldn't make a big deal out of Grandpa being missing. *Missing.* Was he? If he was; why? Craig surely couldn't think Grandpa ran the guy over.

But why not? That other annoying voice in my head taunted me. *They weren't shy about looking at him for Frank's murder, even if they said it was just checking off a box.*

"Maddie?" I jolted back to my parents' table. The whole room stared at me.

"Are you all right?" my father asked. "I know you've had a hard couple of days. Do you need to lie down?"

"No," I said. "But I think JJ and I are going to head home, if you don't mind. Thanks so much for dinner, Mom." I scooped up JJ.

"Wait, honey. Take some chili for you and Grandpa." My mother went to the counter to pack some chili in a glass container. "And call me once you get home to let me know he's there." She thrust the container at me and gave me a fierce hug. "Tell him I will make a routine, whether he likes it or not!"

I promised I'd tell him. As I was making my rounds saying good-bye the phone rang. My mother hurried to answer it. "Lilah! Hi, there," I heard her say.

I cringed. If Lilah Gilmore was calling, Tate's alleged murder had hit the airwaves. Bracing myself, I looked over at my mother. Her mouth was an *O* and she wasn't speaking. I could hear the rise and fall of Lilah's excited voice on the other end of the phone. Val looked at me and frowned.

My mother finally hung up, looking troubled.

"What's happened, Soph?" my father asked.

She came over to the table and sat back down. "There's been a hit-and-run a few streets away. Possibly a murder."

"What?" my father and Gil said in unison.

"That's nuts." Sam stared at Mom, wide-eyed. "Who got killed?"

"A contractor," my mother said, her voice faint. She avoided looking at me, so I knew she knew exactly who Abe Tate was. I wondered if they'd contacted his next of kin already and his name was public knowledge. Lilah knew it, but she knew ninety-five percent of things before they were public.

"Which contractor?" Gil wanted to know.

"Tate," my mother said. "Abe Tate."

Gil frowned. "My God," he said softly. "What's going on here?"

Two murders, two towns, four days. This island was feeling smaller by the minute.

Chapter 43

I floored it on my way out of my parents' neighborhood, sending a quick apology to JJ as he scrabbled for purchase on the leather seat. I winced, hoping Grandpa would be too distracted to care about claw marks.

I knew I shouldn't go over to Tate's office. Craig would kill me if he saw me. On the other hand I knew something the police didn't. Someone was giving large quantities of cash to Abe to help my grandfather. Besides, it wasn't technically his crime scene. I wound my way through the residential streets of Duck Cove until I turned onto Main Street. Tate's office was about a few hundred feet down on the left. I could see flashing lights ahead. As I inched closer, I saw police barricades preventing traffic from going any further. I could also see the same yellow crime scene tape that had encircled Frank's crime scene a few nights ago. The sight made my stomach turn. The body must have been removed, because it would've been visible on the street.

I pulled to the curb and got out, locking JJ in the car, and ventured down the street, trying not to be noticed. The local news truck was parked haphazardly at the curb, and a small crowd of press gathered on the lawn. Two cops stood at the barricades to make sure no one on foot crossed them. I inched a bit closer, then bit back a scream as someone grabbed my arm. I spun around to face Craig.

Perfect.

"What are you doing here?"

"What are *you* doing here? I thought you worked for Daybreak Harbor." I deliberately removed my arm from his grasp.

His face darkened. "Don't, Maddie. You have to leave." He glanced around. "I don't want Ellory to see you."

"Ellory's here too?"

"Yeah. I got the call so he brought me as a courtesy. And I called you as a courtesy, so don't make me regret it."

I looked around again, but couldn't see much beyond the lights and some cops talking. Then I noticed people coming out of the building also. If Tate had been killed out in the street, why were they looking inside?

"Why would Ellory care?" I asked. "I was at my parents'. I saw all the commotion and stopped. Is he going to arrest me for that?"

Craig turned me around and propelled me back to my car. "I'm telling you," he began, but we both turned at the voice calling his name.

"We have to go," Ellory said. "Mancini agreed to—" He broke off, realizing who I was. "Ms. James," he said. "Fancy meeting you here."

"I . . . was at my parents'," I said lamely. I wasn't saying a word about the money until I knew what he was saying about my grandfather. "Were you looking for my grandfather?"

Ellory gave me a long look, like he was gauging whether he should or shouldn't tell me something. "Your grandfather has agreed to meet us at the station to talk." He turned back to Craig. "Let's go."

"Wait," I called after them. "Talk about what?"

"My case," Ellory said without turning back.

Furious at getting blown off, I ran after them, pulling slightly ahead and turning to face them so Ellory had to either stop or go around me. "Unless you're about to tell me Grandpa is consulting on this . . . situation as your former police chief, I'm sending a lawyer down there."

Ellory stopped and looked at me with interest. I ignored Craig, who looked like steam was about to burst from the top of his head. "Now why on earth would you think he needs a lawyer, Ms. James?"

I opened my mouth, but nothing came out.

"Unless," Ellory continued, "you're worried about something?"

Now I kept my mouth shut. We engaged in that stare-off until his phone buzzed. He glanced down, then back at me, then walked away.

Craig looked over his shoulder to make sure Ellory wasn't watching. "Go call your mother," he said. "Tell her to send Val's husband. Or better yet, his father."

Chapter 44

I stood rooted to the spot, watching them go. They had to be kidding, right? They were all over my grandfather about Frank, now they wanted to question him in the death of Abe Tate? Why were they targeting him? And I'd given them extra ammo by texting Craig to ask if he'd seen him. *Stupid, stupid, stupid.* I turned and ran back to the car. I barely remember driving back to my mother's. Thank God—Gil was gone. I didn't need this getting around any sooner than it surely already would.

I careened into the driveway, grabbed poor JJ and raced inside. When I burst through the door my mother looked up in alarm from where she still sat at the table with her coffee and my dad.

"Maddie." She jumped up. "What's happened?"

"Grandpa." I could barely get the words out. "They're talking to him about Abe Tate's death."

"What?" I think she would've been more apt to believe me if I'd told her the shark from *Jaws* had just jumped out of the water and was swimming down Main Street. She looked at my father. "How can that even be?"

"Is Val still here? Can Tanner help?"

"Val!" my mother yelled.

Val appeared in the doorway. "What's going on? Maddie. You're back."

"Can you call your father-in-law? It's an emergency. Grandpa needs him."

The color drained from Val's face. She grabbed her cell phone, said a few terse words into the phone, then handed it to my mother. "He's coming."

My mother disappeared with the phone. I sank into a chair, hugging JJ to me.

Val looked at me. "What . . . ?"

"Is he at the police station now? How did you hear this?" my father asked.

"Police station?" Val looked confused.

I hesitated. I didn't want to tell him I'd driven over to the crime scene. "I talked to Craig. He gave me a heads-up. Grandpa's meeting them there."

My father shook his head and stood. "We should get over there."

"Is someone going to tell me what's going on?" Val demanded.

"We're not sure yet, honey," my father said. "I think your mother is taking some precautionary measures getting Grandpa a lawyer, but better to be safe."

"Why on earth would Grandpa need a lawyer?" Val asked, bewildered.

My mother rushed back into the room. "Erik's meeting us there. Let's go."

I turned to Val. "Can you please watch JJ?"

"Yeah. But—"

"Thanks." I blew her a kiss and rushed out with my parents.

My father drove, thank goodness. My hands were shaking and I had a terrible headache. I leaned my head back against the seat and closed my eyes. What a nightmare the past few days had been. And it didn't look like it was ending any time soon.

"Did you guys know Tate?" I asked.

"I knew his name," my father said. "He's been part of some charity events at the hospital. Is this the man you told me about, Sophie? Who was helping your dad?"

My mother nodded. "Yes. Maddie spoke to him."

I sure did. And saw a case full of money someone had allegedly given him to fix my grandpa's house. I remembered thinking how Jason Bourne that whole thing was, and it was even sillier to imagine that had anything to do with his death. But still, I couldn't keep my mind from wandering there.

When we got to the police station, I saw Grandpa's truck parked out front. A shiny, midnight-blue Jaguar was parked next to it. I guessed that was Tanner's car. My mother jumped out before my dad even had the car in park and raced inside. We were close on her heels. She went up to the window and picked up the phone you needed to use to communicate with the officer behind the glass.

"I'm looking for former Chief Mancini," she said, enunciating the word "chief." "And Erik Tanner," she added.

The cop inside said something and my mother hung up and turned to us. "They just brought Erik in to see him," she said. Her hands were clasped together so tightly the knuckles were white. My father went to her and put his arm around her.

"We'll get it figured out, Sophie," he murmured.

We didn't have to wait long. Less than ten minutes later a door from the inner police station opened and Erik Tanner and Grandpa emerged. Tanner's head was bent close to Grandpa's ear and he gestured as he spoke. They huddled near the door for a minute finishing their conversation then Grandpa shook Tanner's hand and they walked over to us.

My mother hugged Grandpa tight. "Let's go outside," she

said, still holding on to his arm. Shooting the cop behind the glass a dirty look, she marched outside. My dad put his arm around me and we followed, Tanner bringing up the rear.

When we reached Grandpa's car, Tanner turned to us. "There's nothing to worry about," he said, looking at each of us in turn. "Leo's obviously well versed on how this all works, and he came in voluntarily and waited for me to get here. Basically, he has an alibi for when the victim was hit. No one actually saw it happen, since that street is fairly quiet, but he was seen alive mid-afternoon, and found deceased right before his assistant was about to close up the office."

An alibi. Interesting that he hadn't said, *Since Leo was volunteering at the soup kitchen when Abe was hit,* or *Leo was over at Damian's Lobstah Shack having lunch with ten other people,* I presumed he didn't want us to know what said alibi was.

"So they weren't interrogating you or threatening to bring charges, then?" my dad asked.

"Correct. They wanted me to come in so they could look at my vehicle," Grandpa said, his eyes darkening as he looked at the building where he'd spent probably the better part of his life. "See if it had blood on it or something. I think they forget I did their job and then told them how to do their jobs."

"But why were they questioning you in the first place?" I asked. "I mean, you made comments about Tate to me, but did you make them to anyone else who could've misconstrued them?"

"Comments?" Tanner looked at Grandpa then shook his head. "I don't want to know. Basically, they knew your grandfather had been to see Tate this morning—"

"You went to see Tate this morning?" I asked Grandpa. "Why?"

My mother covered her face with her hands. "Dad," she said, her voice muffled. "We have to talk about what's going on."

"It was early," Grandpa said to me, ignoring my mother and avoiding my other question. "Long before the incident."

"What, did they think you came back and ran him over?" I laughed nervously. Tanner didn't. Guess that answered my question.

"Do they think this is related to Frank?" I asked, looking from Grandpa to Tanner.

Tanner frowned. "Why would it be related to Frank?"

Shoot. My parents were both staring at me. So was Grandpa. "I . . . don't know," I said. "Just a thought. Since we never have murders and now there've been two in four days?"

"Well, they haven't said it's murder," Tanner cautioned. "They're treating it as a suspicious hit-and-run. It could've been something as simple as a teenager texting who's now terrified and hiding out."

My exact thoughts when Craig had told me the news earlier. But my gut chastised me for trying to take the easy way out. These two deaths were related. I was positive.

Chapter 45

I wondered if sleep would ever come easily to me again. It didn't seem so at four A.M. Or five, or six. I finally hauled myself out of bed at seven, feeling like I'd been out drinking all night. Grandpa's bedroom door was shut when I walked by. I resisted the urge to knock. Let him sleep. He'd had a rough night. We'd all had a rough night.

I brought JJ downstairs, boiled myself an egg, and put food on his plate. I waited for the coffee to brew while I stared out the window, wishing I'd just wake up and find out everything since Saturday had all been a horrible dream brought on by the stress of losing my grandmother. But every time I tried closing and opening my eyes, nothing changed.

At least the coffee was almost finished brewing.

Who would've run Tate down? More importantly, why? I desperately wanted to hold on to my original texting-teenager theory like Tanner had said, but my childhood Nancy Drew studies told me that would've been too much of a coincidence. Maybe if the guy across the street from Tate had been run down. But the fact that it was Tate, who'd been involved with Grandpa's house, the subject of a bunch of controversy, with a mystery man and some cash mixed in, screamed of a link. And I wasn't even a cop. If Grandpa had been at Tate's yesterday morning, he'd probably gone over there to confront him about the anonymous person and the repairs. If it got ugly and someone heard them they'd have a perfect reason—in the cops' minds, anyway—to think Grandpa could've come back and done something rash. And what was up with this mysterious alibi? The security gig? He had some explaining to do. If it killed me I was going to get him to do it too.

The doorbell rang. I went to the door, peering through the side panes of glass. I didn't recognize the man standing there, but he didn't look like a killer in his dress pants and a short-sleeved dress shirt with tasseled black loafers, so I opened the door. And realized he wasn't alone on the porch.

Debbie Renault moved into view from her spot to the left of the door, waggling her fingers at me. "Hello again!" she cooed.

The man fixed a cool smile on his face and held out his hand. "Morning. Ms. James? I'm Gareth Ward of Pyramid Builders."

Gareth Ward. The celebrity builder. All the initial fears I'd had about Frank O'Malley's allies came crashing back.

"I'm Maddie James," I said, shaking his hand.

"I believe you know Ms. Renault," he said, motioning to Debbie. I nodded.

"We wanted to stop by and speak with your grandfather. Is he available?" Ward continued.

I folded my arms and leaned against the door frame. "May I ask what this is regarding?"

"Of course. My apologies," Ward said. "I'm with O&M Transportation. We've been in discussions with your grandfather about his land and we'd like to see if we can finish those conversations."

As if. "Sorry, Grandpa's not available right now," I said.

"Nor do I think he's changed his mind from your last conversation, Deb." I used the nickname she hated on purpose.

Debbie's eyes narrowed. Ward kept that smooth smile pasted on his lips. "That's something we'd be interested in hearing from him directly. Can you have him give me a call when he . . . becomes available?" He handed me a card. "Oh," he said, as if he'd almost forgotten. He handed me the newspaper that was in his other hand. "Here's your newspaper. I hope last evening's events didn't take too much of a toll on him," he added, handing it to me. Then, with a nod, he turned and walked down the front steps.

With one last nasty look over her shoulder, Debbie followed Ward. I sent a childish wish to the Universe that she would trip or something in her platform shoes, but then hurriedly took it back. My luck she'd break something and sue.

I took great pleasure in slamming the door behind them, then leaned against it and unfolded the paper. A loose paper fluttered out and fell to the floor. I bent to pick it up and frowned. Another clipping about a cat café—this one opening in London, the proprietor a formerly homeless man with an orange cat who had found fame and fortune and was putting it to charitable use. Aside from the orange cat, I wasn't sure about the parallel, but it was a cute story.

Another mystery—who wanted me to learn about cat cafés?

But I didn't have time to worry about it now. I pocketed the piece and focused on the front-page headline. "Local Contractor Dead in Hit-and-run, Police Calling It 'Suspicious,'" it screamed. "Jeez, Becky," I muttered. "Are you running the *Enquirer* over there?" I knew that wasn't entirely fair. Becky certainly wasn't the last word about what got printed, but she did weigh in on it.

I continued scanning the story. Mostly facts—Tate was hit by a car on the street in front of his office, driver left the scene, being treated as a suspicious death, one person voluntarily interviewed at the police station last night. And they named him. Great. I blew out a breath and considered throwing the paper on the floor and stomping on it, as if that could blur the ink enough to make the words disappear.

Chapter 46

The doorbell rang again before I could give in to my desire. Pauline Crosby stood outside with a casserole dish. I breathed a sigh of relief. "Thank goodness. I thought they were coming back." I pulled her inside.

"Who?"

"Gareth Ward and Debbie freakin' Renault. Just who I needed this morning." I led her down the hall into the kitchen, tucking the paper under my arm. Silly, I knew. The entire island had probably seen it already. Many had probably conversed about it over coffee.

"Gareth Ward?" Pauline exclaimed. "My, my, my. They're pulling out the big guns, eh?"

"They really want this transportation center moving. It's to be expected—Frank was bragging about it Saturday when we were setting up the stroll."

I was hardly listening to her, my mind already jumping ahead to how I could take on someone like Gareth Ward. I knew Frank had to have some big-money backers. Which meant this couldn't just be about his loser son— there had to be something bigger going on here.

"Who's pulling out the big guns?" I focused on Pauline.

"Frank's team, of course. I should've known he was in

cahoots with one of *them*. No wonder he was bragging about new chamber benefactors this weekend. He must have been expecting a nice reward."

"Cash is king, right? Want coffee? Hey, why aren't you at your store?" This was an odd time for Pauline to be out and about. Usually she was at her store every day from six A.M. to at least two.

"I'd love some coffee. I have Miles watching the counter. It was very slow this morning. Guess everyone went for their gluten-free doughnut at Bean." Pauline wrinkled her nose.

"No way," I said. "People love your doughnuts."

"Eh." She shrugged and tried to wave it off, but I could hear the underlying hurt in her voice. "Anyway, I wanted to bring your grandpa this." She offered me the food. "It's his favorite. Lasagna, with an extra layer of mixed cheese."

"Thank you. That's so sweet." I took the dish and put it in the fridge, then poured her a mug of coffee and motioned for her to sit while I put out cream and sugar.

She did. "How's your grandpa?"

I hesitated, my own coffee half poured. "He's getting by," I said.

Pauline sighed. "I read the paper. I'm horrified. Absolutely horrified. I don't know what this island is coming to. How could anyone think your grandfather, such a sweet, sweet man . . ." She trailed off and took a breath. "Abe was a decent man, God rest his soul. I feel terrible. But why would they want to talk to your grandfather about that?" She leaned forward. "Do you think it had anything to do with Frank?"

I hesitated. I didn't want to get into the whole Tate-helping-Grandpa-funded-by-a-good-Samaritan thing. "No idea," I said. "But why do you ask?"

Pauline drank her coffee and drummed the fingers of her free hand on the table. "Two murders back-to-back?

We never have murders here. There's a good chance they're linked, no?"

Something niggled at the edges of my distracted brain, but I couldn't quite put my finger on it. "I suppose anything's possible," I said.

"Did your grandfather give you any details?" she persisted.

"Details about what?" Grandpa walked into the room, looking much more dapper than I'd expected after being questioned about a murder by people who used to work for him.

Pauline brightened, then rose and threw her arms around him. "Leo! So happy to see you. Are you feeling okay?"

Grandpa raised his eyebrows at me over Pauline's shoulder. I shrugged.

"I'm fine, Pauline," he said, patting her on the back a little awkwardly. "It was all a big misunderstanding."

Once Pauline let go of him, I went over and hugged him. "Glad to see you looking so happy," I murmured.

He kissed the top of my head. "Can you fill up a travel mug for me? Have to go for my walk," he announced.

Jeez. If I didn't know better I'd think he was avoiding me. But since I did think he needed to stay active and healthy, I let it go and grabbed his mug.

"I brought you some lasagna," Pauline said to Grandpa, and I swore her voice sounded like a dreamy teenager's. I stifled a smile. Did Pauline have a crush on Grandpa? I remembered her husband had passed away years ago. Was she in the market for a new man?

"You did? Aren't you wonderful." He made a big show of opening the fridge to check it out, proclaiming how delicious it looked and how he couldn't wait to eat it tonight. Then he took the mug I handed him, thanked me and left. I watched him go, resigned. I knew he didn't want me to ask him why he'd been to Tate's place, but of course that would be my first question when I could corner him.

Pauline looked happy enough, though. She drank her coffee and smiled. When JJ came in, yawning and stretching, she scooped him up onto her lap.

I took my seat again. "Hey. I wanted to ask you something."

"Of course, dear." She continued stroking JJ, smiling.

"I heard something about a petition that was started a year or so ago to remove Frank from the presidency at the chamber. Did you know about that?"

Her smile faded a little. "Wow, that was a long time ago," she said. "I was only on the fringes. I didn't really want to get involved. I tried to keep my head down and just do my thing, but." She shrugged. "It was a big push for a while. There were about twenty businesses that came together to propose appointing someone new."

"Who was involved?"

She rattled off a few names, some I recognized, some I didn't. "That fella who took over for the Rice family down the street here"—she jerked a finger in the direction of Damian's Lobstah Shack—"he was the instigator. Threw a bloody fit when Frank publically dissed him in a chamber roundup of new businesses on the island. He left the chamber after that and started this movement."

So Damian dreamed it up. I drank my coffee and pondered that. I wouldn't have pegged him as savvy enough. Maybe his mild-mannered appearance was simply an act. Then again, he'd been the one to contact the paper to draw attention to the petition, according to Becky's reporter.

"So why didn't it go anywhere?"

Pauline drained her mug and set it down, pushing it away. "There were a couple of conversations with board members to gauge buy-in. The reception was cold, even from ones who were on the fence about Frank, or less enthralled with him. In the end it was decided it might do us more harm than good to pursue it. So it died on the vine."

And Frank stayed in place, and the businesses he didn't favor got less and less support because nothing changed. I rose and rinsed out my mug, wondering if one of those business owners had simply gotten sick of waiting for karma to come around. "But he knew about it? Frank?"

"He knew," Pauline said. "In the end it didn't really matter that it never went forward. Someone tipped him off, so he knew anyway. He never let anyone involved forget it either. We may as well have just gone ahead with it. At least we might've had a shot."

Chapter 47

After Pauline left, I channeled Cass and tried to sit quietly with my thoughts. But I felt too overwhelmed to sit still. I grabbed JJ's harness and leash. He came running like any good dog would. We strolled down the street among the ever-growing crowd of tourists. JJ got a couple of oohs and aahs and a head pat or two. I paused as we walked past Damian's, but two college-aged kids were manning the counter at the shack. Bummer. I'd kind of wanted to poke around and see if I could casually drop a few hints about the petition to remove Frank. Maybe on the way back. We continued on to the ferry docks. A bunch of people milled around, waiting for the next boat, which was due to come in shortly. We walked down by the water's edge for a bit until JJ got bored with that, then we went up to street level and made our way through the crowd, turning back toward Grandpa's house. JJ stopped to sniff the remains of someone's fried clams that had ended up on the ground. I paused and scooped him up so he couldn't inhale it.

"Hey. Maddie. Heading over to the mainland?"

I turned to find Rick, my sister Val's ex-boyfriend, who worked on the ferries. "Hey," I said. "No, just taking a walk. Are you off today? Heck of a place to hang out, if you are."

He laughed. "No, I'm jumping on the next boat. Doing an extra shift today. I've been working straight since last Thursday. Full boats too."

"That time of year," I said. JJ squirmed in my arms, but Rick was feeling chatty.

"It's going to be a busy summer. Even with all the craziness going on." He wiggled his eyebrows to make sure I understood what he was talking about.

"Ferries are still full, then? People aren't scared yet?" I asked.

"Nope. Lots of journalists been coming over too," he said. "TV crews and all."

Becky would be beside herself over that.

"We're gonna get lots of publicity. I bet this will bring even more people over. But it's too bad about Mr. O'Malley," Rick said. "He was a good tipper."

With his wife's money, I thought, but put on an agreeable smile. "I bet. He'd probably be happy that he was still doing his part for tourism," I said.

"True story." Rick nodded.

"He rode the ferry a lot?" I asked.

Rick shrugged. "Every now and then. When he was going to Boston to see his kids, or on a trip. You know. Mrs. O is a regular, though. With all her charity work and stuff."

I hadn't even thought of that. If she was seeing someone else—like Gil—would she have taken public ferry trips with him?

"Does she usually travel alone?" I asked.

"Mostly. Sometimes with some of her charity peeps."

"But not, like the town selectman?" I asked.

He gave me a strange look. "Not that I've noticed."

"So you worked on Sunday, then," I said. "Mrs. O'Malley must've been pretty upset on that ride over."

"What do you mean?" he asked.

"Sunday morning. The police had to call her in Boston, they said. To tell her what happened."

Rick shook his head. "Nope. Mrs. O came over on the early morning ferry Friday."

On Friday? That would mean she was here when Frank was killed. So why did the police think she wasn't? I frowned. "I heard she wasn't in town when Frank died."

"Maybe she left again, but I'm sure I would've seen her," Rick said. "We all walk the entire ferry when we work. And I know for a fact she was on Friday's, because she told me how she wanted a quiet ride without a lot of people."

Right. So people she knew couldn't do exactly this and out her for not being where she said she was going to be. "Really," I murmured. "That's so interesting."

Rick looked upset. "I didn't get her in trouble, did I?"

"No, of course not," I assured him. *Unless she did kill her husband after all.*

Rick turned his attention to the ferry as it pulled up to the docks, and JJ and I walked home. Damian still wasn't at the shack when we walked by, but my mind was occupied with Margaret O'Malley. Why did the cops think she wasn't in town? Wouldn't it be fairly easy to tell if she was? Heck, the ferry was small. Someone had to have seen her. Rick had. So why would she lie about it? It seemed everywhere I turned, someone wasn't telling the truth about something.

Chapter 48

When we got back I called Katrina again. I still needed to get JJ to the vet and she hadn't gotten back to me. I left her another message, then texted Craig.

Can you talk?

He responded almost immediately.

In a few. I'll swing by and get you? We should talk.

I hoped that was a good "we should talk," not a bad one. Still, I wanted to know what was going on. *Definitely,* I replied. Maybe he was getting close to some answers. Maybe he would even take pity on me and tell me, given what had gone down last night. He had to feel bad about that. If he didn't, then he'd changed into someone I couldn't care about.

I slipped down the hall to the bathroom I'd commandeered as my own during my stay and stared at myself in the mirror. I'd been neglecting my normal self-care routines, and my skin didn't have that California glow right now. I could do a quick travel mud mask to freshen up a bit.

I tied my hair back and mixed up some mud and water, then smeared it over my face, my mind going a mile a minute. But with the mess of the past few days, I was good and stumped. Maybe because I was just too close to it. I leaned against the counter and set my phone timer to let my face dry while I focused on Frank and his would-be killers.

Margaret. Piper. Gil. They all had strong motives. But what about the other people who had issues with him? Reluctantly, I put Jade on the list. Motive—Frank thought she owed him for waiving her dues and was drinking her out of house and home. Kind of weak, but still possible. Alibi—not really. She'd been back and forth to her tent during that time period, most likely, and no one would've blinked an eye.

And what about Damian Shaw? Allegedly spearheading the petition to oust Frank, making no secret of his issues with Frank. Plus, he'd have been mad about the stroll because he didn't even get a tent without having to beg someone to let him squat. Alibi—I'd never asked, but if he was at the stroll setting up his shared booth, probably not.

I added Aidan O'Malley to the list. I'd seen his drunken-rage capability firsthand, and he'd been seen taking a tongue-lashing from his father at the stroll. Maybe he'd figured he could do better without the old man cramping his style.

Sheesh. My head hurt. This happened every single time I tried to narrow the field.

My timer dinged. I grabbed a facecloth and turned on the faucet.

No water came out.

"What the?" I jiggled the handles. Still nothing. Had Grandpa come home and shut the water off?

My mask was hardening by the second. I tried to grimace but it didn't work well, plus I was afraid my face would further harden in that expression. I yanked open the cabinets under the sink, not sure what I was looking for, but it seemed the right place to start. But nothing obvious jumped out at me. I tried the shower. I got a spurt of water, then a dribble.

"No way. How can this be?" I gritted my teeth and counted to ten. I could kick something, but I was barefoot so I'd just break a toe and *that* would be inconvenient.

Cursing, I went downstairs to the kitchen and tried that sink. Nothing. "You have got to be freakin' kidding me," I said to JJ, who'd come out into the kitchen staring at me curiously. I grabbed the phone and called Becky. As I waited for her to answer I tapped my cheek. Great. Soon I'd need a chisel.

She finally picked up. "Hey."

"Do you know any plumbers?"

"Yeah. Hey, Santina," she called out. "What's your father's business called? Case Brothers," she said back into the phone. "One of my copy editors' father."

"You rock. I'll call you later." I hung up and looked up the Case Brothers, then made the call. No one answered so I left a message with the emergency service, which promised a call back within ten minutes.

While I waited I tried to quash my panic about Grandpa's rising home repair costs, and by the time the phone rang I was past annoyed and well into frustrated. Not to mention, stiff. "Hello," I snapped, snatching it up. "How fast can you come?"

Silence. Then a man's voice asked, "Is this Maddie?"

I paused. Was this not the plumber? I pulled the phone away and looked at the screen. It showed a number I didn't recognize.

I cleared my throat. "Yes, this is Maddie."

"Hey. It's Lucas. Is everything okay?"

I cringed. "Lucas. Hey. Sorry about that. Yes, all good. Well, I'm sort of having a plumbing issue and the emergency line at the plumber didn't work too well."

"Really? I know a little plumbing."

That, I wasn't expecting. "I thought you were a dog groomer?"

"I am," he said, and I could hear the smile in his voice. "But I was supposed to be a plumber and take over the family business. I didn't want to spend my life trying to fit under sinks or installing toilets, but I can do it when I need to."

I could see his point. But right now, I'd take a retired plumber. "How fast can you get here?"

Chapter 49

An hour later, I stood in the kitchen trying not to stare at Lucas Davenport's cute backside as he crawled around under the kitchen sink. He'd brought me a couple bottles of water so I could attempt to wash the mud off my face. He hadn't even laughed at me when I'd opened the door, which resulted in major points for him.

I heard Lucas muttering to himself. He backed out of the small space and disappeared down to the basement. He reemerged then went upstairs, then outside. I had no idea what he was doing. I went to the counter to make coffee, then remembered I had no water and grimaced. I leaned against the counter and rubbed my temples. I needed a vacation.

Lucas came back down the stairs, looking deep in thought. "Okay," he said. "One of the connectors on your pipe upstairs is broken. I can fix that, no problem. The rest of the pipes look okay. But that means the issue has to be your well."

"The well?" I repeated with a sinking feeling. "That doesn't sound good."

"I don't know. I've never done much with wells, but I went out and took a look anyway." He paused.

I itched with impatience. "And?"

"Were you guys out there trying to fix it at all? Playing around with it or anything?"

"I sure wasn't. The only reason I even know where it is is because I've seen the water bubbling out of it. Why?"

"The cover is broken off, for one thing. Which means all kinds of things could've gotten down there and clogged it up. Possibly even contaminated it. You need to get a well guy here. ASAP."

I felt like crying. Or punching something. "How expensive is that?" I asked, my voice sounding far away even to me.

Lucas hesitated. "Honestly, I have no idea. And I don't know enough people yet on the island to recommend someone. Maybe your grandfather knows someone?"

"Maybe," I said. And maybe this would be the thing that sends him over the edge and into Debbie Renault's office to sign an agreement.

"But Maddie," he said. "Ask them what they think about how this happened. It doesn't look to me like the well cover is old. Everything looks well maintained."

It took me a minute, then it dawned on me. "Are you saying someone did this on purpose?"

"I don't know," he said, holding up his hands. "But it looks like there used to be a lock over the cap. There are holes and rust spots where it looks like there used to be bolts. I don't know why someone would try to tamper with your well, and I could be just thinking about all the conspiracy theories we were talking about the other night. But I do know well caps usually have locks on them to prevent tampering."

My doorbell rang and I froze. I'd completely forgotten about Craig. "Wait here," I muttered, then raced to the door.

Craig waited on the porch, staring out into the distant ocean. He wasn't in uniform.

"Hey," I said, swinging the door wide. "I thought you were working."

"If I was working, I couldn't be here," he said with a wry smile. He glanced inside. "Your grandfather home?"

I shook my head. He looked relieved. "Whose car?"

I glanced at Lucas's Subaru. "I had an issue with the plumbing," I said just as Lucas appeared in the doorway.

"I'm going to get this connector so we can at least get that fixed." He stopped when he saw Craig. "Oh, hey."

"Hey," Craig answered. He didn't smile.

Lucas looked from him to me. "Okay, then. I'm going to the hardware store," he said. "Will you be here?"

"Actually," I said. "I need to leave for a bit. But here." I grabbed the key off my ring in the kitchen and handed it to him. "Do whatever you need to do and I'll catch up with you. I have another key. And here." I reached for my purse and grabbed some cash from my wallet. "For the supplies."

He waved me off. "We'll catch up later. Don't worry about it. Maybe you can give this guy a heads-up about what we were talking about. Good seeing you, man." He nodded at Craig as he walked by us out the door.

Craig watched him get in his car and drive away, then turned back to me. "Dog groomer *and* plumber?"

"Guess so," I said. "I had an emergency." I felt guilty for some reason and pushed it aside.

Craig watched me for a minute then said, "What do you need to give me a heads-up about?"

"I'll tell you in the car. Are we leaving?" Suddenly I couldn't wait to leave the house.

He nodded. "Let's go."

Chapter 50

Craig hadn't even pulled out of the driveway when he asked me again what Lucas was talking about.

I wasn't sure if I should tell him Lucas's theory about well tampering without having it confirmed first. Who knows—maybe Grandpa had been having an issue with the well and someone had come to start a project, and it never got finished. I didn't want to start a whole big thing if it was as simple as that. And if there was a problem with the well, I highly doubted Grandpa would let us shower in it, cook with it, and drink it.

On the other hand, given the weirdness surrounding Grandpa's house these days Lucas could be exactly right and everyone joking about conspiracy theories would have to eat their words.

I told Craig what happened today, leaving out the part about the extended facial. My skin did feel nice, though.

He listened in silence while we crawled through the downtown streets. He parked down a side street and turned to me. "You know that sounds crazy, right?"

"No crazier than some alleged good Samaritan handing over a briefcase full of cash and telling some random guy to fix Grandpa's house!" *Oh, shoot.* I wasn't supposed to mention that.

Craig's eyes narrowed nearly to slits. "What did you say?"

"Nothing. I need to leave Grandpa a voice mail." I picked up my cell phone but Craig snatched it out of my hand. "Hey!"

"Maddie. Do you have information on Tate that you didn't share? In case you forgot, he's dead. Murdered."

I flinched. "I haven't forgotten," I said, my voice deadly quiet. "Neither has Grandpa."

We stared at each other, then he handed my phone back. "Tell me."

What did I have to lose now? At least Tate wouldn't get a tax bill out of it. I told him about my visit to Tate's office, his odd story about the anonymous call and the money left in the van. When I was done, Craig looked like he had a headache.

"Where was the money?"

"He had it locked in his file cabinet. In the locked case."

"Why didn't you tell me?"

I shrugged. "Tate asked me not to."

"And you didn't think his being dead might negate that promise?"

I gave him a dirty look, then left Grandpa a voice mail in case he came home and tried to turn on the water.

"Grandpa. There's a well problem. There's no water in the house at the moment. I have a friend fixing one of the pipes in case you get home and find him there. Dad's getting a well guy. Call me." I hung up. "He's harder to get a hold of than the cable company," I muttered, then glanced at Craig.

He still watched me, his jaw set, then he sighed. "You're mad at me."

"Why on earth would I be mad at you?" I asked coolly. "You and Sergeant Ellory are just doing your jobs, right?" The truth was, I didn't want to be mad at him. I had no right to be mad at him. He *was* just doing his job.

"Yeah. We're just doing our jobs." He drummed his fingers on the steering wheel and looked around at the people milling about, enjoying this beautiful day. "Is your grandfather okay?"

"He's peachy," I said.

My sarcasm wasn't lost on him. "Maddie. He was at Tate's office yesterday morning. I know he wasn't thrilled with Tate and the good Samaritan thing. We would've looked like amateurs if we hadn't talked to him about it."

"You look insane, actually," I said. "The law is in his blood. You really think he's going to start running people over because he's mad?"

He sighed. "Come on, Maddie."

"Come on, what?" I asked. "It's true. Can we just go inside and get coffee before my head explodes?" I tossed my phone in my bag and got out of the car. Craig followed reluctantly. We walked around the corner to the main road and paused at the door.

"Do they have booze here?" I asked, only half kidding.

Craig smiled and held the door for me. "You been here yet?"

"Yeah," I said. "I stopped in yesterday, actually." I didn't tell him what I'd been doing.

He followed me up to the counter. The barista tossed his asymmetrical hair out of his eye and smiled at me. "Afternoon. What's your poison?"

"Cinnamon latte with soy and a double shot," I said. "And a cheese Danish."

He nodded. "You got it. And for you, sir?"

Craig ordered a no-sugar vanilla latte with skim.

"And to eat?" the barista inquired.

Craig held up a hand. "I'm all set, thanks."

I shot him a dirty look.

"I'll have a bite of yours." We collected our drinks and my food and Craig steered me to the door. As I stepped out onto the street, I almost bumped into Leopard Man, heading into Bean. Guess he liked the good coffee too.

"My dear." He bowed low and stepped out of the way so I could pass, tipping his hat at me.

I smiled at him. "Afternoon coffee?"

He thought for a moment. "The Bard had nothing to say about coffee, but that doesn't mean I don't enjoy a cup," he said with a wink, then nodded at Craig. "Afternoon, Officer."

"Afternoon," Craig said, eyeing him suspiciously as he held the door for him.

I rolled my eyes at Craig. "Is he a criminal too? He didn't even have his tail on."

"Just get in the truck," Craig said, but a hint of a smile played across his lips.

I climbed in and sipped my coffee. He headed west out of downtown. I rolled my window down and sat back, unwrapping my Danish and handing him a piece. He raised an eyebrow.

"Hey, you said you'd have a bite."

He opened his mouth. I rolled my eyes and stuffed it in. He managed to swallow without choking. "Still a romantic, I see," he said dryly.

I laughed. "I think I'm even worse now than I was back in high school," I admitted.

He glanced over at me. "So what's the deal with the dog guy?"

"What do you mean?" I avoided his eyes.

"He got a crush on you or something?"

"You'd have to ask him."

Craig didn't have a good answer to that. He clenched

his jaw and kept his mouth shut. A few minutes later, we left Daybreak Harbor, crossing into Duck Cove. I knew exactly where we were going—Bluff Point Beach, where we used to play volleyball—among other activities—back in the day.

It was one of those nook-and-cranny places that wasn't apparent to the untrained eye, small enough that sun-hungry vacationers missed it in favor of the massive beaches jammed so full of people and paraphernalia that you couldn't walk without getting an umbrella in your eye or stepping on someone's lunch. Places like Bluff Point Beach were the best part about living somewhere like this. And every day you prayed that no one new would discover it, so it would stay sacred.

This one had, so far. When we rolled into the parking lot there were only two other vehicles and they both looked like they belonged to fishermen.

"It's still a well-kept secret, by some miracle," Craig said, reading my mind.

"That's awesome." I opened the car door and jumped out, opening my arms wide to take in the sunshine. This was one of those days I thought Mother Nature only had our island in mind. The sun turned every surface into something sparkling, shiny, and new. The breeze teased my hair and sent the ocean's sea salt perfume into the air. It was just as invigorating as the coffee. "This was a good idea." I reached in for my coffee and shut the door. "Let's go."

We headed down onto the sand, the memories of growing up here overwhelming. I took off my flip-flops, sinking my toes into the sand. In that moment, I would've given anything to be eight years old again, running to the water with my boogie board. But it wasn't happening. We weren't kids anymore. The island was different. Grandpa might lose his house. I lived across the country. I blinked back tears and kept a few steps ahead of Craig so he wouldn't notice.

He caught up with me, though, and we walked in silence. I felt a moment of guilt thinking of the other walk I'd taken on the beach this week—different beach, different guy, but probably the conversation would go the same way. A downward spiral into murder.

Chapter 51

We made our way down to the water where the waves reached up and lapped around our ankles as they rolled in. I stood and looked out over the miles of ocean ahead of me, thinking about how small we all were next to it. After a few minutes of silence, I turned to Craig. "Look. I'm sorry. I don't mean to take my frustrations out on you. Honest. I'm just really at a loss here. Please tell me you don't really think Grandpa would kill Tate."

Craig shook his head slowly. "Apology accepted. And no. I don't."

But someone else might. I read between the lines. "Do you know where he's been working? He told me he got a job but wouldn't tell me where."

Craig plopped down on the sand. "Shouldn't you ask him?"

"He's never around long enough!" I exclaimed.

"He'll kill me if I tell you," Craig said, then cringed. "Sorry. We definitely use that phrase too easily as a society. He'll be very upset with me," he corrected. "And he's already upset with us, I'd imagine."

I made a face at him. "Now you're worried about making

him mad?" I grumbled, plopping down next to him. "You really aren't going to tell me?"

"I don't know for sure. I only have a hunch."

"Please tell me it isn't illegal."

Now he did crack a smile. "Not that I know of."

"Thank goodness for small favors." I sighed. "So what's next?"

"With what?" Craig asked.

I shot him a look. "With everything. Your investigations. Frank, Tate?"

"We're still investigating."

"It's been five days for Frank."

"If you have any information we're happy to take it."

"If I have any information?" I almost shouted, indignant. "I gave you a whole list. As a matter of fact, I was going over my list just this morning. Margaret. Piper. Gil . . ." I trailed off, realizing that I probably shouldn't have said that.

Craig frowned. "Gil? Gil Smith? Maddie, have you completely lost it?"

I sighed and kicked at sand with my toe. "I love Gil. I never in a million years would've said that, but I heard some things."

"What things? And why are you keeping a list of possible suspects? I didn't realize you were consulting for us."

"Oh, stop being snarky. Clearly you need the help," I snapped.

"Ouch. If this was my case I'd be hurt. So what about Gil?"

I started walking along the water's edge. He followed. "Frank was considering a run for first selectman." I took a deep breath. "And I heard Gil was seeing Margaret O'Malley. Romantically. I don't know if that's true," I cautioned. "Piper Dawes said it."

He narrowed his eyes. "When did you talk to Piper Dawes?"

"I bumped into her the other day," I said dismissively. "But she had motive too. A couple of them, potentially."

Craig shook his head. "No go. Piper was in plain sight of about fifty people from noon that day through the time she came running over screaming after we got there. She had to walk with the DPW guy to do an inspection for all the tents. And I already told you Margaret was not on the island."

Margaret. The ferry. Rick. "Jeez, with the well and the drama I forgot why I called you in the first place. What the heck is wrong with me?" I jumped up, almost spilling my latte, and paced around the sand.

Craig stared at me, worry drawing his eyebrows together. "Are you sure you're okay?"

"Listen! I saw Rick. Val's old boyfriend? He works on the ferry. He said Margaret O'Malley was on an early ferry over to the island on *Friday*, not Sunday."

Craig stood now too, his face hardening into a cop stare. "Is he absolutely positive?"

"Yup. He rides most of those ferry shifts and knows all the locals. He said he even talked to her that morning. She wanted to come over on a ferry that wasn't crowded, he said. I told you! Maybe she was seeing Gil."

"Why would she lie?" he muttered, more to himself.

"Well, it's either that or she killed Frank." But even as I said it, I didn't really believe it. I just couldn't picture Margaret stabbing her husband in the back with an ice pick. And no one had seen her at the Food Stroll—she'd never have been able to fly under the radar there, unless she was in deep disguise.

"Well, now you can go check out Gil," I said. "And maybe the business owners who thought Frank was cheating them. Apparently there's a whole list. What the heck has Ellory been doing, aside from chasing my grandfather all over the island? Plus, Margaret was mad at Piper. I guess she was staying at their house and Margaret caught her."

Craig muttered something that sounded like "bunch of whack jobs." "I won't ask how you know that."

"Good," I said.

We started walking again. "There is something interesting about Piper," he said casually.

"Oh, yeah?"

"Yeah. She reported her car stolen on Monday afternoon."

That intrigued me. "Really? What's she drive?"

"A black Lexus."

"Well, she got it back," I said, remembering seeing her car fly by me leaving Margaret's house. Unless someone else with a Lexus had lent her one.

"How did you know?"

"I saw her driving it. On Tuesday afternoon." My heart almost stopped. I slowed and looked at Craig. "And there was a huge dent in it."

Craig looked at me sharply. "Where?"

"Front. Driver's side." I'd had a prime spot from Stewart's shrubs, but I didn't tell him that.

"She said it showed back up at the chamber office on Tuesday. Apologized for what she called a false alarm. Said a friend had borrowed it, and she'd jumped the gun calling us."

"Really." I thought about that as I drained my coffee. I tapped the empty cup against my leg. "But you don't actually know that for a fact."

"Nope."

I frowned. "So really, it could've come back at any time. If it was even stolen at all."

Craig and I looked at each other. I knew we were both thinking the same thing.

"If she knew Tate was fixing my grandfather's house, she might have worried Grandpa wouldn't have any reason to listen to their offer," I said slowly.

"But she wasn't involved in the deal, I thought," Craig said. "It wasn't a chamber thing."

"No, but she somehow ended up responsible for Aidan O'Malley." Excited now, I picked up my pace as I talked it out. "She showed up at the bar the other night and tried to talk Jade out of calling you guys. You know, you were there. She even tried to sweet-talk you."

Craig made a face. "Don't remind me."

"But if she called on Monday night about the car, that would mean she planned the whole thing," I said. "And how would she know when Tate would be outside his office? That kind of kills that theory. Shoot." I sighed.

"Did she say who the friend was?"

Craig shook his head. "But someone needs to ask her." He checked his watch. "I should go. Ellory has to hear this."

I nodded.

"I'm sorry," he said.

"Don't be. I'd rather this mess get cleaned up so everyone can get back to their lives." We turned and began walking back in the direction we'd come.

"You mean so you can get back to California?" he asked.

I shrugged and didn't answer.

"Do you ever miss home?" he asked. "Like, this home?"

I thought about that. "I don't think about it much when I'm out there. I mean, I miss my family, but I don't think of the physical place much. I don't miss snow, honestly." But it was scary how quickly I'd fallen back into a routine here, even despite the craziness.

"I don't blame you," he said.

"What about you? Do you ever wish you'd left?" I asked.

Surprise drew his eyebrows wide. "Left? No. I mean, I enjoyed going to the police academy in Boston. But I didn't want to work in an urban area like that, I figured if I was going to work in a suburb, I'd rather work here. Who wouldn't want to work on the island? And for a position to open so soon after I graduated was like fate."

"It never feels too small? Like you can't grow here?"

"No. I think it's only a positive, having the history and the roots." He shrugged. "I guess I'm just different from you, Maddie. I never had that 'gotta get out of my hometown' angst."

"It wasn't really like that," I said. "I wanted to go to college in New York. Always did. San Fran just kind of happened. I fell in love with it on a trip and figured if I was going to try it, that was the time."

We reached the path we'd taken and turned left to exit the beach. But he took my arm to keep me from walking farther. "Sometimes I wish you hadn't left," he admitted.

I felt my heart do a little flip. This was such a strange conversation, given the timing. I mean, I didn't know if I would've even run into Craig if this murder hadn't happened. It wasn't like I thought much about him on regular days. We hadn't parted on bad terms or anything. We'd just kind of fizzled out, as young-love long-distance relationships often do. There wasn't anything dramatic about our breakup conversation. We'd done it over the phone, which took a little of the emotion out of it. I didn't even recall who'd started the conversation. We just agreed that since I was away at college, we were moving in different directions, and it would be better to call it quits. I knew even then that I probably wouldn't be back. I just hadn't been sure where I'd go.

"If I hadn't left, we might've stayed together longer and had a really bad breakup," I pointed out. "Then we wouldn't be here right now."

"No," he said, moving closer and pulling me against him. "And that would be a shame." Then he kissed me.

Wow, he kisses way better now than he did in high school. I kissed back, my arms automatically pulling him closer. Then my second thought rained on my parade: *I'd be enjoying this a lot more if he wasn't trying to arrest my grandfather.*

I sighed and dropped my head to his chest.

"What?" he whispered, his lips against my ear.

"Bad timing," I said. It took a lot of willpower to step away, but I did.

He didn't disagree. He raked a hand through his hair and sighed. "Tell me about it. Come on." He took my hand and tugged me back toward the parking lot. I let him, trying to figure out what I was doing. I'd agreed to go out with Lucas tomorrow night. Now I was kissing Craig on a beach. What was wrong with me?

I hadn't figured it out by the time we got back to the car. He didn't say much on the way home, but halfway there he reached over and twined his fingers with mine. I stared at our hands for a second. What was I doing? Starting something up with Craig again was unwise for a few reasons. One, I had a cardinal rule about never going backward. Two, I was leaving. Soon. Back to my life on the West Coast, which I loved. There were plenty of guys out there. And three, he was investigating a murder in which his superior suspected my own grandfather. The whole thing was a recipe for disaster.

And yet, his hand over mine felt . . . nice. So did the breeze blowing through the truck, the salt air, the whole moment, really. I left my hand there until we pulled into Grandpa's driveway.

Chapter 52

Lucas had come and gone. He'd left a note on the counter telling me he'd fixed the broken connector; he hoped the well thing got sorted out quickly and inexpensively, and he'd pick me up tomorrow at seven. JJ had slept through most of the drama, and now he lay sprawled on the kitchen floor in front of his empty food dish.

I gave him a snack then suited him into his harness. I was feeling guilty about not getting him to the vet for his ear yet, so we were going to go corner Katrina. We drove to the animal control center and parked out front. I gazed at the building with some trepidation. Katrina'd warned me it was nothing to look at, but I wasn't prepared for the municipal brick building that appeared windowless.

"Jeez," I said to JJ as we paused out front. "I'm glad you didn't end up here, bud."

He didn't comment. His nose twitched a mile a minute. It could be the food aromas wafting around the island, or perhaps the squirrel that sat a few feet away munching on a discarded pizza crust.

We went up to the door and I turned the knob. The hall reminded me of a prison. "Katrina?" I called.

A cacophony of barking ensued. Some came from all

around us, the rest from a distance, presumably the out-
door runs. Katrina appeared a minute later from a back
room. She looked disheveled, her hair falling out of a clip
she'd used to keep it out of her face.

"Hey," she said. "Don't mind the dogs. They like
visitors."

"Is this an okay time?" I scooped up JJ. "I really wanted
to get him a vet appointment."

"Yeah, sure, I just got back from a call. Come on in,
we'll call the doc." She led me down a hall. The walls
must've been white once but now appeared a light gray.
Plaster crumbled in a couple of spots, and the linoleum
floor was worn in too many spots to count. "Welcome to
the Waldorf for pets," she said wryly, following my gaze,
then shrugged. "At least they have food here. Hi, JJ." She
scratched his chin. He lifted his head to give her easier
access, looking disappointed when she stopped. "Want a
quick tour?"

"Absolutely," I said.

"Forgive me if it gets cut short," she said. "I'm sure I'll
get six phone calls while we're talking."

I studied my old friend. She looked even more tired than
when I'd seen her the other day. I remembered her as being so full of energy. Now she looked like she had a leak
somewhere in desperate need of plugging.

I followed her into the main room of the pound, which
was nothing more than a big empty space with dog cages
on one side and supplies stacked up on the other. The
dogs—a mix of small and big—gazed balefully at me from
their cells. They all seemed to ask, *Are you getting me out
of here?* A boxer shoved his nose through the chain link,
trying desperately to sniff me. A little spaniel-looking dog
in desperate need of grooming opened one eye and looked
at me from the folds of her blanket. Every cage had a
face.

"Shoot," she muttered. "The food bowls haven't been filled."

"Nothing like making the stray animals feel like criminals." I hadn't been inside the human jail cells in many years—Grandpa used to take me and my sisters down to scare us when we misbehaved—but I was willing to bet the conditions were better. JJ didn't seem fazed by the dogs, so I went over to the boxer and let him sniff me. "Are these all strays?" I asked Katrina.

She looked up from where she scooped food into bowls. "Some. A couple are surrenders." She nodded at the spaniel. "Like that one. She's sad."

"She needs a haircut." I moved over to get a better look at the pup, who curled deeper in on herself. "Have you talked to Lucas? The guy who opened the grooming place?"

Katrina gave me a look. "You think our budget allows for grooming?"

"Well, doesn't that vet you told me about do it when they're seen? I mean, if they need it." It seemed like a no-brainer to me.

"She hasn't been to see him yet. I just got her in yesterday." Katrina began sliding food into the cages, a sign that this conversation was over. I made a mental note to talk to Lucas myself. Maybe he'd donate his services, even if it was just a couple hours a week when needed.

Katrina finished and rose slowly to her feet. "Next stop, cats," she said, and led me through another supply area into a back room.

I wasn't expecting what I found when I stepped in behind her. The tiny room barely allowed any breathing room between us. Cages lined both walls, and in some cages cats were doubled up. None of them looked happy.

"I know, I know," Katrina said. "It's way too small. You're singing to the choir, Maddie."

I reached in to pet the head of a calico kitten desperately rubbing against the bars. "Where are they all from?"

Katrina shrugged. "Strays, surrenders, you name it. Some are kittens from a pregnant mother rescue, like the one you're playing with. We're overloaded, and it's not slowing down. It was already bad, but it's gotten way worse since Safe Paws closed. Especially for the cats. They used to take in a ton of the strays and even help with ferals when they could. There's a bunch of them down by the ferry docks. But now . . ." She sighed. "I think some of the people who used to work at Safe Paws are still feeding the ferals, but there's no one to really care for them. Lord knows if I tried to fit one more thing into my day I'd probably drop dead."

"Was it really just funding that shut them down?" I asked.

"Just?" She laughed, but the sound was humorless. "It's not as easy as you think for a nonprofit to stay alive out here. I think they got discouraged. And underfunded. The donation pool isn't big, and once you've exhausted your options, you have to keep people coming back. I don't think they had enough people to do the kind of continuous campaigning you need. Heck, we can't get a donation to save our lives. Everyone thinks we just get a nice budget from the state and then go spend it on Louis Vuitton purses when they see this dump." She pursed her lips. "Sorry."

"Don't be sorry. It stinks. Do you have help to take care of these guys?" I noticed one kitten playing in its nearly empty water dish. "Like volunteers?"

She shook her head again. "There were eight volunteers over the winter. Now we're down to four."

"People getting jobs for the summer season?" I asked. That's usually how it went on the island. Winter was everyone's slow time, when work was nonexistent and they could fit other things in. Like volunteer work.

"Who knows. Too busy, I guess. Which means I end up taking them home when we're overfull, or if they need more regular vet care." She slipped past me, signaling our time in the cat room had ended.

I followed her into an office smaller than my closet at Grandpa's. "Does the police chief still run this place?"

Katrina nodded. "Your grandpa tried to get funding to fix it up while he was chief, but it kept getting bumped for other priorities. Every time he'd come here to tell me in person." She smiled. "He'd tell me to stay positive, that we'd get it next time."

"What about the new chief?" I didn't know much about Grandpa's replacement, just that he was some guy from Virginia who'd lasted beyond the two years I'd predicted when I heard that he wasn't a local.

Katrina made a face. "He couldn't care less," she said, then immediately clapped a hand over her mouth. "Sorry. I totally shouldn't say that. He's my boss," she said, looking around as if expecting him to pop out from behind a wall and yell *Aha! I caught you bad-mouthing me!*

"That's too bad," I said. "If the police aren't making it a priority to treat the town's animals well, it's going to hurt them in the long run."

"Yeah, well, I don't think he sees it that way. Or cares. Anyway, let's go call Dr. Drake."

She picked up her desk phone and dialed. "He's kind of a pompous guy. He's got a monopoly here. It's the only vet hospital on the island, can you imagine? I don't even think he gives me that great a discount, but that's one fight I don't have time to take on—Hey, Nora. It's Katrina. I have a favor. I need a cat looked at. He was just picked up off the street a couple days ago and he's got some ear issues. You do? Well, that would be great. Thanks." She hung up. "They have an opening this afternoon. At five. Not with him, though. With Dr. Myers. She's much nicer."

"Sweet," I said.

"Just have them put it on my tab," she said, scribbling the address on a sticky note and handing it to me. Her cell phone started ringing, and the dogs barked, and from the front of the building someone called her name. She looked at me apologetically and grabbed the phone. "I'll call you later, okay? Sorry."

"Don't worry about it," I said, but she'd already answered the phone and turned away. I grabbed JJ and we left, promising the man waiting impatiently at the door that she'd be right with him.

"Yikes," I said to JJ once we'd gotten outside, setting him down. "I think Auntie Katrina needs some help."

JJ looked up at me with those big green eyes, wide with unspoken agreement.

"What do you think we could do?" I asked.

He squeaked, then propelled me toward the car.

"That's not the best solution I've ever heard," I grumbled, but I followed him.

Chapter 53

By five-thirty, JJ and I were back in my car armed with antibiotics and ear medicine. The vet visit had been fairly quick and painless. Katrina had been right about JJ's ear mites, a hazard of street living. While the vet couldn't promise his ear would go back to normal, she didn't think it would get any worse as long as we got rid of the problem.

I'd just turned the car on when Becky texted me.

Frank's services tmrw. Cops released body early this morning. Family keeping it quiet. Burial private but there's a service at Moriarty's, 10 A.M.

Margaret must not want to deal with a big crowd and a long, drawn-out good-bye for her beloved husband. Interesting. I texted a quick *Thanks* to Becky. Guess I knew where I'd be at ten tomorrow. I dropped my phone back in my bag and put the car in reverse. A car pulled into the lot and parked a few spaces away. The driver's door swung open and Gil Smith emerged.

I slouched down in my seat and put the car back in park. Gil had no animal with him. What was he doing here? "Should we wait?" I asked JJ. He didn't seem to care. He'd taken his vet visit in stride, but now he looked exhausted. I knew how he felt. We'd all had a busy week.

I sat, tapping my fingers against the steering wheel and singing along to the nineties station on Sirius radio. It was kind of funny to think of Grandma's car with satellite radio. From the presets, she'd listened to a lot of Frank Sinatra and the oldies stations, but she did have NPR as one of her prime channels.

We didn't have long to wait. Gil emerged a few minutes later with a white bag bearing the vet hospital's name and logo, just like the one JJ had gotten with his medicine. Gil must have a pet. I had no idea.

He got back in his car and pulled out of the parking lot. I pondered for a couple seconds, then followed him.

"You're really losing it, Maddie," I told myself. "Tailing the first selectman? Where do you think he's going to take you?" He was probably on his way home from work, heading to his little house in Daybreak Harbor. He lived on the other side of town from Grandpa at the northern end, nearer to Turtle Point.

He did drive toward Daybreak Harbor. But he didn't take the turnoff that would lead him through downtown and toward his house. Instead, he stayed on the outskirts, keeping to the road that followed the ocean along the perimeter of the island. Thankful I had sunglasses to partially hide my face, I let one car get in between us.

My cell phone rang. Grandpa. Thank goodness. I hit the speaker button. "Hey."

"Hi, doll. What happened to the well?" he asked.

"I'm not sure. Mom is sending someone out. Did you try to fix it recently? Or replace the lock or the cover?"

"I haven't touched the well. It's never given me a problem," he said. "Other than regular maintenance, I haven't had to do anything." He laughed a little. "Figures that would catch up to me now."

"When did you get the maintenance done last?" I peered into the sun glare ahead of me, trying to make sure I didn't lose Gil. He was slowing down, taking a turn I didn't recognize. The car in between us kept going straight. I stomped on the brake and let him get a little ahead of me before turning the corner.

"It's been at least six months. Why?"

"My friend came over and looked at it. Said it looked like the lock had been removed. The cover was busted."

Silence. I could hear noises in the background, but couldn't make them out. I glanced around, but this street wasn't familiar. It was a residential area, and I thought we must've crossed into Turtle Point by now. "Grandpa?"

"I'm here. When is the person coming?"

"I don't know. You'll have to check with Mom. I'm kind of in the middle of something." I didn't mean to be short with him, but I had enough to worry about just trying to keep him off Ellory's suspect list. "I'll see you later, okay?"

I disconnected without bothering to ask where he was. I realized I didn't see Gil's car anymore. Shoot. I hit the gas as I went around a bend in the road.

And almost slammed into Gil's car, which had slowed almost to a stop.

Crap. He'd seen me. I debated blowing around him and hoping he wouldn't recognize the car, but that was silly. Of course he'd know the car. With a sigh, I put my blinker on and pulled onto the shoulder of the road. Gil did the same. Then he got out and walked over to my window. I went to roll it down, then froze. What if my crazy theory about him had been right and he *had* killed Frank? And now he thought I knew and was about to turn him in? I tried to see if he had a weapon. It didn't look like it, but who knew if he had something hidden? I cracked the window just enough that I could hear him and grabbed my phone, half hiding it under my leg so I could hit the emergency call button if I needed it.

Gil strolled up to my window and smiled. "Maddie."

"Hi, Gil," I said, hoping my nerves weren't showing in my smile. "What's up?"

"I was going to ask you the same thing."

"Oh?" I feigned innocence. "Hang on one second." I picked up my phone, pretending to answer a call. "Hey, Becky. I'll be there soon. I'm chatting with Gil out on . . ." I squinted at the street sign ahead of me. "Wavy Lane. Okay." I put the phone aside and smiled sweetly. "So what's up?"

He leaned forward, puzzled. "Can you even hear me?"

"Oh. Sorry." I buzzed the window down further.

"Maddie. Were you following me for a reason?"

I guess I wasn't as good at detective work as I thought. "No," I said, widening my eyes in fake surprise. "Just out for a drive."

He gave me a skeptical look. I sighed and threw up my hands. "Whatever. Fine. Yes, I was following you. I don't know where I thought you were going, I just wanted to see."

"But why?"

My father would be mad at me when he heard this story, but I didn't have the patience to beat around the bush anymore. "Because I heard you might be seeing Margaret O'Malley," I said bluntly. "And I also heard Margaret was on the island when Frank died and wasn't supposed to be." There. I stared at him defiantly, watching for any sign that he could've committed this murder and praying that I didn't see one.

Gil didn't look angry. He didn't even look surprised. Nor did he look like he might have to kill me for asking. Instead he said, "Do you want to go over to the park and talk? It's right down the street and there are some benches."

Ten minutes later, we sat on a bench in a lush, green park with plenty of people around. Kids played on a jungle gym and swing set. Adults gathered in small groups, one eye on the kids, the other on their grown-up conversation. JJ was in my lap and a few of the kids had already come over to play with him. I wasn't scared of Gil anymore. But I did want to hear what he had to say.

"I knew people would find out I was seeing Margaret," he said finally, when the stream of traffic to JJ had died down.

I didn't say anything. I had no desire to tell him how I'd found out.

"Her marriage to Frank was a sham. He cared nothing for her. Well, aside from her money." The words held not bitterness but bewilderment, as if Gil couldn't imagine how Frank could've overlooked the treasure he had. He stared out into the distance instead of looking at me. "She was divorcing him. She'd just started the paperwork when . . . this happened."

"Did he know about you two?" I asked.

Gil shrugged. "I don't think he would've cared if he did, but Margaret was cautious about her own reputation, of course." Now Gil turned to face me. "She did come back early. To stay with me for a couple of days. Obviously I had to be at the Food Stroll that night, but she was at my house. And she does have an alibi. My assistant was there. I'd trust Lucy with my life. She and Margaret were working on my campaign, because Frank had told her he was planning to run."

"But she told the cops she wasn't here," I said. "That makes her look guilty."

Gil looked pained. "She showed bad judgment. It was her knee-jerk reaction to try to keep our relationship hidden. I wish she hadn't done it." He held my gaze, his own more intense than I'd ever seen it. Gil didn't look like "Uncle Gil" right now. "Maddie. Margaret didn't kill her husband. I'm not sure I would've blamed her if she had, but she didn't."

I leaned back against the bench, more relieved than anything. Of course I wanted this to be over, but I hadn't really wanted Gil to be the killer. My dad would've been devastated. Heck, the whole island would've been devastated.

"Thank you for telling me. I'm sorry I followed you," I said. "I'm just worried about Grandpa."

Gil nodded. "I understand."

"Will you tell my dad?"

He smiled. "Not if you don't tell him."

"Do my parents know about you and Margaret?"

He shook his head. "I told no one. Margaret didn't either. So anyone who knows would have to have found out through other means." He glanced at me, curious. "How did you find out, if you don't mind my asking?"

I reached over and squeezed his hand. "I hope you and Margaret are very happy together. Honestly." I left him sitting there and got back in my car.

I hadn't mentioned Piper, but I wouldn't doubt she'd hired someone to get her information. Probably to use as leverage to get Frank to leave Margaret.

But what if he still hadn't left her, even with proof? Craig insisted Piper had been in plain sight all afternoon last Saturday, but really, it wouldn't have been hard to slip away for ten minutes. She had to use the bathroom at some point, after all. And like Becky said, Piper wasn't the smartest person I'd ever met. Maybe she'd even brought Frank some evidence that day and he'd blown it off. And maybe she, too, had just had enough.

Chapter 54

I could barely keep my eyes open the next morning as I sat in the back row at the funeral home with my parents for Frank's service. Since the well repairs were still under way, I'd retrieved my clothes and gone to my parents' for the night. Grandpa had finally showed up too, and he didn't have good news. Apparently Lucas had been right, and someone had cut the lock off the well. The well guy had cautioned him that maybe the last person who serviced it had done this, though he couldn't find a good reason why, but also suggested to Grandpa that he alert the police. Just in case. Grandpa had slipped out first thing this morning, promising he'd see us here, but so far he hadn't showed.

My mother and father had reached the worried stage now. The well news had sobered all of us. I wondered if it had been Tate. Maybe his story had been a big, fat lie. Maybe someone had paid him to wreck things at Grandpa's house, rather than salvage them. Maybe Tate had been on Frank's payroll.

So then who'd killed Tate, and why?

I slumped in my seat, watching as people streamed in. I saw Jenna, Becky's reporter, moving through the crowd with her notebook, getting comments. Piper came in with a bunch of younger people—I guessed the rest of the chamber staff. They took seats in the front row at Piper's direction. An act of defiance, perhaps, so she could face off with Margaret.

Margaret sat on a chair to the side of the casket. A handsome young man sat next to her. The artist son from Boston, I guessed. Aidan hadn't appeared yet.

The room had filled up. I listened to snippets of conversation: *"I heard they're close to an arrest." "Whoever it was must've needed to get in line." "Why do you think they're having a private burial?" "Probably so no one pees on his grave."*

Gil Smith came in. I watched as he went up to Margaret and shook her hand, kissed her cheek, all the polite things people do when paying respects. They were both good. I wouldn't have suspected anything based on their interaction. Gil took a seat in the middle of the room after nodding at my parents and me. His eyes lingered on mine for an extra second, then he sat.

Leopard Man appeared right behind him, wearing a black fedora today, with a black shirt and black pants. I was relieved to see he still wore his leopard boots. I would have no idea what to think if he changed his wardrobe too much.

I could see Margaret checking her watch as the funeral home attendant and priest hovered nearby, clearly anxious to get started. Margaret whispered something to her son, then he excused himself and went to the lobby. She smiled apologetically at the priest and said something.

Her son returned a moment later, looking like he might throw up. Sergeant Ellory followed him. I could see Craig and another cop, standing just outside the door to the viewing room. I nudged my mother and sat up, interested now. We watched Ellory take a seat in the front row, close to Margaret.

Now my mother looked alarmed. "What's going on?" she whispered.

I shook my head slowly. "No idea." But inside, I cringed. I'd told Craig that Margaret had been on the island on Saturday, even though she'd lied to them and said she wasn't. Craig had probably gone to Ellory with the information.

My gut told me this would end badly for Margaret.

The son sat, whispered something to Margaret. She closed her eyes, shook her head, then went to the priest and conversed quietly. I could see her trying not to meet Ellory's eyes. The priest turned to the room while the funeral attendant shut the door. Craig and his counterpart stood on either side, like guards.

Ellory waited until the brief service was over, after the funeral director had thanked everyone for coming and let them know there'd be a private burial. He stood by while people went up to Margaret again and said a few last words of condolence.

I made a beeline over to Craig. "What's happening?" I asked.

He shook his head. "Don't worry about it, Maddie."

"But listen. If this is about our conversation yesterday—"

"Not now," he said, and I could hear the warning in his voice.

"But Craig. You should talk to her. And Gil," I said urgently, but he wasn't listening. Behind me, I could hear ripples of voices moving through the crowd, building in excitement. Something was going on. I turned to find Ellory leading Margaret O'Malley away, one hand gently on her arm, through the door Craig held open. Gil Smith started to follow, but the other cop held up a hand to stop him.

Gil's eyes met mine. They were full of pain and fear and something haunted. I couldn't bear to look at him, so I turned away.

Chapter 55

I went home to get ready for my date with Lucas, even though I really wanted to crawl into bed and sleep until this nightmare was over. On the other hand, I could use a drink. Even though I knew it was silly, I felt responsible for Margaret's fate. My rational side understood that I wasn't the one who'd been having an illicit affair with the town's first selectman, or lied about my whereabouts to the police. They would've found out eventually. The fact it had stayed a secret this long was miraculous, given the speed at which gossip and rumors traveled around here.

And I didn't dare tell my parents about my conversation and Gil's true confessions, so basically I had to hide away and hope people started talking about something else. And the cops found someone else to arrest.

Meanwhile, I had to go out and pretend to be in date mode. Good thing I'd borrowed one of Sam's flowy dresses the other day—a turquoise one that would match my killer strappy silver sandals. I dressed and put on my party face.

Lucas picked me up from my parents' promptly at seven and we drove downtown, which was crazy packed tonight. "What's going on?" I asked.

"It's Small Business Night," Lucas said. "A chamber event." He glanced at me apologetically.

I grimaced, but tried to turn it into a smile. "You can mention the chamber. I won't dissolve into a puddle of PTSD, I promise." It wasn't entirely true. I did get anxiety every time someone mentioned it, but didn't want to tell him that. "So what happens at Small Business Night?"

"Everyone stays open late, they have sales, prizes, refreshments, whatever. The chamber stays open, too, to help promote the event. They have maps to hand out. Usually we'd do a custom map with each person's sale or give-away, but the chamber couldn't do that this week, obviously. But they have the general map of downtown they're giving out."

"Nice idea," I said. And it was. Definitely good for business—as long as you were on the map. "What about your shop?"

"We're doing a raffle for a free grooming. Everyone who comes in gets a dog collar with our name on it. I have my backup groomer working tonight. I wanted to do the gig."

I nodded. I could respect that.

"Hey," he said. "How's your grandfather's well?"

"No idea," I said. But Grandpa hadn't showed up at Frank's service, and we hadn't heard from him the rest of the day. I was running out of patience with everyone.

Lucas got the message and changed the subject, telling me about the Scurvy Elephants' set list for the night, how they were doing a mix of covers and originals. "Any requests?" he asked as we pulled into Jade's parking lot next to the van with all their equipment.

I thought about that. I was kind of in the mood for Tom Petty.

"Petty, huh?" He grinned. "I think we can accommodate. As a matter of fact, I know just the song."

* * *

I stood near the bar an hour later with my second margarita and thought I might be falling hopelessly in love with Lucas Davenport. Or at least his voice. I couldn't remember hearing a voice like that on a local stage in a long time. Throaty and rich but rough, like he'd just walked through a room full of smoke. Darn him. I'd hoped they weren't very good.

Strumming his guitar, he stepped over to converse with his bandmates quickly, then turned back to the mic. "So we're doing an oldie but goodie now," he said. "Who loves Tom Petty?"

A cheer went up. I raised my drink, trying not to spill it.

"And who loves Stevie Nicks?"

An even louder cheer. I think I led that one. Stevie Nicks was my idol. What was Lucas doing now?

"Awesome." Lucas strummed a few chords. "I'm gonna need some help with this one. Maddie? Can you come up here?"

Stunned, I froze. Then someone—I think Jade—took my drink out of my hand and shoved me forward. I climbed the two steps to the stage, my heart pounding in my throat.

"Whaddaya say?" he said, grinning at me. " 'Stop Draggin' My Heart Around'?"

Oh, man. For a minute I wanted to melt into the floor, but then I remembered I loved to sing. Just not usually with this many people around.

"I'll even get you going," he said, then the band launched into the song.

Thank God I'd had two margaritas. I channeled my inner Stevie and jumped in on the second line. By the time we got to the first chorus, I'd forgotten I wasn't in the shower with no one listening and was belting out the song. When we hit the second verse, I didn't even notice Lucas had stopped singing. I did notice the crowd though—they were all singing along.

I didn't want the song to end. When the last notes trailed off, Lucas kissed my cheek, then held my hand up in the air with his. We took a bow together while the crowd cheered us on, then I jumped off the stage, feeling pretty proud of myself. I'd never sung on an actual stage before, only in the shower. And people had even cheered for me! Lucas and I had done a pretty sweet harmony, if I did say so myself.

Exhilarated, I headed to the bar while they launched into their next song, shoving my hair out of my face. Jade offered me a grin. "Nice voice. Didn't know you had it in you."

I smiled. "Thanks. I've been a closet singer forever."

"Well," Jade said. "Maybe you and your guy can start doing duets." She winked at me and moved down the bar to take another order.

My guy. I hadn't bothered to correct her. Didn't really want to. Right now, I didn't have to care about tomorrow. I could pretend I was in Lucas's band, singing at a local club once a week, not a care in the world. I'd started compiling a list of the other sexy duets we could do when Jade came back down the bar and stopped in front of me, jolting me out of my daydream. "Hey. Can you do me a favor? You're buddies with Pauline, right?"

"Crosby? Sure." I focused on her, reluctantly leaving my new stage career behind.

"Can you give this to her? I'm sure you'll see her before I will. I've been holding on to it since I found it Tuesday. I think she must've dropped it in one of my boxes Saturday when she was helping me set up for the stroll." She reached over the bar, turning her hand over to drop something in mine. Wordlessly, I opened my hand to accept it.

Jade dropped a pearl bracelet into my palm.

I stared at the bracelet, then at Jade, my mind working furiously to connect all the puzzle pieces that were just now starting to line up perfectly. Jade cocked her head, looking at me curiously.

"What's wrong? Are you not going to see her?"

"Did you say . . ." My voice sounded far away. I cleared my throat and tried again. "Did you say Pauline helped you on Saturday?"

Bewildered, Jade nodded. "One of my bartenders was out unexpectedly. He broke his ankle on Saturday morning while he was out running. So I was short a person to help set up. Pauline offered to help."

"And you let her."

"Of course I let her." Jade looked at me like I was insane. "I had things to do here, so I gave her a couple boxes to bring over. They weren't heavy, and I wasn't trying to take advantage—"

"No," I interrupted. "It's fine. What time was this?"

Jade considered. "I don't know what time she actually got there. She picked up the boxes from here around two, two-thirty. I didn't get over to the tent until—well, until much later. After . . . everything. I suppose she was lucky as far as timing, though. She could've walked in on the whole Frank thing. Which would've been horrible." She shuddered. "Anyway, thanks for getting it back to her. I appreciate it."

"Welcome," I murmured as she started to walk away.

I looked down at the bracelet in my hand, then looked over at the stage. Lucas and his crew were still going strong. One of my favorites. I wanted to stay and watch. Maybe go home with Lucas and forget about all this crap. Then I thought of Margaret O'Malley. And Gil. And Grandpa.

I closed my fingers around the bracelet, then turned and slipped out of the bar.

Chapter 56

The warm air hit me in the face when I stepped outside. I pulled out my phone and dialed Craig. His phone went straight to voice mail. I smothered my scream of frustration and shot off a text instead.

Call me!!!

I wished I wasn't wearing my killer silver shoes right now. I wanted to run straight to the police station, but I'd break my neck on the way. I also needed Craig to meet me, and he wasn't answering my text. I didn't want to talk to Ellory. He would think my theory was off-the-wall nuts and throw me out. Or arrest me for accusing someone of murder when I'd just pointed them toward Margaret. But the more I thought about it, the more convinced I became that I was right.

Pauline had been at the Food Stroll. I'd seen her the next morning and she'd been looking for this bracelet. She'd never once mentioned helping out at Jade's tent. That was a big detail to leave out, especially given the circumstances. She'd told me when I saw her on Sunday that she hadn't actually talked to Frank at the stroll. But then when she'd showed up at Grandpa's house yesterday, she'd made an offhand comment about Frank bragging about the transportation center *on Saturday*. And, I realized, the final piece falling into place, she'd known about his plan to try to get Grandpa's house. Something Grandpa didn't think anyone knew. Granted, this was a small town and secrets were hard to come by, but I believed someone proud like Grandpa would try to keep it as quiet as he could, because he certainly wouldn't want pity.

But maybe a very old friend who cared about his dying wife, and who now possibly had a secret crush on him, had found out. Maybe he'd even told her. If she'd already been angry and frustrated with Frank, that could've put her over the edge.

This was insane. I felt like crying. I'd known Pauline Crosby my entire life and I was ready to accuse her of murder. What if I was just nuts? She'd never speak to me again. She'd sue me. She'd be upset with Grandpa, which would be worse. I slogged down the busy sidewalk, my mind racing frantically through my options to try to land on the best one before I made a fool of myself at the police station.

I glanced up as I passed the chamber office building, then paused, stepping out of the crowd of people moving by me in both directions. The blinds were pulled in both front windows, and the front door was shut tight. But in the tiny cracks of the shade, glimpses of light filtered through. But Lucas had said the chamber was supposed to be open tonight. Handing out maps for the event. Every other shop on Bicycle Street was open. The chamber should've been right in the middle of the fray.

So why were the blinds drawn? Were they just closed because of the memorial service? Something told me that wasn't the case. Bad timing, sure, but in a business like this you had to roll with it.

I checked my phone. Nothing from Craig. I should call Grandpa.

Instead, I stepped to the door and knocked. Put my ear

against it and waited. Nothing. I knocked again, louder this time. "Piper?"

Still no response. I jiggled the handle. Locked. A young couple walked up behind me. "I thought you could get maps here?" the woman asked.

"I thought so too," I said.

The guy shrugged. "They have them down the street at the coffee shop. I could use an iced coffee anyway," he said to the woman, and they walked away.

I pondered the locked door for another minute. Then I remembered the back door Piper had nearly shoved me out of the other day. My brain told me to walk away. Find Craig, let him handle it. But my gut told me otherwise.

I went down the alley and around the back of the building. It wasn't well lit back here. I pulled out my phone and used the flashlight app to locate the door.

It was open a crack.

I hesitated. Something seemed off. Any rational person would presume that, given Frank's untimely death, the chamber staff simply didn't have the ability to be here tonight for this event. Except Piper didn't roll that way. Especially if she wanted Frank's position. She'd move mountains to prove to the board that she could keep it together under pressure.

Maybe she'd run out of maps and was busy hand-drawing some, I thought, then covered the hysterical giggle that nearly erupted from my throat. I needed to get off this island. Fast. Before I really lost my mind.

If I went in there and nothing was wrong, Piper would probably have me arrested for breaking in or trespassing or something. Or maybe I'd find myself face-to-face with Aidan O'Malley. Who hadn't showed up for his father's funeral. I wasn't sure I was up for that tonight. I turned to walk away, then heard it. A cry of surprise, followed by a thud.

My heart jackhammered in my chest. That couldn't be good. I whipped out my cell phone and dialed 911 as I made a snap—probably stupid—decision to go inside. When the dispatcher answered, I said, "Please send someone to the chamber offices on Main Street. There's an intruder."

I hung up before she could ask a question and stepped up to the door, pushing it open just a smidgen. The lights were off back here, so I cupped my hand around the phone to dull the flashlight's glare and shined it through the crack. I couldn't see anything.

"Hello?" I called, pushing the door wider and stepping inside. I stood in the small back hall, next to Frank's office. The noise had stopped. There was no noise at all, actually. It smelled musty in here, as if this end of the office wasn't aired out regularly. Worse than that, I knew I'd been right—something felt wrong.

I only caught a glimmer of movement from the doorway next to me. Before I could even turn, something crashed down on my head. All I saw were stars.

Chapter 57

Stunned, I fell backward, trying desperately to find the wall to hold me up while not passing out or whacking my head even harder on the floor. The darn shoes weren't helping either, and I lost my purchase and crashed down. I felt the back of my head connect with the floor. Carpeted, but still. The stars were back in full force, dancing in front of my eyes. I almost gave in to the beckoning blackness. I reached up and touched the top of my head. My fingers came away sticky. I cringed. Blood. It might be easier to pass out right now. But then a figure burst out of Frank's office, jumped over me and ran for the door.

Rolling onto my side and stifling a curse, I grabbed wildly for the person's foot, leg, any body part I could get my hands on. I couldn't let the assailant get away, but since I was pretty much seeing double, I doubted this would work out well.

But my aim was better than I thought. My hand closed around an ankle. I tightened my grip and yanked, then heard a crash as my assailant also went down. Ignoring the room spinning around me, I kicked off one of my sandals and held it, heel facing out like a weapon, delivering a blow that connected with something. Something important,

I hoped. And given the howl of pain, I had heard. It registered that the voice sounded female.

"Stop!" I yelled. "The cops are on their way so don't bother trying to run!" I prayed it was true, even though Craig would have no idea where I was. My text only said to call me. He'd have no way of knowing I'd put in the anonymous call about the chamber intruder

My assailant kicked at me, delivering a blow to the side of my leg that sent me falling again. Then I felt something sharp sink into my thigh and screamed. She'd stabbed me with . . . something. She jerked it out of my leg. I felt blood trickle down. I pressed my finger against the wound, hoping it wasn't gushing out. I hoped Sam would forgive me for ruining her dress.

Squinting in the darkness, I forced myself to my feet even though my legs felt like they'd been weighted down, and turned, intent on making a run for the front door, fumbling for a light switch. When my fingers finally closed around one and flooded the hall with light I thought I might cry with relief. Then I realized who I'd just mauled with my shoe.

Pauline. Blood poured down her cheek where my stiletto had stabbed her. She stepped over and slammed the door all the way shut. She hadn't been trying to get out. She'd been trying to keep me in. I could see now that she'd stabbed me with a letter opener, one that had my blood all over it. Not an ice pick, but close enough. She was good at finding weapons of opportunity, I had to give her that.

My fear kicked up a notch as I realized my latest theory had been right. Too bad it was probably too late. "No!" I cried, backing up, still holding my shoe. "Pauline, why?"

She turned to face me, drawing the back of her hand across her cheek and frowning when she saw the blood. "Maddie, why did you have to get involved? You've ruined everything." Her voice, which I'd been expecting to be full of anguish, sounded eerily calm. Not like the woman I'd known my whole life.

"What are you talking about, Pauline? What did you do?" I moved back again, then realized with a jolt there was a figure lying in Frank's office. Piper. She wasn't moving.

I stared in horror at Pauline. "Did you . . . did you kill her?"

"Not yet. I could've hit her a little harder and probably done the job but you had to barge in. Honestly, you couldn't leave it alone? I was going to get away with it. They arrested Margaret O'Malley!"

I didn't bother pointing out that Margaret couldn't have done this to Piper while she was locked up. "You . . . you killed Frank," I said, sliding back another step, gauging my ability to make it to the front door. I didn't think she had another weapon but I wasn't sure. Plus, if the front door was locked she might get to me before I could undo it.

"So what?" she said. "He was evil and he wanted to take over the island. Besides," she continued. "I did it for your grandfather. I did it for all of us. He was going to make this place cheap and ugly. And this one." She nodded at Piper's still silhouette, just visible beyond the doorway. "She was just as bad. They had it all planned out."

"Did you go there to kill him? Did you plan it?" Back another step, then another.

"Of course not. I'm not a murderer! You, of all people, should know that. I was helping Jade. Frank was there, taking advantage of her as usual. Drinking her wine, helping himself. Telling me how his new transportation center was going to be the next big thing out here, and all us little mom-and-pop crap stores would soon be a thing of the past." Her eyes glittered with anger even now. "He made me so mad. I couldn't even hold it in anymore. I'd tried so hard to be politically correct, to do things the right way. To rally others and get support. But nothing was changing. He had too much money. Too many friends." She sagged against the wall now, suddenly looking exhausted. "I was so tired of fighting him."

I almost felt sorry for her. Almost. If she hadn't nearly bashed my head in and stabbed me in the leg, I might. But I had to figure out how to get out of here first. I could hear voices outside, the sounds of a town event in full swing. Why couldn't anyone hear what was going on in here?

"It's no use, though. They'll figure out it wasn't Margaret," I said. "You should just turn yourself in, Pauline. They'll go easy on you. Just tell them your story. Anyone would agree how hard this must've been for you, for anyone who's put their heart and soul into the island." I babbled now, just trying to buy time as I kept taking tiny steps backward.

But she wasn't stupid. She watched me, a resigned look on her face. "They don't care. No one cares. Come in here with Piper." She moved forward, reaching for me with her free hand, the other poised to stab again if she had to. "I have to figure out what to do with the two of you."

My heart nearly stopped. Could this woman kill me? She'd treated me like her own family. As if reading my mind, she shook her head regretfully. "I don't want to, Maddie. But you stuck your nose in where it didn't belong. I'm sorry."

I felt my eyes fill with tears as I thought about JJ. Lucas. Ethan. Craig, even though I was mad at him. My grandpa. My juice bar. I couldn't die now. I had way too much to do. I let her take my arm, then reacted without even thinking about it. With the foot still clad in my sandal, I stomped as hard as I could on her foot. The heel went through her sneaker and she cried out, her leg immediately buckling. I reached for my discarded shoe bringing it up like I was swinging a tennis racket and smashed her in the side of the face. She fell. I bolted to the front door, threw it open, and fell out onto the front steps, screaming, just as Craig and Sergeant Ellory rushed up the steps.

Chapter 58

"How did you figure it out?"

I sat in the ER waiting for the doctor to come back and finish stitching my leg. They'd insisted on bringing me to the hospital more because of my head than my leg, but had pronounced me concussion-free. Pauline, though, hadn't been as lucky. My sexy shoes packed a punch in more ways than one. Craig had come with me.

"Jade. She saw you take off after she asked you to return something to Pauline and put two and two together. When you didn't answer my text I pinged the GPS on your phone. Are you sure you're okay?" Craig asked, squeezing my hand.

"I'm fine." I really wanted to get out of this bed. But then my entire family rushed in. My father wasn't used to seeing any of us in his hospital as patients, I could tell by his white face.

"Maddie! My God. I can't believe this happened." He and my mother were hugging me so hard I could barely breathe. Sam and Val joined them. "I'm sorry about your dress," I told Sam.

"I don't care about the dress, silly." She hugged me too. "I'm so glad you're okay. I can't believe Pauline did this!

I told you. Doughnuts are bad for you. They addle your brain."

We all stared at her, then Grandpa squeezed in and reached for my hand. "Honey. I'm so sorry. Craig told me . . . what she said."

"It wasn't just because of you, Grandpa," I said. "She was mad for herself too. But I think she had a crush on you."

"I know she did," he said miserably. "We've been spending some time together, just talking . . ." He trailed off. I exchanged a look with my mother. There was one reason why he'd been out of the house so much.

"Tell her the rest of it," Craig said.

Grandpa tried to look innocent. "What rest of it?"

"Your grandpa got a job with a PI," Craig told me. "They've been working on Aidan O'Malley. They got us proof that he killed Abe Tate."

My jaw dropped. "*What?*"

Grandpa nodded. "He was also the one who robbed him. Kill two birds with one stone—he'd heard about Tate's mandate to fix my house and knew it could screw things up for him. He also knew there was cash to be had."

"And he used Piper's car, didn't he," I said slowly.

Grandpa raised an eyebrow. "How'd you know?"

I didn't answer. "How's Piper?"

"Got a good crack on the head, but she'll live," Craig said. "Listen, I have to get back to work. I just wanted to make sure you were okay." He bent down and kissed my forehead. "I'll call you."

I nodded and watched him walk out of the room, almost colliding with Lucas. They nodded at each other. Craig turned back to me, a questioning look on his face, then slipped away.

Crap. I focused on Lucas, who had come right from the club, it appeared. "I'm so sorry I took off like that," I said, then realized my entire family stared at me. "Everyone, this is Lucas. We were out tonight. His band was playing."

"Then she took off to be Nancy Drew?" Val suggested.

Lucas hovered, unsure what to do with my family around. My mother caught the hint. "Let's give Maddie some room to breathe," she said, pushing my father out of the room. They all filed out, pulling the curtain behind them.

Lucas picked up my hand. "I'm so sorry," he said.

"Why are you sorry? I took off."

"I should've gone with you."

"You were busy," I pointed out. "And didn't know I'd left."

"Still," he said. "I was freaked out when Jade told me something was going on."

Aww. Sweet. I squeezed his hand. I didn't see it coming when he bent down and kissed me, lightly, on the lips. "I really enjoyed our duet," he said softly.

"Me too," I managed, then the curtain flew back and Becky barged in.

"Are you giving me an exclusive or what?" she demanded, then stopped short. "Oh. Sorry."

Lucas grinned. "No problem."

"Are you okay? What the heck happened? How'd you figure it out? Jenna's on her way. I hope that's okay."

The curtain opened again and the doctor came in. "She can tell you all about it in a bit," he said.

Chapter 59

One week later

Grandpa and I sat in his living room, facing the attorney who'd rung his bell half an hour before. This time, she hadn't been sent by Gareth Wade, or an O'Malley. This woman, Lydia somebody, was here on behalf of an un-named benefactor, with an offer neither of us could wrap our heads around. The amount of money being offered to Grandpa could've just built him a brand-new house in line with today's island prices.

"So you're telling me this person wants to donate money to completely fix up my house?" Grandpa stared at her like she'd dropped from an alien spaceship onto his couch.

"That's right. With certain conditions."

"Conditions," Grandpa repeated, and I could see a spark of fury in his eyes. "Who thinks they can offer me money and give me *conditions* on my own house?"

"What are the conditions?" I asked, before he had a chance to blow the whole thing. I sure wanted to hear the whole story.

The attorney looked amused. "It's actually very interesting. The benefactor would like to see the house used to make a positive impact on the lives of animals. Cats, specifically." She handed Grandpa a folder with a wink. "Here's a suggestion."

Grandpa took it with a shaking hand and opened it, then frowned and looked at me.

I took it and perused the contents. Articles. All about cat cafés. A few copies of the ones that had already been left for me, others that I hadn't seen. Cafés in New York. Japan. London. An article about a café that had to close for a week to "restock" after all the cats had been adopted.

I glanced at Lydia. "So in order for Grandpa to get this money, he has to turn his house into a cat café?"

Lydia nodded, a smile spreading across her face. "There didn't seem to be a concern that he'd want to live with cats. Think about it," she said. "Let me know your answer. I know it's a lot to digest."

I let Lydia out the front door. Grandpa followed me out and now stood staring, like he had no idea what to do.

"Do you have any idea who's doing this?" I asked. "I mean, this is an awesome deal, Grandpa. You don't need to have fifty cats in a cat café. Just a few is fine. And if you did some renovations and turned a couple of the rooms into a space for them and made them separate from the rest of the house . . ." I jumped up and walked around, the space already taking shape in my mind's eye. There was enough money to turn this into a really cool space for cats, with nooks and crannies and places for them to climb, hide, and play.

As if in agreement, JJ sauntered into the room and squeaked at me. He looked faintly smug. I wondered if he'd had any input into this situation.

Grandpa still looked perplexed. "Why would anyone think I could do that? I don't even know what a cat café is."

Ah, but he was missing the point. He didn't know. But I did. "I don't think they want you to do it. Alone, anyway." I took a deep breath. "I think whoever it is wants me to stay and do something with animals. A cat café, to be exact." I scooped up JJ and walked over to the counter to pick up the folder Grandpa had dropped. "Someone was leaving these articles for me," I said. "I thought it was just a fun thing and didn't pay attention. But apparently they're stepping it up a bit."

Grandpa looked at me and wrinkled his brow. "But you have your own business."

"I do." And I needed to call Ethan. "My business partner and I might be open to a change of scenery, though," I said. "That's if you want to share your house with me and a bunch of cats."

Grandpa broke into a smile bigger than I'd seen in weeks. Months, maybe. "I haven't heard a better idea in years," he said.

Wow. I sat down at the kitchen table, still clutching the clippings and my new cat. This was crazy. Ethan and I had an awesome business. I had an awesome life out West. But something was telling me this was where I needed to be, for a little while, anyway. We may have lost my grandmother, but we were getting to keep this other part of our family. And I knew she was close by. I thought of that day in the cemetery, when she'd brought me JJ. That had been the start of it. My gut never failed me, and right now it told me I was right where I was supposed to be.

I smiled at Grandpa. "I have to go call my business partner. See how he feels about a trip to New England."